He held out his hand. "So, are we fake married or not?"

Nichole placed her hand in his. Her voice firm and determined. "We're in a business arrangement."

"We've been friends too long to ink our marriage with a handshake." And because he'd never quite learned to heed his chances, he stood and tugged her toward him. "Let's seal the deal correctly."

His arms wrapped around her waist, he leaned forward, almost catching that hint of an adrenaline rush. Her eyes closed, her long eyelashes fanned across her tinted cheeks, her face softened. And that chance tripped Chase up. He completed a successful hook route, shifting at the last second, and pressed his lips against her forehead.

A reminder to himself their marriage was only a sham. Hearts were not included in any deal. And all adrenaline rushes were best avoided.

Dear Reader,

As a child, our family moved quite often. I was always envious of my cousins who remained in the same small town within bike-riding distance to my grandparents' houses. Fortunately, we took many family vacations to my parents' hometown in the Upper Peninsula of Michigan. My grandparents were such a big part of my life and share an even larger space in my memories.

Her Surprise Engagement celebrates grandparents and the joy, wisdom and love only they can bring to families. Nichole Moore and Chase Jacobs have special relationships with their grandparents. And with guidance from their families, Nichole and Chase discover that opposites can attract and build an even stronger foundation together.

If you live close to your grandparents, give them an extra hug and even more of your time. To those who've been promoted to grandparents, we cherish you.

I love to connect with readers. Check out my website at carilynnwebb.com to learn more about my upcoming books and sign up for email book announcements, or chat with me on Facebook (carilynnwebb) or Twitter (@carilynnwebb).

Happy reading!

Cari Lynn

HEARTWARMING

Her Surprise Engagement

—

Cari Lynn Webb

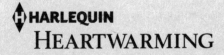

HARLEQUIN®
HEARTWARMING™

Recycling programs for this product may not exist in your area.

ISBN-13: 978-1-335-88977-5

Her Surprise Engagement

Copyright © 2020 by Cari Lynn Webb

This edition published by arrangement with Harlequin Books S.A.

For questions and comments about the quality of this book, please contact us at CustomerService@Harlequin.com.

Harlequin Enterprises ULC
22 Adelaide St. West, 40th Floor
Toronto, Ontario M5H 4E3, Canada
www.Harlequin.com

Printed in U.S.A.

Cari Lynn Webb lives in South Carolina with her husband, daughters and assorted four-legged family members. She's been blessed to see the power of true love in her grandparents' seventy-year marriage and her parents' marriage of over fifty years. She knows love isn't always sweet and perfect—it can be challenging, complicated and risky. But she believes happily-ever-afters are worth fighting for. She loves to connect with readers.

Books by Cari Lynn Webb

Harlequin Heartwarming

City by the Bay Stories

The Charm Offensive
The Doctor's Recovery
Ava's Prize
Single Dad to the Rescue
In Love by Christmas
A Heartwarming Thanksgiving
"Wedding of His Dreams"
Make Me a Match
"The Matchmaker Wore Skates"

Visit the Author Profile page
at Harlequin.com for more titles.

To my grandparents for teaching me the power of love and the strength of family. I miss you every day.

Special thanks to my writing tribe. To my family for understanding that I'm really *not* listening to you when I'm on deadline and that *my head is in my story* is actually a real condition. I love you guys more than you can know!

CHAPTER ONE

SUNDAYS WERE RESERVED for church. Family brunch. And football. Always football.

Only this Sunday was anything but typical. Prayers were too late. Family brunch had been rescheduled for next weekend. And Chase Jacobs's football season had ended three weeks ago in overtime to Oklahoma City.

One field goal kick—three simple points—had broken the Bay Area Pioneers' eight-game winning streak, ending their playoff run. Chase and his teammates had returned home to clear out their lockers, contemplate where exactly they'd gone wrong and watch their longtime rivals step onto the field for the most important game of the season: the Super Bowl.

Chase climbed out of his SUV in the empty parking lot of San Francisco College of Medicine. He locked the car doors, headed toward the entrance of the five-story office building and pulled his baseball cap lower on his head.

The tinted double doors swung open.

A woman stood in the entrance, her brunette hair contained in her usual practical, sleek bun. She lacked Chase's height, barely reached his shoulders, yet her perceptive hazel eyes and fearless posture commanded his full attention. That trait she'd inherited from their mother. He shortened his greeting to a simple: "Mallory."

"I wasn't sure you'd come this morning." His oldest sister tilted her head as if assessing him.

Chase stuffed his hands in the pockets of his jeans. Certain his baseball cap shadowed his face and his guilt. He'd considered skipping their appointment, but his mother and two sisters hadn't raised him to be a quitter. Besides, Mallory would've tracked him down like a defensive lineman sacking the quarterback. "As if that was an option."

"Glad you saw things my way." Mallory nodded and locked the doors behind him.

The medical offices were closed. Normal business hours resumed tomorrow. Chase shouldn't be here either. If not for his persistent sister.

"Does this mean you're finally ready to listen to all my very valuable life advice?" Mallory asked.

Chase shrugged. "If I start listening to you, I'll have to listen to the others too."

"It wouldn't hurt you." Mallory shook her head. "Your family knows best."

"But it might not be as entertaining as listening to myself," Chase teased and followed his sister around a wide reception desk, down a long hallway.

"Perhaps if you listened to us, you wouldn't keep making the news." Mallory stopped and unlocked an office door. The placard read: Mallory C. Jacobs, MD. Assistant Professor of Anesthesiology.

A familiar jolt of pride pulsed through Chase. His big sister was a doctor and a professor. She was well respected, well-liked and successful. Everything he'd always known she'd become, despite setbacks and difficult times. Chase stepped into her large office.

"Mom brought Nonna breakfast and the Sunday newspaper this morning." Mallory turned on the lights. The warm glow did nothing to soften the annoyance in her tone. "Nonna enjoyed reading the article about your golf cart incident at that private club last night."

Chase swiped his hand over his mouth, disrupting his grin. He could count on his nonna to be entertained. As a kid, Chase had to weed his grandmother's garden and mow her lawn every Sunday. It was supposed to have been punishment for whatever infraction he'd caused during the school week—there was always something he'd managed to do in class that landed him in trouble. And yet, Sundays had quickly become his favorite day. His grandmother had taught him to cook and garden. She balanced her criticism with affection, disapproval with support. But mostly, she loved Chase fiercely. He loved her even more fiercely. He'd head to the store after this and pick up the ingredients to make Nonna her favorite dinner.

His sister dropped her purse on one of the twin high-backed leather chairs. "Mom was not as impressed with your golf cart racing skills. You should call her when we finish here." A warning wove through his sister's words.

Judging from the dozen voice mails and texts Chase hadn't yet opened, his agent and the entire Bay Area Pioneers' coaching staff were not impressed either. The off-season always became more complicated than the regular season. During the season, Chase kept his focus on football. Mostly.

Now, less than a month after the Pioneers had lost in the divisional playoff game to

Oklahoma City, Chase had already made headlines. And not the kind the coaches and team owners wanted to read. If only that was all Chase had to face.

His sister rolled her leather chair toward her desk. Her keen gaze leveled on him. "You need a wife, Chase."

As if a wife would solve anything. Marriage was win or lose. His mother had lost after their father had walked out, leaving their mom with three kids under the age of eight to raise all alone. His middle sister had lost too. Ivy had chosen the wrong guy and only recently begun to enjoy her life again. Two years after she'd signed the divorce papers. Chase preferred to remain single and secure. "Why would I ever want a wife?"

"You need someone to speak on behalf of your conscience." Mallory booted up her computer and typed on the keyboard. "Maybe you'd listen to your wife."

"Hey." Chase lifted his hands in surrender. "The golf cart race was…"

"Not your idea." His sister finished for him. "Nothing is ever your idea. Not climbing into a life-size inflatable hamster ball at that party. Or kayaking over a waterfall in a national preserve. Or powerboat racing in a restricted area. Yet you're the one who always makes the headlines."

Chase shifted in the chair. The stiff leather creaked. He forced himself to sit still. He'd squirmed less in the principal's office. "That's the problem with the spotlight—it's hard to get away from it once it catches onto you."

Mallory frowned at him. "Maybe you should try harder to avoid it."

Chase teased, "Where's the fun in that?"

"There's nothing funny about your shoulder, Chase." His sister turned the computer monitor toward him.

Mallory had arranged an MRI on Chase's injured shoulder. Thanks to her colleague, Chase was getting the results early. Right now. In private. Before the Pioneers' coaching staff and team doctors. Chase squeezed the armrests, digging his fingers into the leather. Pain throbbed through his right shoulder. He lowered his voice, flattening out his wince, and avoided looking at the computer screen. "I just need to rest it."

"It's not that simple this time." Mallory's face tensed.

He'd seen that look before. When Mallory had explained the complications about Nonna's osteoporosis and the poor outlook for their cousin's cancer diagnosis. But Mallory had never directed that specific look at him before.

Chase scrubbed his palms over his face, catching his beard. He should've shaved before he met his sister, put himself together better. That was the key, wasn't it? Looking composed and confident made it so. He'd read that in a men's magazine on the plane to Oklahoma City for the divisional playoff game. He'd had a career high for touchdown passes. It still hadn't been enough to secure the win. Maybe if he hadn't taken that hit in the fourth quarter. Maybe if…

Pain arced through his shoulder into his chest and down to his hand. Chase focused on his big toe like his physical therapist had taught him two days after his injury. Nothing ached there in his left toe. The pain sensation was only temporary. The air released inside his lungs. His concentration returned to his sister. "Is this Dr. Jacobs talking or my big sister?"

"Your big sister is ordering you to call Mom when you leave here." Mallory set her folded hands on her desk and eyed him, her gaze solemn. "The anesthesiologist, on recommendation from her orthopedic surgeon colleague, is telling you that you must have surgery on your shoulder."

Not another shoulder surgery. Not now. "But the hit wasn't that bad."

"Perhaps not." Mallory leaned back in her chair. "But your entire shoulder was already compromised. Three prior surgeries tend to do that."

"I played the entire fourth quarter and over-time with this injury." He rolled his shoulder as if that proved he was fine and completely negated the need for an operation.

"Your shoulder needs to be fixed as soon as possible." Mallory pulled the monitor toward her and studied the screen. "You're going to need an extended recovery time."

"Extended." His shoulder throbbed as if in agreement. The wince cinched his voice this time. He cleared his throat. "That hasn't been the case in the past."

"Those weren't the same injuries." Her fingers tapped on the mouse, her gaze remained fixed on the monitor. Hesitation lingered in her voice. "You need every day of the off-season and some of the preseason to recover this time."

Wariness crawled through Chase. His oldest sister never avoided confrontation. Never sidestepped an issue. Mallory had been their mother's right hand growing up. He crossed his arms over his chest and frowned. "What aren't you telling me?"

She blinked, slow and steady, and considered him. Her face softened. "How much do you love football?"

"You already know how much. It's my life."

"Then you better schedule surgery soon if you want to continue living your life."

"I can't have another surgery." His contract was up for renewal. Without a new contract, he wouldn't have a team to play for. Negotiations were about to begin. An op and tons of rehab would not work in his favor.

"You have no choice," she said.

He matched the unyielding edge in her tone with his own rigid voice. "But the Pioneers have a choice."

"You've played your entire professional career with the Pioneers," she argued. "You led the league in touchdowns this season alone."

"Is that enough?" he asked. He was thirty-three and injured. There were younger, faster, healthier guys prepping right now for the draft. If the critics were to be believed, fourth in the league was a generous rating for the aging Pioneers' offensive line. Chase's body felt less than mediocre. He took longer to get out of bed and loosen up his muscles. His shoulder seemed to have given up. But he would overcome all that in the off-season with rest, determination and diligence like he always had.

"If you'd quit dinging your reputation every chance you got, it just might be." Mallory stood and walked around her desk. "Now go and call Mom."

He quickly anchored his most persuasive smile into place. "Can you call Mom for me?"

"I stopped covering for you in high school." She opened her office door. "But I'll put in a good word for you when I talk to her."

"You're my favorite sister." He hugged her.

"You told Ivy the same thing yesterday after she brought your favorite sandwiches for lunch." Mallory laughed.

"Fine." Chase released her and grinned. "You're my favorite doctor sister."

"I'm the only doctor in the family," she said. "And it's a good thing for you."

Chase loved his sisters. Yet Mallory and he shared a close bond. She'd moved in with him during a difficult breakup. Pleased he could finally take care of his independent and capable sister, Chase had kept an endless supply of tissue boxes in the linen closet and a freezer full of cookie dough ice cream. And he'd kept Mallory's secrets safe.

The same as Mallory kept his confidences.

He knew Mallory wouldn't share the details about his current situation. He just wasn't sure how long he could keep the secret from his team or the press.

CHAPTER TWO

"MOM, THAT GROCERY store over there is open." Wesley pointed across the street at Tally's Corner Market. "Should we go in and meet the owners?"

Nichole Moore followed the direction of her son's gaze. Guilt pinched in between her ribs. When had her eleven-year-old taken on the responsibility of pointing out potential vendors for Nichole's fledgling business?

"Josie is waiting for us at Next Level." Brooke Ellis, Nichole's best friend, wrapped her arm around Nichole's waist and urged her toward the women's clothing store nestled deep inside the city's shopping district. "There's no time to waste."

Time. That already remained in too short supply. Every time Nichole turned around, Wesley had grown another inch. Every time she checked her work calendar, her one-year deadline to launch her business crept closer to the end of the month cutoff date. And that money she'd set aside to fulfill her dream dwindled even faster.

But her year wasn't up yet. Wesley wasn't off to college for another six years. She still had time to spend with her son and to secure a better future for them both. Nichole pulled out her cell phone and snapped a picture of Tally's Corner Market midstride. "Sundays are important..."

Wesley peered into Next Level's extra-large window, displaying an array of intimate apparel, and frowned. "Because according to Mom, Sunday nights are when kids like me remember class snack day, forgotten school supplies and bake sales."

Clearly Wesley had been listening to Nichole rehearse her pitch. The one she planned to give tomorrow night to potential investors who could help launch her business.

That pinch became a squeeze inside her chest. Wesley should be playing video games and concentrating on soccer drills, not reciting her presentation word for word.

"You know what else?" Wesley positioned himself spread eagle across the door to Next Level, blocking their entry. "Mom really hates bake sales and when her son is embarrassed by being seen in a women's clothing store."

"I don't hate *hate* bake sales." Nichole disliked good-nights that started with: *Mom, I forgot to tell you…* "I created the *In A Pinch* app for families who have handed out sticks of gum for class snack. Or used stale Halloween candy for the class Valentine's Day exchange. Or sent in grapes on toothpicks for the bake sale."

"Don't remind me," Wesley mumbled. "But the bubble gum was awesome, even though Ms. Warner confiscated every piece."

"It was against the rules." Nichole grimaced at Brooke.

"Well, shopping is not against the rules." Brooke motioned to Wesley. "Now let us get inside so we can dress your mom for her next level of success."

Wesley never budged. "But I'm in a pinch and in need of saving from being seen in there."

"You're in luck. Your rescue squad is almost here." Brooke checked her phone. "Ben and his dad are a few blocks away."

Wesley pumped his fists and grinned.

"But you still have to come inside the store until they get here," Nichole said.

"Ugh." Wesley shuffled away from the door.

"Nichole. Brooke." Josie Beck waved and

rushed toward them. Her smile was wide and welcoming. "Nichole, I'm thinking this must be your son. He looks like he's working on passing you up."

"Mom says no matter how tall I get I won't outgrow her heart." Wesley choked as if he couldn't believe he'd recited such a girlie sentiment out loud.

Nichole poked Wesley's arm to remind him to shake Josie's hand and prayed his hands weren't too dirty. "Wesley, Josie designs her own wedding gowns at her bridal boutique. I'm sure she'd give you a tour." And with luck, Josie would know how to dress Nichole for that next level.

"I'm not getting married." Wesley stepped back and waved his hands out in front of him. "Ever."

"Good to know." Josie touched her cheek as if stopping her grin. "We'll talk again when you're in college and see if you've changed your mind."

"Not happening." Wesley shook his head so hard his bangs swayed.

"That leaves your mom and Brooke to walk down the aisle." Josie clasped her hands together. The velvet scrap of fabric tied in her blond hair shifted in the wind.

"Uh." Nichole stepped back, bumping into

the brick ledge framing the window display. Her pulse raced. Brides were the center of attention. Nichole never wanted that. She'd elope and skip all the fuss. Or even better, she'd follow Wesley's lead and forgo marriage altogether.

"My mom says she'll only get married when she finds someone who eats peanut butter and pickle sandwiches too." Wesley grabbed his stomach and released a burst of laughter. "Last night she ate the whole sandwich herself."

Now Nichole was the center of the attention. "It's a good sandwich."

"That's a rather specific requirement in a partner." Brooke grinned at Josie. "It sort of sounds like a challenge to me."

"There's someone for everyone the same way there's a gown for every body." Josie glanced at Nichole and her smile widened. "We just need to find him for you."

"My friend Adam Tanner will eat anything. He ate an earthworm one day after school." Wesley grimaced. "But even Adam won't try Mom's sandwich."

"I think we've gotten off track," Nichole said. "I'm perfectly happy not sharing my pickle and peanut butter sandwich." She was perfectly happy without a so-called better half. Or rather, she was content. Besides, raising Wesley filled her life—he was everything to her.

"Mom and Brooke dumped Mom's entire closest all over her bedroom floor. Then Brooke announced a fashion emergency." Wesley stepped closer to Josie and flung his arms wide. Disbelief lifted his voice an octave higher than usual. Wesley added, "Mom made me walk all the way here because I can't stay home alone. Even though I'm almost twelve."

Josie rubbed her forehead as if unsure how to console Wesley. Then she looked at Nichole, both eyebrows raised. "Nichole, your text didn't say you wanted to redo your entire wardrobe."

"I need an outfit for only one business meeting," Nichole clarified. A potentially life-changing meeting. Less than an hour earlier, Brooke and she had determined Nichole owned nothing suitable to wear to her upcoming *life-changing* meeting. Still, an entire fashion overhaul seemed a bit much.

"One career-making or breaking meeting." Brooke's voice lowered into dismal and dreary. "With corporate gurus who can smash Nichole's dreams into pieces." Brooke ground her palms together.

Nichole raised an eyebrow. "That's rather dramatic."

"But sadly true." Brooke waved at Nichole, presenting her with the flourish of a game show hostess. "Nichole needs an outfit to put her in control and in charge."

If there was such clothing. Nichole gravitated toward comfort. And anything that helped her blend in. She never wanted to stand out. Not as a child. Not now as an adult. She touched her tunic sweatshirt and tights. "My wardrobe consists of leggings, sweatshirts, jeans and sweaters."

"Mom works on her computer all day. Every day, even the weekends." Wesley scratched his cheek. "Then she wears the same work clothes to the grocery store and on the basketball court when we play at Ben's house. But I have to change my school clothes all the time."

For the past year, Nichole had worked on her home computer to build the *In A Pinch* app. Determined not to go back to her old nine-to-five working life, Nichole had donated her business clothes after she'd quit her full-time job. Now she had no clothes to reenter the job market and a bit more regret than anticipated over her donation exuberance.

"When is your meeting?" Josie tilted her head and eyed Nichole.

"Tomorrow evening." Nichole bit her bottom lip. She needed more time to shop for casual active wear online. How was she going to find an outfit in one afternoon?

"This is my first emergency retail session with girlfriends in...well, ever. I can't wait." Pleasure sparked from Josie's grin up into her eyes and brightened her voice. "There's no time to waste."

What if Nichole was wasting Brooke's and Josie's time? And the investors'. Nichole locked her knees and blocked the doubt leaching into her. The moment for doubt had passed when she'd handed in her resignation letter.

A large pickup truck pulled into the no-parking zone and honked. Wesley shouted, "That's my ride." At the curb, he yelled to Ben and his dad, "Hurry! We need to leave before they make us go shopping too."

The passenger window rolled down and Dan Sawyer leaned over from the driver's side. "We're off to do important boy things. Enjoy your afternoon."

Brooke blew a kiss to Dan, her boyfriend. "We plan to have more fun."

"Not likely," Dan said. The boys' laughter

burst from the truck. Dan grinned, rolled up the window and pulled away.

"Time to shop." Brooke opened the door to Next Level and waved them inside. She whispered to Nichole, "Stop overthinking this and at least try to have fun."

"Overthinking is what I do." What Nichole had always done her entire life. Overanalyzing allowed her to make solid decisions and avoid risks. She'd never discovered any kind of reward in risks. But she'd risked with her app. And now she had to find the reward.

ONE HOUR LATER, the dressing room of the department store looked more like Nichole's chaotic closet, making her reconsider not having joined the boys for their version of fun instead. Nichole slipped on a blazer and stepped out to face Josie and Brooke.

Brooke tapped her chin. "It's better."

Nichole tugged on the sleeves. "They're too short." Like the dress before. And the slacks before that.

Josie moved to Nichole's side and rolled the sleeves in neat folds toward her elbows. She ran her fingers over the exposed silk inner lining. "Now it's functional and fun."

Nichole turned toward the mirror. Her leggings and sweatshirt had been replaced by a black pencil skirt, tailored blouse and blazer. The red pin-striped lining offered a fresh break in an otherwise conservative outfit. Nichole looked like an executive. Sweat beaded against her lower back.

Looking and being were not nearly the same thing. She was supposed to take charge at her meeting. Seasoned leaders delegated. Inspired. And had grit.

Nichole's grit was more like the pebbles in Wesley's fish tank: slippery and easy to rinse down the drain. "This blazer will be too hot."

"Not likely in this weather." Brooke rubbed her hands together as if feeling chilled.

"You could remove it at dinner." Josie unbuttoned the blazer and adjusted Nichole's blouse. "That's the advantage of layers."

"I sweat when I get nervous. It's not a good look for a silk blouse." Which was why Nichole preferred to layer moisture-wicking sportswear. She fiddled with a button on the blazer. "I passed out before my graduation speech."

Brooke grimaced from one of the chairs. "Those gowns and stage lights are really hot."

"I was backstage. Sitting down." Nichole shook her head. She'd frozen and panicked on the theater stage once too and disappointed her mother, the choreographer of the show, and her father, the director of the entire production. Nichole had moved in with her grandparents the following week, permanently. True, she'd only been six at the time. Still, Nichole had avoided the spotlight ever since. She'd always lacked her mother's grace and poise and hadn't inherited her father's charisma. "Who passes out sitting down?"

Brooke and Josie exchanged a look.

"Then I introduced myself as Michole Hoore to the entire graduating class, their families and friends. Not Nichole Moore." Nichole slapped her hands over her hot cheeks. "Who does that?"

"Be serious," Brooke said.

"I am." Nichole pressed her palms against her skin, pushing the old mortification back inside her.

Why had she ever believed she could negotiate the sale of her computer program to a pair of savvy business investors? She should've learned her lesson two years ago at that fiasco of a sales pitch. Of course, back then *In A Pinch* had only been an idea. Regardless, she'd failed to get the investors to see her vision. To believe in her. Now she had an actual program, built and functioning. What if they still couldn't believe in her?

She'd have to tell Wesley and her grandparents she'd failed.

"I'm a train wreck around strangers." Nichole sighed into her hands. "I don't think I can do this."

"You can do this." Brooke wrapped her arm around Nichole's shoulder. "We just need to find you some reinforcement."

"Like a bodyguard. To protect me from myself," Nichole said.

Brooke met Nichole's gaze in the mirror, her voice serious. "Or even better, a personal negotiator."

"That could work. Just like this." Josie lifted up a fitted dress and pressed it into Nichole's hands. "We saved the best for last."

"It's red." Chili-pepper red. Nichole avoided spicy food. It made her face crimson and her stomach hurt.

"It's bold," Josie countered.

"Confident," Brooke added.

"Everything I'm—"

Brooke cut her off. "Everything you're going to be. You're going to make those investors pay double for your program. Use the extra money to pay off your grandparents' mortgage fund, Wesley's college account and take us all on an exotic vacation."

"That's an excellent plan," Josie said. "No one ever takes enough vacations."

"There's only one problem." Nichole removed the blazer and revealed the twin sweat marks on the lovely blouse. "I'm panicked right now. With you guys! What's going to happen tomorrow?"

"We already told you." Brooke pushed Nichole toward the dressing room. "You try the dress on, and we'll find you a personal negotiator."

"It's sleeveless." Josie called out. "No embarrassing sweat marks. Oh, and I also found the perfect overcoat."

Nichole sighed. "We aren't leaving until I try this on, are we?"

Josie and Brooke laughed.

Nichole took the dress and stepped inside the dressing room. Meanwhile, Brooke and Josie tossed out names of friends for Nichole's personal negotiator like pennies in a wishing well.

She hung the skirt, blouse and blazer back on the hangers, then sank onto the small bench. Her head dropped between her knees. A position she'd found herself in more than once growing up. Every time she'd been forced to step onto a stage for a holiday show in elementary school or a choir performance in middle school. Finally, in high school, she'd learned to raise her hand first to make her presentation to her class and then she'd excuse herself to the bathroom, until the urge to faint had passed.

The only time she'd truly fainted had been before her valedictorian speech. She'd opened her eyes to find herself cradled in the arms of the one person she'd never known to be intimidated by anything: Chase Jacobs. She'd been his tutor throughout high school. He'd been her…

Nichole shoved off the bench and reached for the dress. She was an adult. A single mother and hard worker. This wasn't high school. This was her life. Chase Jacobs was a successful professional football player. He'd accomplished his dreams, despite the obstacles. Surely, Nichole could do the same.

She slipped on the dress, maneuvered until she reached the zipper on the back, then zipped her long hair inside the teeth. Her head tweaked backward at an uncomfortable angle, Nichole shuffled out of the dressing room. "This is why I like wearable workout clothes."

"But life is more than a workout." Brooke freed Nichole's hair and directed her toward the full-length mirror. "This is the dress that's going to get you everything you want."

"The dress is its own accent piece. Add earrings or a bracelet, but not both." Josie handed her a fitted black overcoat. "And beautiful shoes."

"Definitely." Brooke nodded. "We'll find those next."

"I have shoes," Nichole argued. The dress was bold. Confident. Everything Nichole was determined to be. The price tag under her arm scratched against her skin, making her squirm.

"Not shoes that say, 'I'm tall and you are just going to have to deal with it.'" Brooke set her hands on her hips and eyed Nichole.

No. She didn't have *those* kinds of shoes.

"You can wear flats or heels," Josie assured her. "But Brooke is right. People are already checking your feet to see if you have heels on or if you are just that tall. If people are looking at your feet, make your shoes memorable."

"I never considered that." Nichole glanced at her bare feet. The ones usually contained in running shoes or boots.

"That's why we're here." Brooke clasped her hands together. "What's it going to be?"

Nichole inhaled, deep and filling like their yoga instructor taught them, and settled into her decision. "Both outfits. I want options."

Brooke and Josie high-fived.

Josie smiled. "Time to shoe shop."

At the third shoe store, Nichole had a pair of stunning flats and a pair of elegant heels in cloth shopping bags. Brooke and Josie declared no shopping spree a true success without a celebratory dinner. Tucked into a booth at Rustic Grille, the debate continued over who could be Nichole's personal negotiator.

Brooke gave her order to the waiter and handed him their menus. Her fingers drummed on the table. "If only Dan wasn't heading back up north with his dad later tonight, he would've gone with you."

"Theo doesn't get back from the east coast until Friday," Josie explained. "And I have dress fittings for my working clients scheduled well into the evening tomorrow night."

"And I'm on babysitting duty. Wesley is spending the night with Ben and me." Brooke's frown intensified. "There has to be someone."

"Not that you need anyone," Josie rushed on.

Nichole nodded. Even she admitted she liked the idea of a personal negotiator. At the very least, someone on her side in case she misplaced her backbone.

"Let's run back through Mia's guest list

from her Christmas party," Brooke suggested. "You don't want a stranger."

"You need to take someone you can trust." Josie swirled her straw in her soda.

Trust. That was a loaded word. Nichole had trusted few people in her past, and even then, each had proven to be a mistake. It hadn't helped that she'd loved those same people and they'd broken her heart too. Had she ever really trusted anyone? One person, but that was in high school. People changed.

The personal negotiator name-dropping paused only to allow them to sample one another's dinner choices.

The table cleared and desserts ordered, Josie stared at her phone and cringed. "My model just canceled for Tuesday morning's photo shoot. The pictures were supposed to be for my new website."

"Can you get someone else?" Brooke asked.

"It's too late. These gowns were designed specifically for a tall bride." Josie squeezed her forehead and paled. "I wanted to showcase that I have gowns for every height and every size, even petite. And I'm scheduled for a dozen bridal expos starting this month."

The waitress set down two brownie skillets with homemade vanilla ice cream. Brooke intercepted Nichole's salted caramel cheese-cake. "How tall does your model need to be?"

"At least six feet." Josie smashed her ice cream onto her brownie.

"Nichole, aren't you six feet tall?" Brooke grinned at her.

Nichole shook her head and reached for her cheesecake. "I'm six feet, one inch."

"That's perfect. You're perfect." Josie latched on to Nichole's arm. "Would you be my model?"

Brooke held Nichole's cheesecake hostage and nodded her head.

"You seriously cannot want me to model for you." Nichole gaped at Josie.

Josie blinked. "Why not? You're beautiful."

She appreciated her friend's confidence boost. "I don't know the first thing about modeling."

"Mia is taking the photographs." Josie's smile lifted into her eyes. "She's an expert at poses and all that. She can show you."

"It's a few hours Tuesday morning to be a pretend bride in Josie's stunning gowns." Brooke sighed.

"The photoshoot is meant to showcase the gowns, not you," Josie promised.

Nichole had mentioned she needed to add more fun to her routine. And Josie's gowns were spectacular. Who didn't want to be a pretend bride for a few hours? "Yes. I'll do it."

Josie wrapped her arms around Nichole and hugged her. Brooke handed over the cheesecake.

Dessert plates scraped clean and the bill paid, the women left the restaurant. Their search for Nichole's perfect personal negotiator remained unfinished, but not yet forfeited. Brooke and Josie promised to come up with more names. Nichole promised to practice her best model poses.

The trio went their separate ways.

Her new clothes hung safely in her closet, Wesley tucked in for the night, Nichole climbed into bed and propped her laptop on a pillow. She studied the profiles of the investors for her meeting. Alerts from her social media page pinged in the corner of her screen. Nichole clicked over to her page. Both Josie and Brooke posted updates about their shopping adventure and tagged Nichole.

More updates from friends scrolled across her page. A familiar name caught her attention.

The one guy she'd trusted in high school.

Brooke and Nichole wanted her personal negotiator to be someone she trusted.

Did she dare ask him?

Nichole tapped her fingers on the keyboard. He was the only person who had never been a pushover, and he owed her. She was well over a decade in calling in the favor. But was there a time limit on favors owed?

She had helped him pass high school, then his college courses long enough to enter the football draft. He'd told her he owed her whatever she wanted. Whatever she needed. She had only to ask.

Nichole's fingers moved across the keyboard and typed. It was one private message. Nothing lost if he never opened it.

But there was even more to be gained if he did.

Nichole pressed the send button and shut down her laptop.

Now she waited. Waited to see if Chase Jacobs would accept her invitation. Waited to see if Chase Jacobs could change her world this time.

CHAPTER THREE

CHASE PULLED INTO a parking space at the state park an hour north of the city, switched off the engine and focused his mind. Thirty-three wasn't old. Never mind that he'd taken more time to get out of bed than usual that morning. He wasn't past his prime. Despite being seven years older than most players on the field. Thirties were the new twenties. He had more experience, more knowledge and more skill.

A quick, succinct rap on his tinted passenger window followed by the words, "Come on, old man. Let's get riding," spurred Chase out of his truck.

Greetings came from half a dozen teammates, a mix of former and current players, waiting near the start of the 12-mile advanced mountain biking trail. One of Chase's favorite postseason workout spots.

Chase waved and ordered his throbbing shoulder to stand down. He regarded the two men leaning against his truck bed. "Didn't think so many people liked bike riding."

"You asked last night on the group chat if anyone was up for a challenge this afternoon." Beau Bradford, Chase's backup quarterback, ran his hand through his curly hair and chuckled. "We all accepted."

"Perfect." Chase cleared his throat. Defiance of Mallory's recommendation for surgery as soon as possible had prompted Chase's impulsive text to his teammates yesterday. He had things to prove to the coaching staff, the team and himself. He had to prove to everyone—especially the doubters—that nothing had changed. He was in fact the same Chase Jacobs: a resilient and capable producer on the field. Not fragile or weak or vulnerable. Not a has-been.

Elliot Cote, his former teammate and good friend, dropped the truck's tailgate and reached for Chase's bike. "Hope you brought extra water and snacks. They intend to do the full trail."

"You said yourself, the other trails on this mountain are for kids and amateurs." Beau laughed and returned to the others.

The full trail involved jumps and steep declines on the return. Chase pressed his lips together and grabbed his helmet from the back seat. He'd always been impulsive. One day he'd learn to censor himself. Unfortunately, today was already too late. Chase fastened his helmet under his chin, accepted his bike from Elliot and rode over to the group. "This isn't your mother's spin class, boys. If you need training wheels, stick to the flats. Otherwise, I'll see you at the top."

Elliot's boom of laughter pushed against Chase's back like a shot of adrenaline, urging him onto the trail.

Having cycled nine miles, Chase dropped his bike in an open clearing and sucked in a deep breath of air. Held it and closed his eyes. He pictured the stadium of his first college football game. The grass freshly painted. The fifty-thousand-plus seats not yet filled. The excited rush of energy racing through his veins. No pain, only anticipation. Chase squeezed his eyes together, concentrated harder. The muscles around his right shoulder refused to relax. The imagery failed to distract his mind. The pain intensified.

Chase cursed. He opened and closed his right hand as if the pins and needles sensation stabbing into his palm was that simple to eliminate. Finished his water bottle as if dehydration caused the intense throbbing in his shoulder, not the rough terrain and tense grip on the handlebars for the past hour.

Elliot dropped his bike beside Chase's. His gaze always perceptive and too intuitive—a gift that had made him unstoppable on the defensive line—was stuck on Chase's shoulder before it centered on Chase. "I saw the hit."

Chase realized exactly what hit Elliot referred to. The one that had occurred with less than thirty seconds on the clock in the divisional playoff game last month. The sack had drawn a penalty flag for roughing the passer and a gain of yards that had brought his team half the distance to the goal line. But the damage had already been done to Chase's shoulder and the game had already been lost. One touchdown would take the point deficit to three, but not change the final outcome. Chase had taken four hits to his right shoulder the past season alone. The last hit had proved to be the most damaging. "Nothing that time won't heal."

"Or a doctor's knife," Elliot suggested.

Elliot knew Chase the best out of anyone on the field, past or present. Elliot had witnessed the sack from the sidelines. And no doubt had watched Chase's awkward recovery on the field. Chase had rushed to the scrimmage line, called the play and waited for the snap. Adrenaline had overridden the pain. Chase had thrown for a touchdown and tied the game. Overtime had been a challenge. He'd overthrown two receivers and suffered another sack. Three plays later, their best receiver dropped a pass. Oklahoma City recovered the ball, moved into field goal range. Chase had watched the clock run out and accepted defeat. And never disclosed his injury. Today his indignant shoulder demanded his full attention and refused to be ignored.

Beau slowed his bike beside them and flashed his trademark grin, easygoing and welcoming. The grin that made Beau the guy everyone wanted to hang out with. The guy every little kid wanted to become. "Tapping out already?"

Chase had only ever wanted to be himself. But would *he*—as he was, injured and past his prime—be enough to secure the Pioneers' starting quarterback position? Doubt chased along his already frayed nerves. Chase pointed at a trail that disappeared into the eucalyptus forest and steepest side of the mountain. "We're hiking to the peak."

Elliot muttered beside Chase.

Beau nodded at the trail, respect on his face and in his words. "We'll take the switchbacks and see you at the top." Beau waved for the others to follow him.

"We don't have to keep going." Elliot wiped the sweat from his forehead. "We've seen the view how many times before?"

Chase hadn't seen the view with surgery and the possible end of his career looming on the horizon. "You can't tap out on the last three miles." He couldn't tap out of the game or his career now either.

One mile in, Elliot broke the silence. "How'd the exit meeting go?"

"Routine." Chase slipped on a rock and grabbed a tree limb with his good arm to steady himself. At least he'd managed a firm, steady handshake at the end of his routine exit meeting with Keith Romero, the Pioneers' general manager. "Keith wished me an uneventful off-season."

Elliot chuckled. "Got a plan for that?"

"Still working on it." Just as he was working on getting up the mountain without face-planting. And working on avoiding surgery.

Dried branches snapped underneath Elliot's heavy steps. His voice came out in a long exhale. "Any word on your contract negotiations?"

"Nothing, but Travis gave me a lecture on my repairing my reputation." His agent, Travis Shaw, had always been more like a father to Chase, despite being only six years older than him. Travis had always been protective and supportive, yet maintained high expectations.

Travis had continued his fatherly role a few days ago on their weekly conference call. He'd lectured Chase for more than an hour about being responsible and showing he had respect for the game, himself and the team. As if Chase didn't leave everything he had on the field every Sunday for the love of his team and the game. *It's your disregard for your health and safety off the field that the Pioneers' coaching staff and entire management question. It's the disregard that's interfering with your contract extension. You do want a new contract, don't you?*

More than anything. Fear clipped him. Panic rushed him and Chase slipped again. A life without football scared him. This time his right hand flailed, his fingers refused to curl around a low-lying tree branch.

Elliot braced his hand against Chase's back, catching Chase before he fell. Chase clenched every muscle in his back, firmed his legs and reminded his entire body that only his right shoulder was impaired. Elliot never commented, never teased his friend, only had

Chase's back the same as he'd done for Chase over the years both on the field and off.

Finally, Chase rallied his body and sidelined his pain, reducing it from all-consuming to a localized dull ache. He pushed away from Elliot and forced himself to finish the rest of the hike on his own two feet.

Together Chase and Elliot stepped out onto the peak and used their shirts to wipe the sweat from their faces. The others had already arrived and posed for photos near the edge.

Elliot jammed his elbow into Chase's side. "Did anyone tell you that Beau is sharing your quarterback coach this off-season?"

Chase dropped his shirt into place and scowled. "They left that piece of news out."

"Figured." Elliot squeezed his water bottle. "Thought you should know."

Russ Stanley, the renowned quarterback coach, and Chase had a rhythm. A routine. A relationship they'd built over several seasons together that included how to win and what to improve. A relationship they always continued into the off-season.

Now Chase would share his off-season prep time with his backup quarterback. Russ could recommend Beau over Chase to the Pioneers' coaching staff and management.

The Pioneers could sign Beau as their franchise quarterback and release Chase to the free agency. Then his career would be over. What other team would take a risk on an injured quarterback, past his prime and put him in an unfamiliar offense? *No one.*

His stomach clenched. That fear, not from pregame jitters, snagged inside him. Chase needed his new contract signed with the Pioneers and soon. "Beau is a good guy."

"Speaking of reputational repair." Elliot nodded toward the group of players. "Beau has the reputation you want."

Chase looked at his friend.

"He's got the pretty wife who is a social influencer with her organic lifestyle products that benefit the environment." Elliot sprayed water from his water bottle over his head. "And they have the adorable little kid and another one on the way."

"He's the perfect family man."

"Hasn't been banned from country clubs, national parks or museums." Disapproval weighted Elliot's tone into a blunt rasp.

Chase could not claim the same. He grabbed Elliot's water bottle and sprayed his own face as if rinsing off the sweat and mud would transform him into a different man. *The only time the Pioneers' coaching staff and management want to read your name in the headlines this off-season is if it's attached to your nonprofit work and things like the Pioneers' upcoming kids' sports camp. Got it, Chase? Avoid adrenaline rushes, challenges and dares if you want your contract renewed.*

Chase rubbed the back of his neck. Surely today's ride didn't count. It was a workout with his teammates, nothing more. So far, no bets had been placed. Chase had to keep it that way.

"Don't worry." Elliot slapped Chase on the back near his good shoulder. "Beau doesn't have your talent."

But Beau Bradford had the reputation the Pioneers wanted. Now Beau had Chase's quarterback coach too and a direct connection to the head coach the entire off-season. How was Chase going to polish his reputation, heal his shoulder and ensure his starting position as quarterback? He had to develop an exceptional game plan and quick.

"Group photo op," someone yelled.

Chase and Elliot joined the others.

"Hashtag team bonding." Beau positioned his camera for a group selfie.

Pictures taken, Chase posted the photograph to his social media pages. Proof for the Pioneers that he was a team player and playing it safe. A private message in his inbox from a familiar name caught his notice.

"Anyone up for trivia night at The Shouting Fiddle once we get off this mountain?" Preston Park, a rookie wide receiver and standout player last year, issued the challenge.

Chase lifted his gaze from his phone. He'd never turned down a game of trivia before. He liked the strategy and finesse involved in winning. Heck, he liked to win.

"Can't." Beau zipped his phone in his jacket pocket. "Have to get home and pack. Cassie planned a babymoon at a spa in Sedona."

The younger players congratulated Beau as if he'd announced he'd won the lottery. Chase glanced at Elliot.

"Got me." Elliot shrugged. "Sounds like a vacation, although I wouldn't be going to a spa. Maybe the casinos in Vegas or the white sand beaches in the Bahamas. I like those drinks with the umbrellas."

The guys looked at Chase. Preston flicked his hand at Chase. "We know Chase is in for sure."

Elliot whispered, "Remember that reputation repair thing."

The last time Chase had played trivia, they'd moved the fun to another player's penthouse suite and launched drones from the balcony. Their erratic flight plans invaded the privacy of other residents and resulted in more than one call to law enforcement. Not exactly the headline the Pioneers or Travis wanted to see.

Even more important, Chase needed an immediate physical therapy session on his shoulder, yet he couldn't admit that, not to his teammates. Chase glanced at his phone and the open message from a former classmate and old friend. The message he couldn't quite read. But he seized on the excuse and improvised. "I have a date."

Now the congratulations heaped on Chase. Along with hopes that this one stuck around longer than the last few. Preston clarified that by *longer* they all meant more than one week. Chase accepted the ribbing and laughed. His dating stats looked worse than a benched player. Yet a benched player worked harder to get back on the field, back into the game. Chase preferred to keep his dating life on the sidelines. The only long-term deal that interested him was football.

Nichole Moore had stuck around longer than a week in high school. She'd stuck around long enough to make sure Chase had graduated from high school and earned a college scholarship. Then she'd stuck around again helping him pass his college courses until he'd been drafted into the pros his junior year of college. She'd been more than a tutor, more than a simple friend. She'd been his confidante and he hers when they'd both needed someone the most.

But they were adults now. They'd moved on and hadn't spoken in years. What could she want? More than intrigued, Chase headed for the trail. He stopped only to send a quick text to JT, his physical therapist, requesting an afternoon treatment session as soon as possible.

It only took an hour and one fall off his bike for Chase to make it back down the hill. He tightened the straps on his bike in his truck bed, called goodbyes to the guys and started the engine. He connected his cell phone to the audio system and pressed the button for the automated voice to read his message from Nichole out loud. In school, he'd relied on Nichole to help him work through his dyslexia and graduate. Now he relied on modern technology and kept the truth of his dyslexia a well-guarded secret.

He listened to the message twice. Nichole was calling in her favor owed. Expected him to honor his promise made a decade earlier. She'd always expected him to be better. Do better. As if she'd always known he could be more. He grinned from the inside out. He hadn't accepted a challenge from Nichole in entirely too long.

He pressed the reply button and agreed to meet her for drinks at Glasshouse Inn. It wasn't one of the city's hot spots. Glasshouse Inn was known more for its exceptional five-star menu at its exclusive restaurant, Sapphire Cellar, than a bar scene. He wouldn't have to worry about damaging his reputation tonight.

Besides, he'd be with Nichole Moore, the high school class valedictorian and his one-time conscience. What could possibly go wrong?

CHAPTER FOUR

"CHASE. YOU REALLY CAME." Nichole exhaled, trying with difficulty to raise the volume of her voice. Now if she could just get out the words: *Can you help me close this deal?* She drew a breath and then choked on it as energy—the nervous, fluttery kind—streamed through her. But this was Chase.

"I had to." Chase tipped his head. "It's the first time ever *you* asked for *my* help." One side of his mouth eased up into his cheek—part smirk, part grin and all parts appealing.

And just like that, the distance of a decade apart dwindled to simple seconds. She recognized that grin. The one that suggested there were wagers to be placed. Apologies to be accepted. Bad decisions to be overlooked. He'd won over high school teachers, college professors, countless reporters and now the public too with that one particular look.

He ordered a soda and sat on the barstool beside her as if he was taking his usual seat at the kitchen table to work on American

Lit. Only their knees collided and remained connected. The simple contact both distracting and reassuring. This was worse than her clumsiness.

Can you help me? "I just wanted to catch up with an old friend. It's been a while."

He'd been her only true friend in high school. He'd once called her fearless and she'd believed him. She'd also believed in true love and happily-ever-afters. How she missed the naive strength and foolish wonder they'd once possessed together.

"We could've played the catch-up game online or over text." He shrugged, only one shoulder and one corner of his mouth lifted. His usual misleading smile eased back into place. "But you told me to come here. In person."

"You've improved at following orders." She smiled.

His grin widened. The wealthy, successful bachelor humoring his brainy, bookish friend. And she completely lost her nerve.

"What is it you need?" he asked.

That deep timbre of a voice always on the verge of releasing a contagious laugh flowed over Nichole. Familiar, though different. "I... this was a mistake. I've read about you." About his philanthropy. His multimillion-dollar contracts. His dates with models and his endless adventures.

He rubbed the back of his neck and cleared his throat. Twice. "You've been following me then. That's nice to know."

His green eyes, sharper and more intense than she remembered, scattered her inner calm. "I follow stock market trends, weather forecasts and the classified ads too." She had to get rid of him, end this awkward walk down memory lane, then step into her dinner meeting and her future.

"But you read about me first," he teased and bumped his shoulder into hers. "Admit it."

"If I say yes, will you join me for dinner tonight?" *No. Wrong question.* Nichole's words hung between them, unretractable.

"This is starting to feel like a date." Chase lowered his soda glass and stared at her like he used to when he'd wanted to distract her from their studies. He'd guess her mood by naming the different shades of brown in her hazel eyes. Now his gaze hinted at more than a silly game.

"This is the favor owed." Nichole grabbed her glass and drank the water fast. The cold water was like splashing ice on a sunburn. Temporary and fleeting. She was aware of Chase like a full body sunburn, uncomfortable and distressing. "Besides, I don't date. I'm a single mom with a son."

"Single parent." Chase nodded. "You have all my respect."

His mom had raised him and his two sisters alone. In interviews, he never missed the opportunity to thank his mom or express his love for her. He understood Nichole's struggle the same as he'd understood her reserve in high school. He knew her secrets and had never judged her for them. "Wesley is eleven and everything a preteen boy is—energetic, funny and messy. Thankfully he inherited his father's one redeeming quality—his physical grace."

"I could get him into the Pioneers' Spring Break camp next week, if you want." He sounded relaxed and pleased to make the offer. "It usually fills up fast, but I know some people. I can make a couple of calls."

"You'd do that?" *Would you also help me close my deal?* Nichole pictured her son: gangly arms and legs on a skinny frame. Too many freckles to count and a laugh that took over his whole body. Her love for Wesley was limitless. Surely her sudden awareness of Chase had to be fleeting. A simple glitch from their time apart. "You don't even know him."

"But I know you." The boy she'd once considered her best friend, now a man, scooted closer. Gone was the attention-stealing, misdirecting full grin. In its place, a soft smile. A strong shoulder to rest her head on and a warm, compassionate gaze that centered on her.

She leaned toward Chase as if they'd seen each other yesterday and the day before that. As if he'd asked what was really on her mind like he'd done so many times in the past and had genuinely wanted to know. She whispered, "I pray every day I'm enough for Wesley. That the void of a missing parent never consumes him."

Her words fell into that familiar space between them. That space she'd never quite found with anyone else.

"You're more than enough." He set his hand on top of hers, steady and secure.

The warmth from his hand spread through her. But the simple touch confirmed their connection had endured despite the time and the distance. "How are you always so sure?"

"I had this tutor once who had refused to let me fail." The affection in his gaze was true. "She made me believe."

"She sounds like an amazing woman." She picked up her water glass and toasted him.

"Well, Nonna always liked you the best." He tapped his soda against her water glass.

"I'm sure that's not true." Although she had adored his entire family. The Jacobs clan had welcomed Nichole into their home and accepted her from the very first introductions. The Jacobs house had been the only place outside her grandparents' farm where Nichole had been comfortable.

"You were my only girlfriend who cleared her plate for every meal at my family's house." Chase chuckled. "Of course, Nonna liked you the best."

The word girlfriend thudded inside Nichole's chest, displacing her ribs and her common sense. She focused on the facts. "I was the only girl you allowed your family to meet in high school."

"It wasn't only high school." Chase rolled his glass between his hands and looked away.

Before she could challenge Chase, two businessmen approached the bar entrance. The only two that Nichole had seen arrive in the past half hour. Only five minutes until the reservation for her meeting. The one that could change her family's lives. So much to gain. So much to lose. Heat enveloped her, followed by a cold, encompassing shiver.

"I do need your help." But only this once.

Then she'd go back to relying on her own shoulders. After all, she was Nichole Moore, always practical, predictable and levelheaded. Chase was fearless, reckless and completely wrong for her. She glanced at Chase. "I need you to help me believe now. To help me fight for my vision and my dream."

He shifted and looked at the two guys who'd just arrived. "I'm going to assume your dinner invitation wasn't for a date."

Nichole stood, swung her tote bag over her shoulder. She swayed and curled her toes inside her new heels to find her balance. "It's a business dinner. A really important one."

He rose and adjusted the strap of her bag on her shoulder. "What kind of business dinner?"

"The kind that could make or break me." Her bag slid off her shoulder toward her elbow, knocking against her knee. Josie had recommended a simple clutch. Brooke had suggested a small sleek briefcase. Nichole hadn't listened. Now her oversize tote and tangled thoughts about Chase knocked her off-balance again.

"What do you need me to do?" He pulled his wallet out, paid for the soda.

"Stand beside me." He'd stood in her line of sight during her campaign speech for class treasurer in high school. She'd lost that popularity contest. She couldn't lose tonight. "I just really need a familiar face."

"I can do that." Chase held out his arm and waited for her to set her arm around his. "Lead the way."

Thankfully, Chase never pressed her for more information. Most likely she couldn't have answered appropriately anyway. She was too busy concentrating on not leaning into his side. Not giving in to the relief snaking through her with Chase beside her. Not letting herself weave her fingers around his and hold on as if he was suddenly her anchor. That was all kinds of foolishness for someone as levelheaded as her.

Nichole greeted the hostess for the restaurant and followed the woman toward a private dining room. Two men wearing black suits and ties rose and stepped around a square table. Floor-to-ceiling wine shelves encased in glass made up two walls. The other two were lined in cork for an intimate setting. A setting for business deals, tough negotiations or romantic interludes. Nichole's four-inch heels failed to stiffen her spine.

"You look really good, by the way." Chase's voice whispered across her neck. "Powerful and in charge."

Nichole offered a quick nod. His hand dropped onto her lower back and propelled her forward. When had she stopped walking? She inhaled a deep breath of Chase's spicy cologne, which scattered her already short-circuiting focus.

The executives she only knew by name after several emails and two phone calls came forward. Neither one bothered to hide their excitement that an all-pro football player stood before them. She had to make this happen. It was now or never for her business deal.

Nichole stepped slightly in front of Chase and blurted, "Gentlemen, I'd like to introduce you to my husband, Chase Jacobs."

CHAPTER FIVE

My husband.

Nichole's matter-of-fact words slammed inside Chase's head like a helmet-to-helmet hit. He waited for the ref's whistle. The shrill sound that would disrupt the momentum and pause the moment.

Two gentlemen in coordinated business suits stepped forward, hands outstretched in greeting, smiles restrained by the boundaries of professional politeness.

Time continued to run down. No one called an audible. No one changed the play—the one that called for a pretend marriage. The moment never paused.

"Congratulations. I'm Vick Ingram." Vick, the stockier of the duo, his midsection relaxed by more than one good meal, shook Nichole's hand. "Pleasure to meet you and your new husband." Vick turned to Chase. Speculation added dimension to the man's plain brown gaze. "Offensive player of the year three seasons straight, four-time Pro

Bowler and more than three hundred and fifty touchdowns. That's quite a career."

"The news of your sudden marriage is quite big too. I'm Glenn Hill." The knot on Glenn's tie was one tug away from sloppy. The unfastened top button of his dress shirt signaled his lack of effort with his attire. As if he wasn't serious about this particular meeting.

"It's a recent development." Nichole's words rushed out.

So recent, Chase hadn't been aware marriage vows were part of the favor owed.

"We're still adjusting to our new status," Nichole rambled on. "There's a lot of details to be worked out."

So many details that they'd need a lengthy one-on-one conversation to hash through them all.

Vick's grin appeared genuine. "Love can be a whirlwind."

Or a complete hoax.

"But it also makes for the best headlines." Glenn rubbed his hands together. "It's surprising I haven't read about the sport's favorite playboy bachelor finally getting hitched. You're one of the internet's favorite topics."

The best headlines were often the most lucrative. Chase wondered about the guy and straightened into his full height.

"Vick and Glenn are senior partners in Fund Infusion." Nichole shifted toward Chase. "Their firm has offered to invest in the app I designed and built."

So much hope swirled in Nichole's hazel gaze. Too much. She trusted these two men with her dream. *Why?* Chase trusted these men about as much as he trusted any defensive player to tag him rather than tackle him during a game. In other words, *not at all.* Concern, not confidence, stiffened his shoulders.

"Aren't you going to share the details of your wedding?" Glenn adjusted his tie as if their wedding news was more than worth his full consideration. "I'd love to know. After all, we're friends."

Friends. Not exactly. Chase wrapped his arm around Nichole, tucked her into his side. "We'd like to keep this affair private. As friends, I'm sure we can count on your discretion until we've made a public announcement."

"Of course." Vick's gaze slanted sideways toward his business partner, making the assurance in his words all the more suspect.

"If you change your mind, we're more than interested in hearing a good love story."

Glenn's smirk was obvious despite the mustache covering his entire top lip.

"Perhaps you'd also be interested in reviewing the business plan I put together." Nichole's crisp professionalism was clear, but the underlying plea caught Chase off guard.

That wasn't a challenge. That was a dropped ball on what should've been a touchdown scoring pass. Chase glanced at Nichole.

Chase Jacobs, you're a cheater.

Yes, I am.

That admission had rocked Nichole's bluster, but she'd never wavered. Never walked away.

Where was the Nichole who'd always challenged Chase's motives and his integrity? She looked like the slightest nudge would topple her over. He secured his hold around her waist and his guard.

"Now that you've married Chase Jacobs, you could simply give your program away for free." Glenn's mustache twitched, revealing his smirk again.

Chase smoothed out his smile. The man had dismissed Nichole's program. Dismissed Nichole. Surely Nichole noticed that slight. Surely Nichole would challenge Glenn now.

"I did not marry Chase for his money." Although the sudden lost thread in her voice hinted at her uncertainty.

Chase searched Nichole's face. What *would* motivate someone like Nichole Moore to marry someone like Chase? He blinked. Definitely not the topic for this evening. But the question stuck inside him like a clump of grass smashed into his face guard. An unavoidable nuisance and difficult to remove.

The doubt and worry lingering in Nichole's gaze reinforced his conviction. For the first time in far too long, Chase wanted to rescue someone other than himself.

Chase took Nichole's hand and pressed a kiss against her knuckles. Color tinged her cheeks, faint and all too charming. The longer she held Chase's gaze, the less put out she looked. Satisfaction pulsed inside him. "Money was certainly my motivation for marrying Nichole. She's my retirement plan."

"Then we should discuss your wife's program and the potential for it to be a profitable retirement plan over a fantastic meal." Vick's good-humored laughter rolled around them, ushering them to the dinner table.

"If I recall correctly, you were quoted comparing the Hail Mary pass to marriage." Glenn dropped into the chair across from Chase, stirred an olive around in his glass and eyed him. "You claimed both had the same success rate—very low."

Chase recalled that particular interview. He still believed marriage and Hail Mary passes were similar in that both failed more often than not. But his views had no impact on his fake marriage. He treated Glenn like any other dogged reporter and neither confirmed nor denied.

"You've never thrown a Hail Mary pass. You've said it isn't part of your game plan." Glenn combed his fingers through his mustache. "Now you have to adjust your outlandish off-field lifestyle to include a wife. How will that work?"

No adjustments required. Fake was fake. And his fake marriage dissolved at the end of the evening. There'd be no glass slipper, no hint that a fantasy would turn into real life. Marriage appealed to him as much as a borrowed helmet. Neither were a good fit. Both disrupted his focus and detracted him from success on the football field.

Still, Chase was adjusting remarkably well to his sudden, albeit temporary, role as husband. Every word Glenn spoke honed Chase's protective edge. He scooted his chair closer to Nichole and rested his arm on the back of

Nichole's. "As with any new team you learn as you go."

And he was quickly learning how much he liked being close to Nichole.

"Let's order!" Vick handed out the menus. He lacked the yellow flag to signal an offside penalty but maintained the professional poise of a seasoned ref. "What appetizers would everyone enjoy?"

Glenn folded his hands together on top of his closed menu and studied Nichole. "Ms. Moore, or rather Mrs. Jacobs, about that business plan?"

"Nichole is fine." Nichole lowered her menu and reached into her bulky tote bag on the floor, pulling out a binder. "I understand an app is not a business. However, the plan includes market analysis, financial projections and a full marketing strategy."

"Nichole has created something of value, or we wouldn't be here." Chase intercepted the binder before it reached either Vick or Glen. "I'd like to know what value your firm brings to it and to her vision."

"Fund Infusion has offered to fully fund the last round of my program revisions." Nichole's hand landed on Chase's arm. A warning infused her words, tempering her tone.

"Is that all?" Chase countered. He could fund that much, although she hadn't asked him.

Vick spoke up. "We believe we will have a strong and fair offer for your consideration, if Nichole presents us with the information we require."

"What more would you like to know?" Nichole tugged the binder from Chase's grip and passed it across the table.

That eagerness was back in her tone. Where was the skeptic who'd always intrigued him? Nichole used to question everything. She'd even made Chase list ten facts to prove the homecoming dance was worth her time. He'd failed to convince her. She'd claimed numbers six through ten had been feelings, not facts. She had always insisted he was illogical because he'd relied on his emotions and gut instinct. *Be rational, Chase. You can't know you'll like skydiving simply because it looks fun on TV.*

Well, he did like skydiving. And he distrusted Glenn from only one unfastened button and the kink in his own gut. She'd called him in to stand beside her and he'd do his part. "Call me old-fashioned, gentlemen, but I never do a deal with anyone until I know what those folks are about."

Menus studied and orders placed: three surf and turfs and one petit filet, Chase eyed Glenn and then Vick.

"I prefer my steaks rare and my drinks cold." Glenn smoothed his hand over his tie, loosening the knot even more, as if talking about himself was his favorite pastime. "As for the business, it's simple. I started Fund Infusion to prove to my father I was better than him."

"And did you?" Chase asked.

"Within the first year." Glenn sipped his drink as if he'd given himself a private toast. "Now my legacy is ensured."

Chase added cutthroat to his description of the man. Nichole would claim that wasn't a strong enough reason not to let the guy invest in her business. Maybe it wasn't, but it still didn't speak well of the man across from him.

"I intend for *In a Pinch* to be my legacy. I've devised a go-to market strategy in Section Four." Nichole tipped her chin toward the binder, pointing excitedly. "I've collected over two thousand test users and identified their preferences and needs. The local vendor list is expanding daily. I've also pinpointed competitors and highlighted their weaknesses. I have an aggressive growth plan that includes launching in several key metro areas prior to going nationwide."

Nichole's strategy impressed Chase the same way he appreciated a good play call by the opposing team. Good or not, Nichole just revealed too much of her game. Coaches called plays from behind laminated paper to avoid giving their opponents an advantage.

Chase grabbed her hand, drawing her attention and pausing her presentation. Advantage: Chase. "I'd like to know what their next steps are before you give them your full proposal."

Glenn placed his palm on the binder. "The first thing we'll do is review your wife's business plan and determine if it's even viable."

"Of course, it's viable." Nichole had written it. Irritation snapped inside Chase, tweaking his frown into a scowl. "You don't think you're the only ones interested in my wife's app, do you?"

Nichole cleared her throat.

"They should know they're only the first to the table. Not the first to show interest." Chase squeezed Nichole's hand. "If you have a go-to-market strategy in place for my wife's program, then we have something to discuss."

Their food arrived, forcing another pause in the conversation.

Vick fumbled with his lobster cracker. Glenn dipped a piece of mangled lobster into the small dish of melted butter and dripped onto Nichole's binder. The disregard grated on Chase. He wanted that binder. Wanted these two vetted. Even more, he wanted the evening with them concluded.

"Let's talk about next steps." Vick sounded as if he were placating. "Once we review the material, we'll meet with our investors to discuss our offer and contract terms."

Chase's first step was easy. He leaned across the table, picked up the binder and set it out of Glenn's grasp. His next step: he'd find someone to research Fund Infusion and determine if they were a legitimate company or not.

"This is great." Nichole's optimism seemed infectious. Chase wished he could get on board. "You're serious about making an offer for *In A Pinch* and launching it nationwide. I'm satisfied."

Vick lifted his glass, but his smile never quite reached his gaze. "To a successful partnership."

"I left nothing behind." Glenn rubbed his stomach, his voice mellowed, his eyelids halfway closed. "Now that the business is out of the way, you can tell us how you two met."

Clearly Glenn's full stomach hadn't dulled his quest for a possible lucrative news story.

"We've known each other for quite a while," Nichole said softly. Her head dipped and she took a quick gulp of her wine.

"Since high school." Chase wrapped her hand in his. He held on to her, his easygoing tone and his lie. "She sat behind me and copied off my biology quizzes freshman year."

Nichole's nervous laughter registered with him as she tapped her shoulder into Chase. The same way she'd used to bump him during their tutoring sessions to get him to concentrate on his schoolwork, rather than memorizing offensive plays.

They both knew the real story. Chase had sat behind Nichole and attempted to copy off her biology exams freshman year. One day she'd confronted him outside the locker room on his way to practice. *You can't want to be a cheater. No one wants to be a cheater.* If it hadn't been her tests, he'd have copied off someone else in their biology class. *Good luck passing biology by using anyone else's work.* Frustrated and desperate, Chase had issued a challenge: *You have a better idea?* With hands on her hips, she'd stared him down. *Yes.*

Nichole had never faltered. Certainty and

confidence sang in her voice and her unwavering gaze. *I'll be your tutor. No one needs to know.*

That had sealed their relationship. First, she'd been his tutor. Then his friend and confidante. But never more. He'd never considered more until he sat beside her, pretending to be her husband.

"My wife and I met in grade school." Vick touched his wedding ring, sounding wistful. "There's something about first loves you can't ignore. I'm going on thirty-four years with my true love."

"I'm currently between wives." Glenn stared into his empty glass.

"Glenn might be taking a hiatus on love, but we can toast." Vick lifted his glass over the center of the table. "To first loves and your new journey together."

Nichole and Chase's journey had nothing to do with love: true love or first love. And everything to do with favors owed to an old friend. The evening had even been enjoyable. Ironic, since he'd spent the entire night sitting in a chair, not seeking the next adrenaline rush. Chase tapped his glass against Vick's. "To love."

Nichole gripped her wineglass, offered a whisper-soft clink against the others with no more force than an air kiss. Her smile wobbled. "To…"

Her sentence died.

Instead, she shoved her chair away from the table. "If you'll excuse me."

She rose and spun around in one swift movement. Too swift. Her momentum carried her right into the waiter. The one holding a very full pitcher of ice water.

Chase reached out. The collision unfolded like a slow-motion instant replay. Fortunately, most of the ice water sloshed onto the floor. Nichole stumbled backward into Chase's arms. Into his lap. Finally, the evening felt completely right.

Chase curved his arms tighter around Nichole's waist and followed his gut. Lowering his head, he caught her next startled gasp with his lips. Then he kissed her until his own gasp claimed him.

Across the table, Vick's laughter spilled through his words. "I think we'll take the check and skip dessert."

CHAPTER SIX

CHASE IGNORED HIS MANNERS. Swerved around common sense. Gave in to instinct and extended their kiss into something that they were no longer pretending. The type of kiss that he'd definitely share with his wife.

Too soon, Nichole broke away. She blinked slow and steady as if clearing the mist from her fog-filled senses. A deep blush seared from her chest to her face. Chase kept his arms around her, seeking his own balance. He'd replay that moment in slow detail later.

The waiter placed a bottle of champagne and two glasses with strawberries resting on the rims on the table. Added a quick whispered explanation: courtesy of the gentlemen who had just left, before he disappeared again.

Just like that, the private dining room became even more private.

Nichole scrambled off Chase's lap, dropped into the chair beside him and latched on to her binder like it was the elephant in the room. "They forgot my business plan."

"You can email the information." *Then kiss me again as if we really were newlyweds.* Chase scrambled away from his own thoughts, wanting to call a false start penalty on himself.

Newlyweds implied a shared connection. A connection that went deeper than appearances, first names and conversations about the weather. Newlyweds promised each other a future together. Newlyweds trusted each other to fulfill that promise.

There would be no more kissing. And apparently no more protecting Nichole from the duo. Frustration over the kiss and his safeguarding had to come to an end. Or perhaps it was the floundering feeling that he'd been seconds away from something astounding, only to find himself sacked one yard from the goal line.

Nichole secured the binder in her bag. Her hands fluttered over the dessert menu. She looked everywhere, except at Chase. Her foot tapped a restless beat against the hardwood floor. Chase shifted his focus to where it belonged: her business deal. "I wouldn't send anything to those guys until they sign an agreement."

"What kind of agreement?" Her fingers stilled on the menu. Her foot slowed.

"The kind that says Fund Infusion won't talk about your idea or steal your program." Nichole and Chase needed an agreement too. Or at the very least an understanding about exactly when his fake husband duties officially ended. Everything had to end.

"You're talking about an NDA." Relief flowed through her words and her shoulders lowered. "I already signed one."

"But did they?" Would she want him as a fake husband for much longer? He couldn't continue their ruse. It was wrong. And yet, like most of his bad ideas, this one had appeal. Too much appeal.

"I never requested they sign one. That was stupid. I'm glad you're here."

What more could he do for her? He was a football player, not a lawyer. Thanks to a long-standing battle with dyslexia, he most likely couldn't get through the first page of her potential contract. People were depending upon her to make smart choices. She deserved a more qualified fake husband. Yet for a fake wife, Nichole was perfect. He should definitely end things here. "So, about this marriage thing?"

"I'm so sorry." Nichole covered her face with her hands. "I panicked and it came out."

"I panicked too when you landed on my lap." Chase chuckled, bringing the conversation back to the light and easy like he preferred. Like people expected from him. "Beautiful woman...heat of the moment... hot kiss."

He bypassed an apology. He wouldn't have been sincere. There was something special about their kiss. The first contact had spiked through him and a different sort of adrenaline rush had overtaken him. He wanted another hit. Still, he should explain.

A variety of red shades colored her cheeks and stained her neck. He wanted to trace his fingers over her skin, discover if her pulse raced as fast as his. His gaze locked on to her hands, the ones blocking his view of her mouth. The temptation to kiss her bypassed his common sense.

He'd earned his reputation for misbehaving over years. Although he'd been well-behaved most of the evening. He couldn't change his entire personality overnight. One more kiss between friends. In private. No one had to know. Surely that would end his sudden fascination with Nichole Moore.

"We should let the marriage stand." *Time*

out. That was completely wrong. However, the idea felt right. The same way a football had always fit naturally in his hand.

"You aren't serious." Nichole gaped at him.

"Maybe." He shrugged.

A pretend wife, specifically one like the stable and steady Nichole Moore, had merit like a trick play on a fourth down and one yard at the goal line. Certainly, a wife like Nichole would help polish his tarnished reputation. The very reputation the Pioneers' staff and his agent had insisted he repair. Immediately.

Fortunately, her common sense remained intact. She shook her head. "Of course, you're not serious. You're never serious about anything."

"I'm very serious about football." And saving his career any way he could. He grabbed her hand and his decision. "And this."

"You can't be." She tugged her hand free in disbelief.

"It makes sense." Except for the list of potential drawbacks, including possibly hurting her reputation. Asking her to lie. Wanting to kiss her again.

Chase abandoned his list of cons and moved closer to Nichole. The connection settled him. "You said yourself you're glad I'm here. Well, I can be right beside you until you sign your contract with Vick and Glenn."

Could he repair his reputation, save his career, help Nichole and keep her in the friend-zone? She had to stay where she couldn't distract him, and he couldn't hurt her. But this was such a bad idea.

"You want to remain my husband." Nichole's eyebrows raised, her mouth pursed.

She was the only one who had ever ignored his charm and always expected more from him. She'd never let him off easy. He'd missed her. He pile-drove that realization beneath the con list, regained the breath trying to hitch inside his chest and raced down the path of no return. "I have my own contract negotiations going on."

"You cannot believe a fake marriage will help." Nichole's voice ratcheted from disbelief to full-blown skepticism.

This was the Nichole he knew. The one who'd always guided back him back to the right path. The one who'd held him to a higher standard. The one who'd let him devise his schemes in full detail and had squashed them. Soon she'd force him to see the error of his ways and present a better option.

"Absolutely. I need a reputation overhaul." He relaxed into the smile he always relied on and warmed to his scheme. Secure in the knowledge that Nichole would never agree. "You said it yourself. I'm never serious about anything. Married men are settled, dull and disillusioned. I definitely don't ever want to be actually married."

"This is a bad idea." Nichole put a hand to her forehead.

"It's only short-term," Chase assured her. Perhaps if his father had told his mother the very same thing—that his wedding vows had an expiration date, his mother wouldn't have been so hurt and devastated when his father had left. "Until contracts are finalized and signed. Then we break up."

"We claim our lives are going in two separate directions, file for a pretend divorce citing irreconcilable differences." Nichole paused as if sorting the details out inside her head. "That's what all those celebrities do and then they go their separate ways. Everyone's happy."

Chase's mouth dropped open. Nichole had never contributed to one of his schemes before. *Never.* "We couldn't tell anyone the truth. No one."

"Of course not." Nichole frowned at her glass of champagne. "Not even our families."

She'd never liked lying. And this scheme

required they lie to the ones they loved the most. This couldn't be happening.

"We only tell the people we need to about our marriage." She nodded. Her voice gaining strength. "We ask for their discretion like we did with Glenn and Vick."

"You do remember that I always come up with horrible schemes." Like when he'd decided to cheat off her test in biology.

"Is it so horrible if my app sells and your contract gets renewed?" Nichole dropped a strawberry in her glass of champagne as if preparing to celebrate. "Is it so horrible if we both get what we want?"

His gaze tracked back to Nichole's face. He could want… Talk about bad ideas. "I'm asking you to lie to save my career." That was all kinds of wrong. And still he never called a time-out.

"I created the whole lie in the first place." She dunked another strawberry into the glass as if searching for clarity in the bubbling liquid. "I started this."

He took both of her hands. "So, we decide together how we finish it?"

"I want my dream, Chase." She squeezed his hands.

I want my dream. I deserve it. He'd confessed that to Nichole after he'd told her about his dyslexia and his struggle to pass his classes. She'd looked him in the eye, conviction in her voice. *Then you'll have it. But only if we do things the right way. My way.* "Shouldn't you be telling me this is a bad idea? That it's wrong to deceive people to get what we want."

"It is a really bad idea." Her gaze fastened on his. Direct and probing. "But I know the kind of man you are."

"What kind is that?"

"The kind who doesn't want a partner. The kind who doesn't trust in commitment." Her intent gaze skimmed over his face. "The one who doesn't believe love conquers all."

She was right. He was selfish. Relied on himself. Loved his job more than anything or anyone else. Her accusation hit more precisely than a targeted sack from an opponent. Chase rubbed his chest, hoping to loosen the airflow and tease her into seeing just how bad an idea this was. "How is that a good thing?"

"I'm the same kind of woman. This is only a business arrangement between old friends." She released his hands. "We aren't deceiving ourselves. Love, promises and vows aren't involved. We won't walk away brokenhearted." She picked up her champagne glass, her tone earnest. "We'll walk away with everything we wanted."

Not everything. He wanted to kiss her again. Another bad idea.

She tipped her champagne glass at him. "Also, we are not making any kind of public announcement."

He knew the media. A mediocre reporter could figure out who had attended a private party from the take-out containers located in the trash. Chase could promise only so much, but nothing more. "There won't be a press release."

"So, no public announcement." She counted off the details on her fingers as if bad decisions were always made with logic and not haste. "We tell only the people we absolutely must that we're married. We close the deal with Fund Infusion. Get your contract renewed. Then end our marriage."

Simple. Less than a handful of steps. But the details... Those complicated everything. "You don't like to take risks."

"I have to take this one." Her expression was sincere and serious. "This is for my family."

He'd do anything for his family too. Chase ran his hands over his face. His family had considered Nichole one of their own in high school. Claimed her as part of the Jacobs family. He held out his hand. "Do we have a deal then?"

She set her hand in his. "We're in a business arrangement."

"We've been friends too long to ink our fake marriage with a handshake." And because he'd always been a risk-taker, he stood and pulled her toward him. "Let's seal the deal correctly?"

His arms wrapped around her waist. He leaned forward, chasing that hint of an adrenaline rush. Her eyes closed, her long eyelashes fanned across her tinted cheeks. Her face softened. Suddenly risk averse, Chase used a successful hook route, shifting at the last second to press his lips against her forehead.

A reminder to himself their marriage was only a sham. Hearts were not included in any deal. And all adrenaline rushes were best avoided.

CHAPTER SEVEN

"You're married!" Brooke shoved the door to the Rose Petal Boutique closed. She scowled and pointed at the large stain on the front of her cream-colored sweater. "Nichole, you owe me a new sweater, too, besides an explanation."

Her friend's accusations jarred Nichole into fully alert mode better than a triple espresso shot. Nichole stumbled beside Josie and spun around to face Brooke. She stammered, "Wh-what?"

"We're clearly late for more than the photo shoot this morning." Josie clutched Nichole's hand and tugged her toward the back of the bridal salon. "Brooke! Get back here. We'll have to walk and talk."

"Does no one want to know how this all happened?" Outrage shifted through Brooke's voice.

"No time." Josie pulled Nichole past the vintage couch reserved for the bride's family and friends, plowing toward the dressing room. "Mia is waiting for us at the cathedral and we're already late."

"But it's all over the news." Brooke rushed after them.

Nichole swiped several chocolates from the candy dish on the side table. *No public announcement. We'll only tell the people we need to.* The internet hadn't been included in the need to know category. Chase had promised. A dull ache pounded behind Nichole's eyes. She fumbled with a candy wrapper. "It can't be."

"Too late for that now." Josie picked up the candy bowl and thrust it at Brooke, then grimaced at Nichole. "You need clean hands."

"Desperate times." Nichole unwrapped two candies, popped them in her mouth and offered Josie a regretful shrug.

Brooke stomped a foot like a frustrated five-year-old. "I dropped Wesley and Ben off at school this morning. We had an excellent sleepover. Dan lost every game we played last night. Then I got my usual coffee. Opened the news on my phone and voilà. Dumped said coffee all over myself." Brooke pinched her stained sweater away from her stomach. "Then I rushed over here."

"It's a good thing too. We need your hands, Brooke." Josie unwrapped Nichole's scarf and tossed it on the couch. "We're getting later by the minute. Mia can only wait so long. She's doing me a huge favor this morning as it is."

"As long as I get all the wedding details." Brooke arched one eyebrow.

Details. Nichole lunged for the candy dish and swiped a handful before Brooke jumped out of reach. Nichole unwrapped several, shoved the chocolates in her mouth and waited for the melting sensation. Something to knock back the dread thumping in her chest.

Josie unzipped Nichole's hoodie and gaped at her. "You're wearing a neon pink sports bra. You can't wear a sports bra under a wedding gown."

Brooke looked on aghast. "Please, tell me you didn't wear a sports bra last night to your own wedding!"

Exposed. Nichole added another candy to her mouth. No sensible bride wore a neon pink sports bra. Nothing about last night had been sensible.

"I...uh..." Josie snatched the candy dish from Brooke as if she could no longer be trusted.

"Has no one been listening?" Brooke raised both of her arms over her head. "It's in the news."

"Explain while you change, Nichole." Josie urged Nichole into the dressing room.

Nichole swiped more chocolates on her way past Josie.

"We have to hurry." Josie motioned. *"Hurry."*

Nichole had to hurry and find a cover story. She shoved more candy in her mouth. Now she had to lie to her friends half-dressed in a sports bra.

"Mia is only free for an hour this morning." Josie scooped the rest of the chocolates from Nichole's palm, dropped them back into the bowl she set on the bench and pressed a wet wipe into Nichole's hand. "You'll have to ditch the bra."

That was the least of Nichole's concerns. Nichole shoved four more candies in her mouth.

Josie reached for Nichole's waist. "Brooke, grab the first gown on the rack."

"What about her marriage," Brooke shouted from the workroom.

"Stop yelling at me." Nichole brushed Josie's hands away, yanked off her boots and leggings, then launched herself at the candy bowl as if one more bite would mean an escape to candy land. "You guys were encouraging me to find romance. So, I did."

Josie swept the candy dish out of the dressing room and Nichole's reach. The designer returned with the entire container of wet wipes. Nichole lifted her hands for Josie's inspection. Her hands were clean. She couldn't claim the same about her conscience.

"Overnight?" Brooke carried an exquisite gown into the dressing room. The crystals on the high halter neckline flashed. The beading on the fitted gown shimmered against the ivory silk. Beautiful, intricate hand embroidery covered the entire dress like shared love letters.

Nichole and Chase shared a secret. "You always accuse me of being too predictable." Her words came out quickly as if she was already in the midst of a full-scale sugar rush. *Impossible.* "Come on. Get me in the dress already."

"Who did she marry?" Josie unzipped the back of the wedding dress.

"Chase Jacobs." Brooke beamed.

Josie gaped. "The Pioneers' quarterback."

"It's not that improbable," Nichole shot back, wished for another chocolate to stall her next words and stepped into the gown. She had said "I do" to a business arrangement. A fake marriage agreement. Her heart raced.

"Of course not." Josie guided the beaded

and crystal straps over each of Nichole's shoulders, then looked at Nichole. Regret in her small smile. "I'm sorry. It's just you're *you* and he's *him*."

"I'm quiet, dull and averse to risk." The chocolate had completely dissolved in Nichole's mouth. Her voice sounded dehydrated as if she'd chewed on desert sand. "He's charismatic, handsome, adventurous and a favorite in the press."

"You're accomplished, intelligent and beautiful." Josie fastened the clasps for the high neck and adjusted the crystal straps across Nichole's bare back. "And the absolute best single mom I know."

Nichole met Josie's gaze. Deception nauseated her. Shouldn't her friends notice her pale skin? Damp palms? Certainly, they recognized she lacked the blissful spirit of a new bride. "Thanks."

"And Chase Jacobs is…" Brooke's voice trailed off.

"My husband." Her marriage was a fraud. A small misspoken phrase had turned into something that now entailed consequences. Consequences she'd face later. "What can I say? Opposites attract."

"So, we all must keep walking and talking. This conversation is too good to stop now."

Josie wrapped a plush shawl around Nichole's shoulders and handed her a pair of fur-lined white boots. "Put these on."

Nichole shoved her bare feet into her fleece-lined boots, searching for warmth and balance. "How do I look?"

"You look amazing." Brooke turned Nichole to face the mirror. "Just like a bride."

She recognized the woman in the mirror from her youth when she'd envisioned being a bride gliding toward her once-in-a-lifetime love. She'd never imagined a gown quite so enchanting, as if she'd stepped into her own fairy tale. Nichole's breath caught. She hadn't lost her breath ever. Not until last night when Chase had kissed her breathless.

"You look better than any professional model ever would." Josie hugged Nichole. It was the kind of hug shared between two close friends. The kind of hug that only made Nichole's deception cut deeper. Josie added, "Now it's time to go. Walk fast, talk faster and don't leave anything out."

The truth supposedly set people free. Or ruined dreams. Nichole exhaled around the guilt and spilled what she could. "Chase and I went to high school together. We reconnected last night."

Brooke set Nichole's phone in her hand and tugged Nichole off the platform.

Josie handed several garment bags to Brooke, added two pairs of strappy heels to a tote bag with her supplies. "Before or after your business dinner?"

"Before." Nichole hurried toward the entrance. "He stayed through dinner and we celebrated afterward."

"All the way to the altar in…" Brooke stepped outside to prop open the door with her foot.

"Reno," Nichole blurted. "At the Hearts Forever Chapel."

"What about flowers?" Brooke asked.

"Mia has a bouquet for Nichole." Josie locked the door. "But what did you carry last night?"

"I had Chase's hand to hold. That was enough." The chocolate clumped together in her stomach. "Besides, the chapel provided a lovely rose bouquet."

"That you brought home to preserve." Josie pointed through the boutique window at the display on her wall. The one showcasing a collection of preserved bouquets in resin paperweights and heart frames, handcrafted by a local artist.

"Of course." The lies backed up in Nichole's throat, quickly working to outnumber the chocolates she'd consumed. "That's what all good brides do."

"Good brides tell their friends they're getting married," Brooke challenged. "Ask their friends to serve as witnesses."

"It all happened so fast." Nichole clenched her phone and adjusted her shawl. "A conversation. A kiss. A wedding."

Brooke brushed her fingers across the back of Nichole's hand. "Where's your ring?"

"Did you miss the part about it happening fast?" Nichole searched the crosswalk for potholes. For more stumbling opportunities. The only fracture was in her rationale for a fake marriage. "There wasn't time to even pick one out."

"Maybe he'll surprise you with one." A sigh wove into Josie's voice as if she bought into the make-believe romance.

Not likely. Chase had already been surprised enough after her outburst last night.

Three blocks later, Brooke hurried through the park gates and hollered to Mia. "I confirmed it. It's her."

Mia lowered her camera, cheered and pointed at the cathedral. "I'll get the details later. Take Nichole up to the top of the cathedral stairs."

"Confirmed what?" Nichole hiked up the dress and lengthened her steps on the wide staircase.

"That you were the one in the photograph on the internet." Brooke matched her pace. "I showed the picture to Mia on my way to the boutique."

"What photograph?" No one at the table had taken any pictures. But the staff could have. *Consequences.* Nichole had to accept those. Make her choices work in her favor, not against her.

"The one of you sitting on Chase Jacobs's lap." Delight filled Brooke's voice. "I couldn't believe the headline and then I saw that hot kiss you two shared."

Everything scrambled inside Nichole's brain like a multiple car pileup on the fog-covered interstate. Logic became lost.

"That kiss was…" *Surprising. Nice.* More than nice. Nichole stopped at the top of the stairs. It was a kiss shared between a couple. Or even a bride and groom. Nichole declared a chocolate hiatus.

"The press only called you Chase Jacobs's new wife." Brooke helped Josie pin a cathedral-length veil in Nichole's hair.

"What?" Nichole could've denied it was her this whole time.

"It's not the clearest picture." Brooke picked up her phone and tapped on the screen. Josie peered over her shoulder.

Nichole shook her head and grabbed her own phone. She typed a text to Chase in all capital letters: CHECK THE NEWS. NOW. She hit Send. She glanced at her friends. "How did you know it was me?"

"We helped you pick that outfit." Brooke high-fived Josie, rambling about everything being meant to be.

Nothing but potential disaster felt meant to be to Nichole. She had to come clean to her friends. To Fund Infusion. Find another way to help Chase.

Nichole's phone lit up, signaling a text. She read Chase's recent reply: What about the news?

Do you check the news?

Not until after my workout, breakfast and physical therapy. Maybe after lunch. Sometimes not at all.

Now his replies came in real time as if she'd finally garnered his full attention. Nichole typed: Why not?

It's depressing.

Make an exception. Then text me back.

"Now you get to kiss Chase whenever you want." Brooke lifted her eyebrows up and down.

Did Nichole want to kiss Chase again? *Maybe.* That sugar rush spiked through her blood. *Yes.* She did. But one kiss led to another and another. Then hearts cartwheeled around chests, and emotions like stardust were sprinkled over the clouds. And she'd start to believe she walked on those clouds. But hearts broke, and those pieces had to fall to the ground sometime. "I have to concentrate on closing my business deal."

"What's more fun than mixing business and pleasure?" Brooke helped Josie drape the long veil down the staircase.

But Brooke was in love with Dan Sawyer—the soul-consuming, forever kind of love. Josie and Brooke had misinterpreted Chase and Nichole's kiss. The fallout from being so in love was misreading other situations. The lovestruck saw love in everything, even a spur-of-the-moment kiss. Besides, Nichole had added a dose of deception too. And that was never a good thing.

Nichole glared at her phone and Chase's response:

You can't boss me around. We're not really married.

She replied. Once again in all caps:

THAT'S NOT WHAT THE PRESS CLAIMS.

"Nichole, you're beautiful." Mia hurried toward Nichole. The smile on her face matched the delight in her voice. She handed Nichole a tall bouquet of calla lilies in white and deep purple. "It's as if Josie created this gown specifically for you."

Josie touched the tip of a lily. "It's better than I could've imagined."

"You're like a real bride, Nichole." Brooke sighed into her hands. "How does it feel?"

Head-spinning. Dizzying. Nauseating. "Thrilling," she said. She'd disappoint her friends soon. But not now. "Let's get started."

"Give me a minute to get my equipment set, then put your phone away." Mia skipped down the stairs. Josie and Brooke moved to the side.

Nichole checked her phone and curled her toes in her boots. Chase had watched the news. He'd sent six texts with different versions of call me. The last one:

Why aren't you calling me?

Nichole grinned.

You're too bossy.

This is serious.

Yes. And you need to fix it.

Call me. Please.

Can't right now. I'm in a photo shoot.

What? Never mind. Where are you?

Nichole sent Chase the address, clutched the bouquet and tossed her phone to Brooke.

One round of photographs finished, Nichole waited on the cathedral steps for Josie. She'd gone inside to ask if they could use the restroom for Nichole to change into the next gown. Brooke stood beside Mia and looked over the photographs on Mia's camera. Morning yoga attendees and several dog walkers paused to admire Nichole and her wedding attire. Several spoke to Mia and asked for Josie's business card.

A movement near the side entry of the church caught her attention. Chase rounded the corner, holding his phone, wearing a crisp, well-tailored suit. He spotted her and his mouth dropped open. His steps picked up until he stood within bouquet-tossing distance.

"You look stunning." His appreciative gaze drifted from her head to her feet and back up again.

Stunning. No one had ever called Nichole stunning. Would Chase tell his real bride-to-be she was stunning? With the same awed wonder in his gaze? The same admiration in his voice? She'd never felt stunning until right now with Chase. She wanted to believe him. But so much was already pretend. And Chase excelled at the charade.

Nichole eyed him.

"Don't you think you're taking this fake marriage a bit too far?" he quipped, obviously amused. He tilted his head and propped his usual grin back into place.

Nichole pulled back. His grin blocked people out, including her. "It's for Josie. She owns the Rose Petal Boutique. Her model… Never mind." Nichole held out her hand, the one holding the calla lily bouquet, for Chase to help her up the stairs. She wanted to confront him eye to eye.

He tugged a little harder than necessary. Nichole swayed on her borrowed heels. The momentum carried her into Chase. She pressed her other palm against his lapel, stopping full body contact. Her heart collided against her ribs. But a worse wreck, like heartbreak, waited ahead if she started to believe her own press. "Why are you in a suit?"

His grin never slipped. "I have a photo shoot for the city's athlete of the year award."

"Congratulations. You look good." Handsome even. Nichole curved her fingers into the soft wool fabric. "We have to come clean. Admit we aren't married."

"The media got the marriage piece, but not your identity." Chase covered her hand with his, drawing her gaze to his face. "We have time."

"Time for what?"

His grip tightened around her fingers. "Time to tell our families."

"You mean tell them the truth." Nichole clenched his hand to ensure he heard her. "That this is all one big mistake. A hoax."

Chase accepted her grip yet never tapped

out. "We tell them we're married like we agreed last night."

"That was before the media blitz." Nichole smoothed her voice into patient and reasonable, the same tone she'd used to negotiate with her preteen son. "They'll figure out who I am. It's the right thing to do."

Nichole tried to adjust her grip on Chase's other hand. The bouquet interfered. The tall flowers reached between them as if growing from their joined hands.

Chase rubbed his chin. His gaze drifted over Nichole again, intense and mysterious.

She'd never trusted mysterious. Mysterious allowed for too many possible theories. Too many different assumptions. Too many opportunities to get hurt. She'd been drawn in by an enigmatic man once before and believed she'd known him. She had a broken heart to prove how completely wrong she'd been.

"You can't see your face in that photo." He reached up and pushed the veil over her shoulder.

His fingers never connected with her skin. His caress never fell against her arm. Still her breath caught and held as if waiting. Waiting for his touch and the warmth she knew would be there. A swarm of butterflies collided in her stomach as if lost. An insistent whisper of *what if* echoed inside her. "You seriously want to keep up this farce?"

"I got you something." Chase reached into his pocket, pulled out a ring.

Not any simple ring either. Sparkling diamonds filled the platinum band that swirled like a halo around a large brilliant center diamond. The ring was vintage, stylish and flawless.

The sigh from her heart skimmed over her. That butterfly swarm flapped its collective wings. Her voice shook. "Now who's taking this fake marriage thing a little too far?"

Chase slipped the elegant ring over her finger. "Now everything looks real."

Nichole pressed her hand below her ribs, silencing those artificial butterflies. Today was make-believe. Just as her childhood dreams had proven to be nothing more than fantasies. Her gaze fixed on the ring. "It's gorgeous. Exactly what I would've wanted."

"Then it's perfect." Chase took out his phone, stared at the screen, then lifted his hand in a fist pump. "The coaching staff just congratulated me. With heart and happy face emojis. Everything is working."

Nichole's debate skills were not working. "We have to tell our families."

"I'll talk to my grandmother after the photo shoot." Chase checked the time on his fitness tracker and frowned. "Timing is going to be tight. I'll get takeout for her."

This wasn't a lunch date with his grandmother to catch her up on the good things in his life. It was a conversation where he fully intended to deceive his own family. He couldn't possibly have an appetite. Surely, he'd choke on his lunch and his own dishonesty.

The idea of calling her own grandparents nauseated Nichole. Thankfully, her grandparents relegated their TV watching to game shows and DIY series. They'd even canceled the newspaper, claiming it had gotten smaller than a forgotten diary. But her grandparents had neighbors and friends, ones overly involved in worldwide gossip. The story would find its way to her grandparents' porch soon enough. Nichole had to finish this photo shoot, change and phone her grandparents.

"I have car pool duty today." She bit into her lip and failed to discourage her headache from thumping. "I have to tell *Wesley*."

"I'm free all afternoon." Chase glanced up and smiled. "I can go with you to pick him up."

"We need a story," she said. "Details. Everyone wants the details."

"Those have to wait for our drive to Wesley's school." Chase tapped his watch. "I have to get to the photo shoot."

"But you don't know what I've already said." This was all wrong. Nichole's phone vibrated on the stone wall she'd set it on. She picked it up and glanced at the screen. Joy swept through her and crashed into a wave of dread. "Vick and Glenn returned the signed NDA. They want to schedule a dinner with us to discuss the next steps as soon as possible."

"See." Chase caught her, swept her off her feet and swung her around. "We can't confess now."

CHAPTER EIGHT

"You're late." Elliot leaned away from the makeup artist and glanced at Chase, the layer of amusement in his tone thicker than the lotion the woman smoothed across his forehead. "Didn't want to leave your new wife, did you?"

"Something like that." Chase hadn't really wanted to leave Nichole at the cathedral.

Him in a tailored suit, Nichole in pure white from head to toe… The sheer brightness should've blinded him. But all he'd seen was her, bringing a wedding dress to life. That'd been his first thought. What magic had she used and how could he be a part of the occasion? Then she had set her hand on his chest and his arms had wrapped around her waist—as natural as the bouquet she'd clutched. He'd almost believed in the fantasy. Believed she was his and their new life was about to begin.

Fortunately, Nichole had grasped his hand, the strength of her voice tethering him to the

present. They weren't starting a future together. They were working together to secure
their individual futures. At least for now.

Chase dropped into the empty salon-style
chair beside his friend and another makeup
artist appeared. Only one path remained: finalize both contracts quickly before Nichole
got cold feet and became his fake runaway
bride. "How long before we start?"

"Few minutes," Elliot replied. "Photographer promised a quick session if we follow
her directions precisely."

"That must mean action shots are out
today." Last year for the same award photo
shoot, Chase and his teammates had tried to
convince the photographer that action shots
portrayed them better. It might've worked,
too, if the guys hadn't moved from light
passes to tackles that had toppled the back-
drop and one startled assistant.

Elliot laughed. "Definitely out."

The makeup artist unrolled a leather case
of brushes and opened a drawer in a plastic
bin. Chase eased back in the chair, preparing to sit quietly and not disrupt the woman.
He needed a fast session. He had to pick up
his grandmother's favorite takeout and get to
her apartment. He would've preferred to cook
for her, but he feared he was already too late

to reveal his wedding news himself. Takeout would, he hoped, at least help neutralize her annoyance.

"My best client gets married and I don't get an invite." Travis Shaw, Chase's longtime agent and the only person who could negotiate Chase's new football contract, walked toward Chase, his steps sure, his expression reserved.

Panic rolled through Chase. He spun the chair away from the makeup artist and toward Travis. Had the Pioneers decided not to re-sign him already? Had his plan failed before it had even started? "Travis, you never come to these things."

"I wanted to see if my wedding invite got lost in the mail." Travis rested his hands on his hips and scowled at Chase.

"His friend and former teammate never got an invitation either." Elliot lifted partway out of his salon-style chair and shook Travis's hand. Elliot added, "Not even a heads-up."

Travis scrubbed his hands over his face and exhaled loud and deep. "Chase, please tell me that this is not another publicity stunt."

Chase lifted his chin, trying to stretch the annoyance from his stiff neck. He could be serious about things other than football. He simply chose not to be. "It's not a publicity stunt."

At least it was never meant to be public. It was however a desperate attempt to repair his reputation. And a stunt that benefited Travis and the contract negotiations. Chase had known there could be repercussions like this. He stammered, unable to scramble fast enough away from the blitz and the impending sack. "You're really here because I got married?"

"Why else?" Travis speared his arms out to either side as if preparing to make that sack. "There are things we need to do to influence the media and maximize the positive PR traction."

Maximize. Chase flinched. Nichole would dislike anything that maximized the PR reach. How could he say no to reaching more fans if it helped his cause?

Travis gave an exaggerated count on his fingers. "Things like a professional photo shoot. Formal press release. A joint statement."

No. Not happening. Chase had promised Nichole no media blitz. "She wants to preserve her privacy for herself and her child."

"Single mom." Elliot nodded his approval

and high-fived Chase. "Does she have a son or daughter?"

"Eleven-year-old son." A son Chase would meet in a few hours. He'd been less anxious for his first ever pro football game. If Wesley disliked Chase, Nichole would end their agreement.

"Pioneers Camp." Travis snapped his fingers and pointed at Chase. His eyebrows boomeranged up his forehead, amplifying his battleship-gray eyes. "You can make your public family debut there. It's the perfect reveal."

Pioneers Camp had appeal, although not for the PR. Rather, to help Chase win over Wesley. Nichole had mentioned Wesley was a Pioneers' fan, hadn't she? His nerves unraveled. "If I bring them to Pioneers Camp, it'll be for her son."

"Right." Travis paced behind the twin salon chairs. His fingers combed through his cropped hair as if testing different hairstyles.

Or running through every possible angle.

Travis always worked through problems and situations the same way: hands in his hair, measured, succinct steps—the same number in each direction. His agent had never broken his stride on the day Chase had entered the pro football draft. Chase wanted to give Travis time, but extra minutes were scarce.

Chase kept himself immobile in the chair for the makeup artist. He had to get to his grandmother.

"Good PR is the bonus," Travis muttered. "We need all the bonuses we can get."

"I'm thinking a formal reception party for the new couple at a certain cliffside beach house would be a big bonus," Elliot suggested.

Chase lurched away from the makeup artist's brush and stared at his friend. Travis owned a beach house on the cliffs. But a party was not necessary. Or a bonus.

"Already working on the details." Travis leaned his hip on the mirrored counter and tipped his chin toward Chase. "Do you want to speak to your family, or should I call them? I know they'll want to be included in the party planning."

Travis refrained from adding, *since they were excluded from the wedding planning*. But the disapproval framing his agent's words seemed to cause a deep frown as if Chase had hurt Travis. Chase hadn't even been included in the wedding. He had to slow everyone down, starting right now. "We already celebrated after we said our vows."

"Not with your friends and family." Elliot scowled. "And by all accounts it was the middle of the night. Where were you again?"

Elliot sounded hurt, too. A cramp twisted his stomach. He wanted to blame hunger. But only guilt gnawed that deep. *Details, Chase. We need details.* What Nichole had meant was more detailed lies. One city catered to eloping couples every day of the year. "Vegas."

"Must have been your bride's dream to celebrate in a casino at the quarter slots." Elliot's voice was sandpaper dry.

Nichole had business dreams. Besides, fake marriages did not have real reception parties to celebrate a couple who had never recited any vows. "We enjoyed it," he told them halfheartedly. It didn't sound true in the least.

"That's great," Travis insisted. "But we are still having a party for you and your new wife."

Elliot smacked his hands together in one resounding clap. "That's what I like to hear."

Chase wanted to hear his contract had been finalized. He wanted to hear the words *sign here*. "I'll talk to my grandmother this afternoon and my wife, of course. I'm sure she'll want to be involved in the party planning." *Or not.*

Chase pretended he didn't have an urge to

clear his throat, that the understatement of the year wasn't lodged in his throat. Nichole had always hated parties. Even more, she'd hated being the center of attention. He'd recognized that after he'd convinced her to run for class treasurer. Nichole had garnered few votes and too much ridicule. He'd blamed himself and guilt had stuck to him like surgical tape.

Travis's gray gaze sharpened on Chase as if he, too, recognized one of Chase's tells.

He slanted his attention to Chase's left hand. "Don't tell me you lost your wedding ring already."

"Now that's a really bad move." Elliot shook his head and groaned beside Chase. "You gotta be better than that, my man."

Chase clenched the armrests and scrambled for a reply.

The cell phone clipped to Travis's waist lit up. The ring split the silence, disconnecting Travis's assessment and Chase's response. Travis lifted his phone to his ear and walked away.

"Lost your ring and kept your marriage from your grandmother." Elliot's disappointment was more than clear in his continuous, slow headshake. "That's just not right."

None of this was right. No one was supposed to even know. At least not until Nichole and Chase had personally told them. "It's all been a bit of a whirlwind."

Elliot stilled and glanced at Chase. "Welcome to married life."

"You're not married."

"Doesn't mean I don't know what it's like." Elliot closed his eyes to allow the makeup artist to dab some kind of thin paper all over his face.

Chase had no idea what married life involved. He had no interest in learning until Nichole had called him her husband and landed in his lap. Then today, seeing Nichole in the wedding gown. He'd been overwhelmed by her beauty, but even more, he'd been proud of her poise. She hadn't crumpled at the unexpected reports of their marriage. Married life had never really been a consideration for Chase. But there was something about Nichole that captured his interest.

Chase grinned and closed his eyes, blocking out the makeup artist holding a massive brush and a container of cream-colored powder.

"You hate photo shoots and all the prep. Always have." Elliot's curious voice broke into Chase's thoughts. "What gives?"

Chase peered at his friend through his half-closed eyes. "I still do."

"Why the silly grin then?" Elliot asked.

"Don't you recognize the expression of a newly married man?"

"You've barely been married twenty-four hours. Now if you're thinking about your up-coming honeymoon and smiling like that, I want the specifics." Elliot punched Chase's uninjured shoulder, jarring Chase's eyes wide-open. "What's your honeymoon plan? Better not be Vegas."

Press releases. Wedding receptions. Hon-eymoons. Chase rocked forward, slammed his feet on the floor in a wide stance. Panic had no place on the field; he wouldn't panic now either.

Elliot laughed. "Now you can take Beau's babymoon and raise it with a stellar honey-moon."

Had Chase's marriage leveled the field with his backup quarterback already? Chase grinned at his friend. "It's going to be quite spectacular." Once he arranged it.

Travis returned. His frown tightened, firm-ing along his jaw. "You skipped your appoint-ment with the team doctor this morning."

He'd been on his way there, then Nichole had texted. He'd substituted a stop at the jew-elry store for the doctor's office. "I'll just reschedule for next week. They want to talk about my therapy plans."

Travis tipped his attention toward Chase's shoulder as if he knew more than he admitted. "How is the therapy going? Making progress?"

Travis had always been honest and straightforward. Never promised anything he couldn't deliver. He'd invested time and money in Chase and had believed in Chase's talent before any professional team. Chase had been loyal to him from their first meeting. Now for the first time ever, Chase broke his own vow to be truthful. "Good. JT and I have an extensive rehab schedule."

One that had included more than two dozen acupuncture needles after Chase's mountain bike ride and subsequent hike on Sunday. He'd gained more mobility in his shoulder and the pain had dulled into manageable. Manageable enough for Chase to join Nichole for drinks and dinner. Manageable enough for Chase to convince Nichole to continue their ruse. But never dull enough to ignore. Or forget. *You need surgery, Chase. Soon.*

Travis's voice was grim. "You can't avoid the team doctors much longer, Chase."

"I'm not avoiding them." How many times could he stretch the truth in one conversation?

He must have reached his own personal record. Chase loosened his smile into easy and relaxed like his carefree tone. "I've been a little distracted with my new wife."

Elliot chuckled beside him.

Travis remained still, from his stiff arm braced on the light bulb–framed mirror to his subdued expression. The lack of movement intensified Travis's voice, ensuring there would be no misheard words. No misunderstanding. No distractions. "This isn't like the last contract negotiation. The last negotiation, you had no injury and your stats obscured your off-field antics."

"I have better stats now than when I started playing. I'm repairing my off-field reputation. Check the social media likes. My approval rating is climbing," Chase countered. Unfortunately, he did not have the same healthy shoulder. Or his youth. "As for my shoulder, I'll be ready to play by the preseason opener."

Travis nodded and held out his hand.

Chase reached out and shook it. "I'm counting on you to take care of me and my career."

Travis clenched Chase's hand and held on like a father about to impart an important life lesson. "Don't let me down on your end."

CHAPTER NINE

HIS TRUCK TIRES SQUEALING, Chase motored into the last empty parking space at Bright Heart Sanctuary. He grabbed the to-go bag from The Panini Parade, hotfooted it toward the entrance and hoped for a onetime miracle. Anything that put a hiccup in his grandmother's typical morning routine: cappuccino sweetened with cream and sugar and a splash of hot milk, two almond biscotti and an in-depth review of the day's headlines both newsworthy and gossip.

Ten yards from the entrance, his eldest sister charged toward him like a defensive back after the receiver. "I knew you'd come to Nonna's first. You've ignored my texts and calls all morning."

Chase deflected to the left, sprinted around her and rushed the glass doors as if the assisted living center was the locker room at halftime and he had twelve minutes to revise his game plan.

Mallory kept pace with him. "When I suggested you get a wife, I didn't mean literally overnight."

The miracle train had obviously departed the station hours ago. He lunged for the door and stretched his grin extra wide. "I was just following your advice."

"You never listen to me." Exasperation creased his sister's forehead. Her voice was curt.

"That's not true." Chase urged Mallory inside the lobby. "I listened in high school and got myself a tutor. Then again, in college, I reached out for tutoring assistance like you told me to do."

"You wouldn't have passed high school without Nichole's help. And she helped you stay in college long enough to get drafted." Mallory wasn't fading. "You had no choice."

He had no choice last night either. Nichole had called him her husband. If he'd corrected her in front of Vick and Glenn, he might've ruined her opportunity to sell her program. As for convincing Nichole to continue their charade, his rationale sounded much less sensible and much more selfish without Nichole glowing in a wedding dress in front of him.

He picked up his pace, hurrying toward the front desk and the check-in station. The receptionist called her congratulations to

Chase. He waved, offered the woman an appreciative smile.

The press had often labeled him selfish. He'd always pretended the label never stung deeper than a mosquito bite. More nuisance than liability.

But the label fit. He was selfish. That truth surged through him like a full body dunk in an ice bath, uncomfortable and cloyingly cold. "Mallory, don't you have classes to teach? Dissertations to read? Or even patients to put to sleep before their surgery?"

"Never mind my schedule." Mallory made a slashing motion with her hand. "What is this about you having a wife?"

"We have to talk on the way. Nonna prefers her paninis hot." And Chase preferred to discuss startling and unsettling news with his grandmother after she'd eaten. She'd always been more receptive to his pranks and mischief between dinner and dessert.

"What's really going on?" Mallory followed Chase down the corridor. "Who is this woman? Someone looking for their five minutes of fame, I suppose."

"It's not like that." Mallory hadn't recognized Nichole in the blurry photograph. He could salvage things. His family had always liked Nichole. "She's not like that."

"Then it's true?" Doubt lingered in Mallory's frown.

Carter Jones, one of the nurses, leaned on his medicine cart outside the elevators and held up two thumbs. Carter's smile hooked from one ear to the other. "Pioneers are going to the big game this coming year. I can feel it already."

The constant ache in Chase's shoulder intensified. The speculation from the staff and the judgment from his sister hurtled toward him, pushing on him to falter. Chase beelined for the staircase, taking two at a time. "Let's get Nonna her lunch."

"You aren't going to tell me anything, are you? That's fine." Mallory rounded on Chase outside their grandmother's apartment door. "Nonna will get the truth out of you. You've never been able to lie to her."

There was a first time for everything. His mother and grandmother had often recited that particular phrase after one of Chase's adventures. How could he deceive Nonna now? How could he not?

If Nonna believed Chase, then surely his fake marriage had merit. If his grandmother called him out, then he'd end the pretense and find another way to help Nichole.

He opened the door and entered the one-bedroom apartment. Everything inside him stumbled. His mother and his younger sister, Ivy, sat beside Nonna at the square kitchen table turned crafting center. News traveled fast in the Jacobs family. He braced the cheer in his smile and his tone. "Hello, everyone. This is unexpected."

"Not so very surprising." His grandmother's wry tone lacked the bright happiness of the pastel pink flowers she clasped. "If you read the news and keep up on current events. Which I might remind you we are obliged to do, thanks to your fondness for always making the headlines."

His mother and sisters nodded, slow and solemn, as if Nonna had just recited the keys to a long life and they were part of her inner council.

Chase dropped the panini bag on the kitchen counter and searched for the key to survive the next half hour. "Had I known you would all be here, I would've ordered more food."

"Now that you're here, you can call the newspaper and demand a retraction for reporting false and harmful stories." His mother wrapped burlap around a large round wreath frame, quickly and efficiently covering the green foam. The same way she'd raised three kids on her own: organized, controlled and tender. Her gaze settled on him. "After all, the mother of the supposed groom should know about her only son's wedding before some unknown reporter."

Chase took off his suit jacket, folded it over a kitchen stool. Guilt clung to him. He'd never wanted to disappoint his mom. *Ever.* If he lost his football career, he couldn't provide for his family and give back through his foundation. Without football, what would he give, but more disappointment?

"What about me?" Ivy waved her hand from her seat at the table. Her mouth, usually set in a wide, open smile that revitalized the most dreary room, flatlined into an unwelcoming grimace. "I only run your nonprofit. I have access to your full financials and tax records. Yet I wasn't even told you had a fiancée."

Ivy's words sliced at him. She'd expanded his foundation and grown its impact in the city and surrounding communities. She was business minded and career oriented. Were those tears pooling in her eyes? Ivy never cried, never allowed anyone to see a weakness. Chase loosened his tie.

"What about me?" Mallory cut in.

Her words stopped Chase from handing

Ivy a tissue. No doubt, Ivy would resent him all the more for pointing out her tears.

Mallory pinned a silk flower behind her ear, the baby blue color enhanced the spark of victory in her perceptive gaze. She'd already suspected foul play. "I know his full medical history. I should've been told too."

And that ended Mallory's case. She wouldn't believe Chase had kept such big news from her. Mallory and Chase had shared too much over the years. Chase released the button on the collar of his dress shirt. If he continued, Mallory would leave Nonna's apartment bewildered and betrayed. If he exposed the plan, his family most likely wouldn't understand or approve. If they spoke to the press, they could accidentally ruin everything.

"A reporter called my house, Chase." His mother walked to him and gripped his hands. She owned every inch of her petite stature and her regal stance alone demanded obedience. "She wanted a comment about my son's nuptials."

His sisters scowled at him. But his mom's dismay and outrage diluted the silence.

"My only son gets married and I wasn't even invited." His mother dropped his hands like a spider's nest and sagged into the chair beside Nonna.

Chase yanked off his tie. When had his family become champions of marriage? His mother had never remarried. Rarely dated in the two decades since her divorce. Ivy and Mallory put their careers first, the same as Chase. Marriage wasn't supposed to be this big of a deal.

Nonna patted his mother's forearm and peered over the rims of her glasses at him. "This family does not work that way, Chase Baron Jacobs."

Chase winced. The hurt on her face fused the guilt deep inside him. His throat tightened around his confession. One admission would end all of this. But the disappointment would no doubt remain for his latest foolish stunt.

"Maybe he's taken too many hits." Ivy sorted silk butterflies by color on the table and avoided looking at him. "Concussion damage is very real."

Mallory tipped her head, her gaze narrowed. He already knew she was making a mental note to order an MRI on his brain.

"You dismissed your family as if we mean nothing to you. You refuse to request a retraction." His mother's voice was as empty and stark as the wreath frame she clutched. "What's happened to my son?"

He hadn't really excluded his family. That truth hardly eased his torment.

"Because marriage and you, Chase…" His mother's voice faded away.

Her apprehension landed like a boulder in one of Nonna's ceramic birdbaths. Chase recoiled. He'd supposedly gotten married, not sentenced to jail. First, he'd upset them for disregarding the sanctity of marriage. Now his own mom refused to believe he could even be married. As if marriage and Chase repelled each other. "Would it be so bad if I was married?"

"Marriage isn't a joke, Chase." His mother stood, set her hands on her hips and stared him down. "Marriage is definitely not something you do on a whim or because it sounds fun in the moment."

He paced away, avoiding the crafting table and the jury seated there. He chose not to commit to a relationship. That hardly meant he couldn't commit. But if he committed to football and to a relationship, then one was certain to suffer. His own father had struggled to remain committed to his marriage and his career. And his family had paid the price. Chase kept his focus on football and avoided the collateral damage of bruised feelings, crushed expectations and damaged hearts, including his own. And that occasional twinge of loneliness he simply stomped beneath his cleats. "I know exactly what marriage means."

His mom brushed his words aside. "It's a commitment that requires hard work, patience and dedication."

Even then, marriages failed. Yet marriage was clearly important to his mother and sisters. He'd never considered how important until now. Not some simple word to be tossed out like confetti to celebrate a win. An odd, uncomfortable sensation rooted between his ribs.

Were marriage vows as sacred to Nichole as his own family? Had he ruined marriage for Nichole too? Dread and regret coiled through him. "I can do all that. I can be a good husband."

He just never had the inclination. He never wanted to divert his attention away from football for a relationship. There it was again. Another checkmark in the selfish column. He'd always referred to himself as singularly focused. That was simple sugarcoating, like the powdered sugar his grandmother sprinkled on her crinkle cookies.

"It's really good to know you can be all that." Ivy walked into the kitchen and unpacked the paninis. Frustration had crept into her voice. "Because you're going to have to do all that and more now that you're a husband."

His sister lengthened the word *husband* as if capitalized and highlighted in bold. Chase pulled plates from the cabinets and debated confessing.

They'd discourage him from continuing a fake marriage. Might even let the truth slip to someone outside the family, believing they were being helpful. Nichole's chances at a sale would diminish. And he had his own contract negotiations to consider. Selfish check mark number two.

He was quickly earning the championship title in the all-about-me category. His phone vibrated in his pocket. He checked his messages: more congratulations from teammates, coaching staff and Pioneers' management filled the text previews. Mission Reputational Repair was in full progress.

Quick beats of pleasure pulsed inside him. The approval proved difficult to ignore.

An image of Nichole on the stairs outside the cathedral flashed in his mind. His breath skipped again. He couldn't remember the last time a woman had made him breathless from nothing more than a brilliant smile and perfectly fitted gown. He'd almost believed Nichole was his...

Chase set the plates on the counter and cast his misplaced thoughts aside. Defeat came when players lost focus. They had a business arrangement and contracts to finalize. Nothing that should make his knees buckle and his heart trip over itself. "Mallory suggested I needed a wife."

"Only to speak as your conscience." Burlap tangled around Mallory's hands. "And not immediately."

"It wasn't a bad suggestion." Nonna unwound the burlap from Mallory's grip and frowned at him. "Yet your methods to achieve such a goal make me consider that Ivy might be correct. You've taken one too many hits to your head."

Chase grinned. His grandmother hadn't questioned his ability to be married. She'd been disappointed he'd excluded his family. He'd be sure to include them if he ever decided to step into marriage for real.

"I'm sorry about this. Really sorry. I know you'll need time to forgive me." He loaded regret and chagrin into his voice, lowered his shoulders, dropped his chin to his chest. "It just all happened so fast." Literally, in one day. With one misspoken phrase.

"At least tell us who you married." His mother held a plain, unadorned wreath frame in front of her as if to protect herself from the answer. "You've excluded us enough already."

Perhaps this revelation would ease the hurt and usher in their forgiveness. His family had adored Nichole. Chase straightened and embraced one truth he could admit. "Nichole Moore."

Four sets of eyes stared at him. Unblinking. Composed. Unimpressed. Surely, they remembered Nichole. She'd been an important part of his life. A vital part. An unforgettable part.

"Nichole Moore," Chase repeated, putting more emphasis on Nichole's name. "From high school."

"Sweet, smart Nichole." Ivy's bold, buoyant smile returned. She set a sandwich on a plate with more flourish.

"Little Nikki." His mom's smile softened into her eyes.

She wasn't Little Nikki any longer. Nichole was engaging and intriguing. And in a wedding gown, captivating. But she'd been captivating on his lap, right before he'd kissed her. *Focus. Focus. Focus.* He would've hit the side of his helmet if he'd been wearing one.

"You married *that* Nichole Moore." Mallory jumped from her chair. Confusion pulled her eyebrows together. Her words came slow and succinct. "Nichole the class valedictorian. Summa cum laude. National Honor Society. And student voted most likely to invent the next generation's iPhone."

His family's collective shock set him back. Or perhaps not. He'd always known, even in high school, Nichole was far out of his league. The idea she'd marry him, a jock without a college degree and a learning disability, was somewhat far-fetched. Chase managed a small nod.

"How did you reconnect with Nichole?" his mom asked.

"She invited me to dinner. I accepted." That sounded reasonable. Plausible. What wasn't reasonable or plausible was Nichole marrying him. "But the marriage..."

"I always liked her," Mallory cut in.

He'd always liked Nichole too. Even when she had frustrated him. Or had pushed him to read more. He'd liked her. Now he'd convinced her to pretend to be his wife. How could she like him? He rarely second-guessed his decisions, even the bad ones. He simply accepted the consequences and moved on. But Nichole not liking him soured his insides. He swallowed but doubted a barrel of water could wash away the distaste. And if that wasn't a bad sign, then he had learned nothing from Nonna and her tales about omens.

Ivy carried a sandwich plate into the family room and set it on the end table beside the couch. "How is Nichole?"

"A single mom. Her son's name is Wesley." Now it was more important that Wesley liked Chase. Now his family was involved. "Nichole created a computer program and an investment firm wants to buy it."

"She always was talented and very creative." His mom's smile bloomed. "I remember walking into the kitchen after she'd hidden the cookie jar with fresh peanut butter cookies inside. She wouldn't let you have any until you had memorized the entire periodic table."

Nichole's methods had been rather cruel. Nichole had known peanut butter cookies were one of his favorites. Still, he'd managed to pass that particular chem test.

"I still can't believe Nichole pretended you guys were only classmates, nothing more than acquaintances at school for all those years."

Ivy leaned against the kitchen counter, amazement staining her cheeks and wide gaze.

"She did it for Chase." Mallory shook her head at him. "I can't believe you asked Nichole to do that for you."

Chase rubbed the back of his neck, catching his flinch. Nichole and he had run in different circles at school. It'd been easy to avoid each other. His family had believed he'd wanted to protect his reputation as a popular football player. But he hadn't wanted to invite questions. Kids would've asked how Nichole and he knew each other. That would've led to even more questions that he never wanted to answer. He'd never wanted anyone to know about his dyslexia. Not his teammates or his friends. Nichole knew about his faults and his weaknesses. At school, seeing her reminded him he wasn't flawless. Was far from perfect. He was *less than,* like his own dad had believed.

Except with Nichole at his house after school, she'd made Chase feel like he could conquer anything and reach his dreams. He squeezed his neck. Had he made her believe she could reach her dreams too? Not likely. He'd been too consumed with his own. He had to help Nichole now. Give her something good. He owed her that much and more.

"Nichole was always so smart." Ivy punched his shoulder, her humor stepping back to the forefront. "Yet she married Chase."

His stomach collapsed as if punched too. He wasn't good enough for Nichole. He should've never started this. "It's not..."

"I'd like to see the woman Nichole has become," his grandmother interrupted. She lowered herself onto the couch and picked up her plate. "When do I get to see this new wife of yours?"

That simple question launched a full-scale debate among the women. Days, times and places were thrown out, discarded and revisited. Chase tried twice to intervene. His sisters and mother ignored him. He sat on the couch beside his grandmother and checked his phone again.

"Something more important on your phone than your family?" Nonna dabbed a napkin against her cheek.

"I'm waiting to hear from Nichole." Chase flipped his phone over in his hands. Had Nichole changed her mind about car pool pickup? About their deal? "This wasn't the way it was supposed to go."

Nonna placed her hand on his arm, drawing his gaze to her wisdom-aged whiskey-brown eyes. "We can plan all we want, but love has its own mind and its own agenda."

Love. This wasn't about love. This was about contracts and reputation repair. Chase rose and stuffed his phone in his back pocket. "I have to go. It's car pool day today, and I don't want to mess that up on my first day." His mind raced to cover any other loose ends. "This weekend won't work for a family gathering."

Conversation stopped. His mother and sisters stood shoulder to shoulder and eyed him. They'd been forming their impenetrable wall since he'd started kindergarten to make Chase squirm. To make him confess to putting hot sauce on Mallory's pasta instead of spaghetti sauce. To make him admit he purposely scared Ivy and her friends during their sleepover. To force him to concede he ate the entire family-sized bag of potato chips in one sitting. Now they wanted another confession.

"Nichole and I are going on a ski-moon." Chase slammed his lips together. *What?*

"Where are you going?" Mallory's arms crossed again, her eyes narrowed, her foot tapped against the hardwood floor.

He didn't envy his future nieces and nephews. Mallory would make a formidable mom one day.

"I've never heard of that." Ivy scowled and considered him as if searching for a weakness. "What is it?"

Chase wanted to know the very same thing too. He ran his hand through his hair. His family watched him, silent and judging. "You know." He rushed on. "It's like a honeymoon. But it's in Tahoe and we'll be skiing. Get it?"

Ivy caved first and laughed. "It can't be a real honeymoon if Nichole's son is joining you guys."

"He is going, isn't he?" his mother asked. Suspicion wove through her words.

"Of course," Chase managed. He hadn't met Wesley yet, but what kid didn't like the snow. "We're family now." *Family*. The idea pinned him in place like an ambush.

His mother's nod remained stiff and small as if she held back her full approval.

"I really have to go." Chase backed toward the door, searching for the handle and some semblance of balance. He'd built a career on his agility and sure-footed skill. What had happened to his poise? Finally, his fingers curled around the brass door handle. But his balance remained off-kilter.

His grandmother's voice stopped his escape. "Honeymoon or ski-moon or whatever, you'll bring Nichole here to see me tomorrow at her convenience."

That wasn't a request. Or an invitation. It was a direct order. Chase agreed and fled the small apartment. And hopefully, the faint whisper of love's arrow.

CHAPTER TEN

THIRTY MINUTES BEFORE the end of the school day and the start of her car pool duties, Nichole pulled into Chase's driveway. She stared at the three-story Mediterranean-style villa hidden behind a pair of lush olive trees. Chase lived in one of the most sought-after districts in the city within easy walking distance of the best the city offered, including bay views. Nichole rented an unremarkable two-bedroom in a dull duplex tucked away in a modest part of town. Nichole and Wesley relied on their bus passes to travel around the city most days.

But today wasn't typical. She turned off her sedan. The four-door car outdated Wesley by a decade, tallied more than one hundred and fifty thousand miles and boasted several completed cross-country road trips. Not the luxury town car Chase was most likely accustomed to. Her *rattleship* as Wesley called it wouldn't become the image booster for Chase. Neither would Nichole.

Why had she agreed to their pseudo marriage? *Opposites do not attract.* No scientific evidence existed to support the theory. Nichole and Chase were about as opposite as possible. Now she had to come up with a suitable explanation for Wesley. *I'm helping out an old friend* was the best she'd devised.

Nichole walked up the stairs to the main entrance and rang the bell. The door swung open. Chase stood in an unbuttoned dress shirt. His wrinkled tie hung loose around his shoulders. He looked disheveled and dashing and drew her in like a magnetic field. She said, "I'm guessing your grandmother didn't take the news well."

"My mother and sisters were there too." Chase opened the door wider and motioned her inside. "They were thrilled I married you."

"But," she pressed. No area rugs softened her footsteps on the worn hardwood floors, nothing dulled the racing pulse buzzing in her ears.

"They have to be invited to my next marriage and be included in the wedding planning." Chase shut the door and walked barefoot past her.

"You're getting married again?" Nichole skipped her gaze from the fitted white T-shirt under his dress shirt to his bare feet and back again. *Opposites do not attract*. She ran her hand across the microfiber couch in a familiar red wine color rather than reach for Chase and conduct her own experiment on the outdated opposites attract theory.

"Definitely not on the agenda, but don't tell them that, please," he said. "What about you?"

"What about me?" *I'm definitely not interested in you. Not like that*. Her hand stilled on the couch as if he'd caught her reading his personal files.

"Do you want to get married for real?" He moved closer, his gaze serious. His tone thoughtful.

"I did." *I could*. Nichole blinked, disconnected her old daydreams and blamed Josie. Had Nichole not put on the stunning wedding gown or carried a bouquet of her favorite flowers or stood inside Chase's embrace, she'd never have imagined again. That old whimsy caught her, and she whispered, "Once upon a time."

"And now?" His voice softened to a murmur. His gaze warmed as if he too saw her in the wedding gown. As if he too imagined.

Stop. She unplugged the illusion. Willed her racing heart to quit. She needed to be

convincing. "I have other priorities." *Her son.*
In A Pinch. *Helping her grandparents retire.*
Never getting her heart broken again.

Chase clutched the ends of his tie as if cen-
tering himself. "One of which is Wesley." He
checked the time. "We don't want to be late."

"I've mastered the car line." She hadn't
mastered what to tell Wesley. Or how to tell
him. Or how to protect her son. "We still have
time."

Chase motioned to his suit pants and
started for the staircase. "Make yourself at
home while I change. I'll be fast."

Nichole wandered into the kitchen, away
from her ill-timed thoughts. The appliances
looked a decade older than the dated ones
in her rental. The cabinets might've been
circa 1930s but the layered paint on the cabinet doors obscured the wood. The kitchen
wasn't restored vintage charm or modern and
sleek. And nothing she expected Chase Jacobs to own. The Chase Jacobs portrayed in
the media should have a high-end bachelor
pad that converted to a swanky nightclub in
the evening. Every extravagant toy from a
speedboat to a 4Runner to a snowmobile in
his garage. Yet she'd glimpsed the tailgate of
an older truck on her way to the stairs.

One lone placemat sat at the head of the

oval kitchen table. Nichole skirted the table and drab eating nook and moved into the connecting sunroom. A floral-patterned couch was the only foliage in the room aside from several small pots of herbs sitting on a TV tray—the kind she hadn't seen since she'd been about six. The bright space begged for a potted palm tree or a fountain. She picked up several CDs from one of the many stacks towering on the floor. Her mouth dropped open.

Not CDs, but audiobooks. Nichole flipped through one stack. Everything from classic literature to biographies to current fiction filled the pile.

"Those aren't mine." Chase's deep voice came from behind her, defensive and guarded.

Nichole spun around, still holding an audiobook, and swallowed her apology for snooping. "You have a roommate?"

"Never. I've always lived alone." Chase bent down, straightened one of the stacks and avoided looking at her. "They belong to an old girlfriend."

Nichole read the title of the audiobook she held. "Your ex liked to learn about how to build the supreme male body."

Chase rubbed his chin. "What can I say? She had rather eclectic tastes."

And Chase had secrets. Ones he refused

to share with her. That shouldn't bother her. Business deals were never personal. Emotions were always excluded. Yet the slight needled her. She set the audiobook next to the herb plants. "Did your ex grow herbs too?"

"Those are mine." Chase checked the soil in one pot, affection in his tone. "Can't cook without fresh herbs."

The man before her was somewhat of a contradiction. She never liked those much. Always wanted to reason through the different layers and make sense of every inconsistency.

The boy she'd known had despised reading. Claimed literature belonged to the select few who could understand it. The man she fake married, the one she knew from the endless media stories, wasn't sprawled out on a sofa, listening to Homer's *Odyssey*, waiting for his fresh herbs to grow. That man was mingling with fans, devising new escapades and winning over the public. "You cook often?"

"As often as I can." Chase carried one of the herb plants to the kitchen sink.

She walked back through the kitchen into the living room and stared at the stained glass windows framing the fireplace. The original glasswork attempted to stand out despite the deterioration around the rest of the house.

The same way Chase stood out. Except now, Nichole questioned who he really was.

"Why haven't you fixed this place up?" Even Nichole, the least qualified DIY-er in the state, could see the potential. Envision the possibilities.

"I don't own this place." Chase sat on the couch and tied his running shoes. "I rent it."

"You rent?" Nichole rolled her lips together too late. The shock already bounced against the scratched hardwood floors.

"It's not that much of a surprise." Chase stood up.

"The details of your current football contract are public." From his signing bonus to his earnings. His endorsement deals were not public. However, she could name four commercial products she'd seen him in campaign ads for. Chase could buy any home he wanted, including this one. He could also buy any image he wanted.

"I bought my mom a house." He walked into the kitchen and pulled two bottles of water from the refrigerator.

Nichole moved to the kitchen table, glanced at the floral-patterned couch on the sun porch and remembered. How many times had she sat beside Chase at the oak table? The couch had been off-limits to food, pets and teenagers. "Then you took your mom's furniture."

"She wanted all new furniture for her new home." Chase ran his palm over the scratched kitchen table. "This stuff is great. Still usable. I wasn't throwing it out."

His fingers lingered over a particular notch in the table. His face relaxed as if the history comforted him. Nichole turned around, scanned the living room, recognized even more from his family's home. "You have all your mom's original furniture, don't you?"

"It fits perfectly for what I need." He folded a hand towel and slid it over the handlebar on the oven.

But he could have a chef's kitchen. Eight-burner stainless steel range. Double ovens. Modern leather sofas. Glass coffee table. He should have that. The headline-making Chase Jacobs certainly had *that* house. Not this. An outdated unit with used furniture that looked more like a college apartment than an all-pro football player's home.

"You don't like my place?" A playful note swerved into his voice.

"It's not what I expected," she hedged. Chase was not who she'd expected. Despite his mother's cozy furniture, a loneliness filled the space. "It's sparse."

"What did you expect? A house that doubles as a nightclub?" Again, that tease swayed through his words.

"Yes," she admitted. That would have made more sense. That wouldn't have made her curious about him. That wouldn't have made her wonder what else he might be sentimental about.

"I have all the essentials." Chase indicated the counter. One plate, a fork and a single cup rested in the steel wire dish rack. "Everything I need."

"You're living like a college student on a slim budget." She'd lived that life for too many years. Microwavable soup for dinner and scrounging together enough quarters for one load of laundry. Her paycheck from her library attendant job would arrive, but the money would've already been spent. Until she'd earned her degree and accepted her first and only teaching assistant job in graduate school. She'd gotten a raise and met the professor she'd believed she'd share her life with.

It was too late when she'd discovered his contradictions were not so easily overlooked.

"Don't underestimate the merits of a good dorm room." Chase set his hands on his hips and grinned. "The dorm room is like a tiny house in a building of other tiny houses. And a built-in entertainment center. There was always something fun going on in our dorm."

Nichole laughed—the good kind, not the nervous or awkward or forced kind. The kind of laughter that rolled from deep inside and speared delight into every cell inside her. Chase had always been able to make her laugh. Even when she thought she couldn't. Finally, she found a real connection between the man standing before her and the boy she once knew. Nichole relaxed, settling back into the comfortable friends-only zone.

Chase rubbed his hands together. "I'm ready to take on the car line."

Nichole chuckled and followed Chase to the front door. "It's not that bad."

"Should we practice what we're going to tell Wesley?" Chase locked his front door.

That conversation could be bad, or at the very least, awkward. "Can we give him the truth? We're two old friends helping each other out."

"What about the marriage piece?" Chase opened her car door and walked around to the passenger side.

"You're supposedly married, but no one knows it's to me." As it should be. She buckled her seat belt and started her car.

"Except my family, your friends and the

Fund Infusion guys." Chase slipped on a pair of sunglasses and drummed his fingers on the center console.

"You think the press is going to figure out it's me in that photograph," Nichole guessed. She had no experience with the media. Chase had achieved expert status. She wanted to hope he was wrong. Wanted to ignore her gut that agreed with Chase.

"In case I didn't tell you before, I never contacted the press." Chase pulled out his cell phone and typed on the screen. "The media wasn't part of my need-to-know category."

"I'm going with the waiter or busboy." Nichole's need-to-know category had consisted of two people: Vick Ingram and Glenn Hill. Then she'd fabricated a story for her best friends. And she feared how much larger her need-to-know category would become. "It's a pretty bad picture. Maybe the press won't identify me." Nichole pinched off that bud of hope.

Hope and wishes were a waste of energy and time. Time that could be spent actively working toward achieving a goal. Nichole had done nothing that morning to help the sale of her app. She'd have to work into the night to keep up with her schedule.

"Local news reporter Vanessa Ryan has

located one of our high school yearbooks." Irritation fueled Chase's tone.

"That's not a problem." Nichole relaxed her grip on the steering wheel. She had more time before the press identified her and more time to enhance *In A Pinch* to ensure Vick and Glenn couldn't say no. "The media won't put us together from an old yearbook."

Chase and Nichole hadn't interacted much at school on purpose. Chase had wanted to preserve his popular status and Nichole had wanted the same for herself. She hadn't wanted her advisors or peers to ever question her dedication to her studies or her judgment. She hadn't wanted her future derailed by a boy. And falling for a boy like Chase could've done that and more. She'd graduated top of her class, gained a full-ride scholarship and earned her freedom from a small town that only ever referred to her as that tall, smart girl. As if she'd had nothing more to offer than in-depth class notes and the ability to reach the chemistry beakers from the top shelf.

"You always were too good for me," Chase said. "Back then and even now."

"Thanks for that." Nichole stopped at a red light. "But we both know the truth."

"Which is what?" His voice lowered as if guarded.

"You're at your best surrounded by people. You're at your best on center stage." Nichole frowned.

Chase was more like her parents than Nicole ever could be. He wouldn't have been banned to live with her grandparents had he been their son. What would her parents think of her now? Claiming to be married to a famous athlete and still struggling to conquer her stage fright. Surely by now she should've grown beyond her fears.

She peered at Chase. He took up the entire passenger seat, and where his body didn't touch, his confidence took over. "I prefer the backstage role and less people."

"So, the press won't connect us because we're too different." Chase nodded, and his usual sideways grin dropped into place. He leaned on the console and wiggled his eyebrows at her. "What about that saying— opposites attract?"

"Be serious." Nichole pushed him back into his seat, pressed on the gas pedal and stalled her own impulse to close the distance between them. She'd earned immunity from his ever-present charisma years ago. She wouldn't fall for it—or him—now. "This was never about attraction. This was about clos-ing our business deals."

She hadn't pushed him far enough away. She still felt his regard. *Don't look. Drive. Don't look.*

Another red light stopped their progress. Silence squeezed into the car like a crowd at the bus stop. And Nichole looked.

One of his eyebrows lifted, the slight-est flinch. His intense gaze dropped to her mouth. Only a quick dip. Quick enough she rolled her lips together. Recalled their kiss. In remarkable detail. Before he focused again on her eyes.

Was that attraction in his gaze? Interest? *No. This was charming Chase. She was plain Nichole.* Still she fidgeted, tugged on the sud-denly too tight seat belt. The city rarely had a heat wave. But she wanted to roll down every window and turn the AC to full blast. Was she attracted to him? She wanted an-other kiss... Just to test her theory. Prove she was right. No attraction existed. Impossible thoughts solved nothing. Actions mattered. Nichole leaned toward him.

A car horn blasted behind them. Then an-other. Nichole jerked away, grabbed the steer-ing wheel and what was left of her common sense. She sped through a yellow light, vow-ing not to waste another red light or minute on the improbable. Kissing Chase proved nothing.

Four green lights in a row kept Nichole's concentration on the road. Finally, the school came into view. Nichole turned into the car line. A familiar man, his usual bow tie in place, waved at her and motioned her into a front row parking space.

"What's happening?" Chase looked outside the window. "I thought car lines were moving. Is this usual?"

"Never. I have no idea what's going on." Nichole turned off the engine and climbed out of the car. Had something happened to Wesley? She reached for her phone. Why hadn't the school office called? Why was Mr. Burton, the school principal wanting her to park?

Chase rounded the front of the car and met Nichole on the sidewalk. He stood beside her, close enough that their shoulders touched, as if he understood her alarm, yet wasn't quite certain how to help.

Mr. Burton hurried toward them, his bow tie tilted. His gaze swept from Nichole to Chase and back. "Ms. Moore, we had a bit of an incident today."

What was a bit? If Mr. Burton was involved, surely that implied more than a minor mishap. Where was Wesley? "You're just telling me about this now. Why?"

Mr. Burton rubbed his chin, his gaze got stuck on Chase like a fervent fan's. He seemed unable to believe his idol actually existed. "It's just that…"

"Hey Dad!" At the entrance of the school, Wesley managed a wave that lifted his feet off the ground. His grin splintered across his entire face. He yelled again. "Hey Mom!"

Nicole swayed and would have given in to her buckling knees if not for Chase's supportive hand on her lower back. Surely, she'd misheard. No one had openly recognized her in that photograph. Certainly, a bunch of schoolkids weren't interested in Chase Jacobs's marital status. Her knees wobbled.

Mr. Burton sighed, almost as loud as Wesley's greeting. He lifted his hand toward several staff members as if reassuring them all was well now. Or perhaps he was holding them off for the moment. The staff members already had their phones out.

Across the parking lot, parents pointed. Teachers huddled together. Then recognition flared, rocketing across the crowd. As if on cue, everyone produced their cell phones.

Wesley sprinted away from his two best friends and raced toward Chase and Nichole.

Before Nichole could fling open the car doors and order everyone to safety, Wesley reached them and launched himself into Chase's arms for a full hug.

"Ms. Moore, call me tomorrow and I can explain." Mr. Burton smiled at Chase and Wesley. Tenderness reached from his gaze to his voice. He touched Chase's shoulder and nodded as if offering his approval and support. The principal added, "Right now, I'm going to get the car line moving."

Nichole wanted to get moving too. Wesley had yet to release his hold on Chase.

"I can call you Dad, can't I?" Wesley's whisper fell far short of a whisper.

Chase's gaze collided with Nichole's, his bewildered and stunned. But in the corner of his mouth, there was a gentle weak quiver as if he was touched by Wesley's unexpected question.

Or maybe that was only Nichole wanting to see what she needed to see. That Chase wouldn't hurt her son. But she'd done this before. Saw what she'd wanted in someone else and not the truth. That careless error had broken her heart and left her a single mom, determined to love her child better than two parents. "No, you may not call Chase Dad."

"Why not?" Wesley released Chase and

rounded on Nichole. "You're married now. That makes Chase my dad."

Nichole tried to gather Chase and Wesley, herd them back toward the car. A crowd had gathered on the stairs outside the school. The car line barely moved. Cell phones were aimed in their direction from every angle.

A gaggle of kids approached. Wesley's two best friends separated from the rest: a red-headed boy, Ben Sawyer, and a blonde curly-haired girl, Ella Callahan. Ella gripped Ben's elbow and kept her walking stick extended. Ben leaned his head toward her as if giving her a rundown of the unfolding scene. Ella nodded every other minute, her face intent.

"I told Mr. Burton I wasn't lying today in his office." Wesley adjusted his backpack and scanned the onlookers. "I knew it was you, Mom, in that photograph with Chase."

"How long were you in the principal's office?" Nichole slapped a hand to her forehead. For one blurry picture, she certainly was recognizable. First Brooke and now Wesley. The press wouldn't be far behind.

"It doesn't matter." Wesley waved at a trio of boys across the parking lot, a smirk on his face. "Now Tyler Mills knows I wasn't lying. That's all that really matters."

Except Nichole and Chase were lying. *To*

everyone. And that mattered very much. Nichole shifted her stance, but the guilt never dislodged.

Chase stepped beside Wesley. "Do I need to talk to Tyler?"

Absolutely not. He was a fake parent. Nichole always protected her own son and hadn't requested Chase's interference. She had to get inside her car. Had to get home. Maybe then her world would right itself and she could think reasonably clearly again.

Wesley rubbed his hand under his nose and grinned at Chase. "That's cool, but it's all good now."

Except it was far from good. It was bad. So very bad. Admiration sparked in Wesley's gaze more and more vivid every time he glanced at Chase. He even edged closer and closer into Chase's side and farther away from Nichole.

"They want pictures with you." Wesley motioned toward the growing crowd. "I might have sort of promised."

Nichole cringed. No more pictures. Pictures got Chase and Nichole in trouble.

Chase's arm bolted up and he waved the crowd over. Once again, he never even considered the consequences.

Ella and Ben joined Wesley and Chase. Ben

hopped from one foot to the other. "We can help too. My dad is going to be so bummed he missed car line today."

Nichole wished they had missed car line too.

A line formed of kids first, then parents followed. Then teachers stepped in. All the while Chase shook hands, laughed and greeted every stranger like a friend. Every picture, every interaction seemed to energize Chase even more. He never tired, never lost his patience. Never appeared anything but genuinely thrilled to meet each person.

Wesley and Ben took the photographs, Ella asked names and called out the correct spellings for anything Chase autographed. All the while Nichole acknowledged parents she knew only from car line and slipped farther into the background. Chase never noticed. Never turned to check on her. He simply surrounded himself with his fans as if they were all he needed. And Nichole took careful notes.

Chase and she belonged in two different worlds. She couldn't afford to lose sight of that fact. If she hurt now, so much the better. The twinge at his disregard in a crowded parking lot was a bee sting compared to the full body misery of a broken heart.

Finally, car line ended, and the teachers returned to their classrooms to finish their workday. Everyone climbed into Nichole's car and they gained some privacy. Two stops later, Ella and Ben were dropped off and Wesley scooted into the center seat.

"This is so cool." Excitement colored Wesley's voice. "Ben has Kyle Quinn as his uncle. Chase, you've heard of Kyle Quinn the inventor, right?"

"Yes, I've heard of him." Chase looked back at Wesley. "We haven't officially met."

"I can introduce you," Wesley offered.

"Kyle is engaged to Ava," Nichole explained. "Ava is Ben's aunt."

"Their engagement is old news, Mom. That's why Ben has Kyle." Wesley waved gleefully at someone they passed on the street.

"Ella's grandmother is Mayor Harrington." Her son rambled on, his voice gained traction and his enthusiasm spilled out. "Now I have Chase Jacobs. Everyone has someone famous to call theirs."

As if it was a game of tag and they were picking teams. Nichole had a solid team with Wesley and her friends. Chase had his own team. The rules were already set. Wesley couldn't claim Chase. Neither could Nichole, even if she wanted to. Opposites did not attract. Besides, Chase couldn't offer anything that Nichole couldn't provide for herself and Wesley.

Nichole eyed Wesley in the rearview mirror. "You think someone as famous as Chase married someone like me?"

"Of course." Wesley never hesitated.

Nichole smiled and appreciated his team loyalty. Her son hadn't completely abandoned her for team Chase.

"The surprise is your mom marrying someone like me." Chase twisted to look at Wesley. "Your mom is too good for a guy like me."

Chase couldn't really believe that. He was making the statement for Wesley's benefit and hers. She peeked at Chase. His usual grin wasn't in place to tease away his claim. His expression was thoughtful and serious. How could he believe Nichole was too good for him? She was a single mom, unemployed and a developer of an app no one wanted to buy. He was *the* Chase Jacobs—charismatic, talented and celebrated.

Wesley slid forward and popped his head between the front seats. His excitement bounced from his smile to his voice. "How long have you guys known each other?"

"Since high school," Nichole said. Even then, their differences had stood out.

Wesley's mouth dropped open. "You never told me that."

Nichole shrugged. "It never came up."

"Is that why you watch every Pioneers game?" Wesley's fingers drummed an animated beat against the seat. "Why you wear your special jersey and Pioneers socks on Pioneers' game days?"

"I'm a fan. There's nothing wrong with supporting my team." Nichole kept her gaze fixed on the license plate of the car in front of her. Specific socks and a specific jersey had been Chase's ritual before every high school and college football game. Nichole had adopted the habit for reasons she couldn't explain now. "There are a lot of Pioneers' fans out there who do the same thing each game day for good luck."

"Is it also good luck because you wear Chase's number?" Wesley asked.

Chase shifted and cleared his throat. Still, she heard his muffled laughter.

Nichole stared straight ahead, willing the light to turn green. The heat burning her cheeks spread up into her ears. Did Chase think she was a silly superstitious fan girl now?

"I have a secret," Chase offered.

Wesley popped between the seats again, shifting closer to Chase.

"Your mom was my tutor in high school," Chase said.

Very few people had known about their arrangement back then. Chase had passed his classes. As for Nichole, she'd gotten out of the farmhouse a few times every week and alleviated her grandparents' concern. They'd been worried Nichole had missed all her potential high school fun spending too much time studying in her room. They'd met Chase and believed she'd discovered a social life.

"She's supersmart. She helps me too," Wesley said. "What subjects?"

Chase slanted a wry grin at Nichole. "All of them."

"Cool." Wesley flopped back into his seat.

If only everyone could've been as receptive back then. But there were those unwritten social rules of high school. Neither Chase nor Nichole had wanted to break them. Nichole had believed she wouldn't be taken seriously if she'd been seen with Chase. Ironic that now Nichole knew Chase was the reason the Fund Infusion gentlemen treated their meeting seriously. After all, they'd requested a second meeting on a night that Chase could attend.

"Have you guys been talking in secret?"

Wesley rushed on before Nichole or Chase could answer. "Ella, she's the one with the walking stick and one of my best friends. Anyway, she said because Chase is famous you couldn't tell anyone, even me. So, you had to put on disguises and make up stories to see each other in secret. Like when you dressed up as the school mascot, Mom. Remember that? You had to put on the Roadrunner costume."

Chase covered his mouth and glanced out the passenger window.

Nichole cleared her throat. Twice. She'd been the only parent tall enough to wear the costume and march in the school parade. She could explain or keep silent.

Wesley seemed oblivious to Nichole's silence and continued on, "Last Christmas, I told everyone what I got them for Christmas. I did the same thing for Ella's and Ben's birthdays too." Wesley chuckled to himself. "I'm really bad at keeping secrets so that's why you couldn't tell me. Mom is really good at secrets. You must be too, Chase. 'Cause it was all one big secret, wasn't it?"

Chase smiled. "Something like that."

"This is *so cool*," Wesley blurted. "Chase Jacobs, the best quarterback ever, is my dad. And I don't have to keep it a secret."

Nichole flexed her fingers on the steering wheel. She'd need more fingers soon to count all the secrets piling up. And she'd need more than hands to heft her guilt.

What happened when the truth came out? Wesley was going to be crushed. One hour with Chase and Wesley was hooked. Wesley had referred to Chase as his dad a second time. What happened if it became a habit? Nichole's stomach rolled, twisting around the secrets, the guilt and her fears.

She'd been diligent about filling the void of no father in Wesley's life. Had she failed? Should she try harder? Chase had mentioned nothing about wanting to be a father, not in any interview, not even in college or high school. He'd rarely talked about his own father. Always laughed off engagement rumors during press conferences. Now he had a fake marriage and pretend stepson. What had he been thinking?

Nichole had thought nothing through. Now it was an avalanche about to consume her. Once she sold her app, she'd have money. Surely money would solve everything this time. This time she was in control. She'd earned her success on her own. Wesley's biological dad had believed money solved any problem. He'd wanted to convince Nichole the same thing. She'd taken his money, faced more problems alone and carried her broken heart like a badge. She turned into her driveway and rolled over the past to focus on the present.

Wesley gathered his backpack. "When are we moving into Chase's place?"

Nichole stumbled and braced her hand against her car. Even more details she never considered. Their home wasn't as large as Chase's, but it wasn't as empty either. Joint living had never been part of their agreement. Nicole liked her home she shared with Wesley. Chase preferred his solitude and no roommates. End of discussion.

Wesley unlocked the front door and glanced at Chase. "Your place has to be better and bigger than our little house."

Chase stepped inside and looked around. "I like your home."

"But your house is bigger, isn't it?" Wesley pressed. As if bigger always equaled better.

"It's being remodeled," Chase said. "So, you'll have to wait to see it until the construction crew clears out."

Or until the pretend divorce occurred and visiting Chase's place no longer became an option.

Wesley dumped his backpack in the entryway and raced into the kitchen. "Who wants popcorn?"

"Hey, I… I should've mentioned this earlier." Chase picked up Wesley's soccer ball and held it between his hands. "Is there any chance you might be able to take a trip?"

Disrupt her schedule. Adjust her to-do list. Not possible. Days off were carefully selected and arranged in advance, according to her budget and calendar. She never did anything on impulse and whim. Except fake marry Chase and the results of her one uncharacteristic move had become more than complicated. Nichole dropped the mail on the side table and studied Chase. "Why?"

"I might've told my family we were going on a ski-moon." He squeezed the soccer ball as if he'd stepped in to coach the team and now had to defend his qualifications. "I did tell them that."

"A what?" Nichole asked.

"They wanted to plan a party for us this weekend. Travis wants to plan a reception." Chase tapped the soccer ball against his head. "It was the only thing I could come up with on the fly."

"What is it?"

"Basically, a ski trip to Tahoe." Chase

peered at her over the soccer ball. A cringe creasing his eyes.

"We're going to Tahoe!" Wesley cheered in the doorway to the kitchen and knocked popcorn onto the floor from the bowl he was clutching.

Something knocked inside Nichole, spinning her even more out of control. She whispered, "This wasn't part of the arrangement."

"I know." Chase sighed. "I panicked."

Now Nichole panicked. Chase wanted to take her to Tahoe. They'd stay in the same house. They'd be together. She could discover the real Chase. Or test her attraction. Her nerves tingled. Anticipation or anxiety, she didn't know.

She did know that she could not go to Tahoe. Not with Chase. A ski-moon sounded too much like a honeymoon. She shouldn't be tempted. First, she wore a wedding gown and saw herself as a bride. Now she saw herself pretending to be married in Tahoe. With Chase. This was what happened when she didn't follow her plan, stick to her schedule. Chaos ensued.

"Can Ben come too?" Wesley buried his hand in the popcorn bowl. "He loves the snow more than me."

"Works for me. Invite Ben's parents, too."

Chase propped the soccer ball against his hip, natural and easy as if he belonged in their house. As if he'd always been in their lives. Always planned their vacations.

But Chase had only just arrived. Barely been invited into Nichole's world. The one she controlled. That was it—she had to take control.

Chase added, "It can be a family getaway weekend."

No. It could not. They weren't family. Nichole muted the buzz in her heart and silenced the part of her that wished. That still hoped for a complete family and love. *Love?* She had no wish to love and find herself set aside. Displaced and forgotten as if her love never mattered. Nichole pressed her hand against her core, pulled herself together, opened her mouth.

"I have to go pack!" Wesley shouted first, and dropped the popcorn bowl on the coffee table. "There's so much I have to remember to bring."

"Wait. Time-out." Nichole raised her hands and regained her focus. Her sharp voice cut into her son's celebration. "You have homework to finish right now. Then school tomorrow."

"So, no Tahoe?" Disappointment crushed

Wesley's eyebrows together. "No fun in the snow?"

"Let me call Brooke and Dan." *Let me think. Let me develop an action plan. Give me more time.* Nichole rubbed the back of her neck. Tahoe was a bad idea. "It's spring break next week. Maybe we can go up there this Friday." She looked at Chase. Another bad idea. Her heart tapped against her chest. "Friday works, right?"

"Definitely." Chase high-fived Wesley. "Fun in the snow is a go."

Wesley whooped and raced away.

Nichole collapsed onto the couch and vowed she'd made her very last misstep. Tomorrow she'd get back on schedule. Back on track with the life she'd already planned.

CHAPTER ELEVEN

CHASE STEPPED INTO his grandmother's apartment and scrambled into the kitchen. "Nonna, what are you doing?"

"Boiling potatoes and preparing my statement." Nonna peered into a large pot on the stove and pointed at her notepad perched on the end of the kitchen counter.

Chase scratched his chin, wondering where to start: the potatoes or the statement. "You're not supposed to cook without one of us here to help."

"Nichole. My dear. Thank you for making time to visit me on such short notice." She elbowed Chase and his declaration aside, then hugged Nichole. "Now, where's my new great-grandson?"

"It's Wednesday and a school day." And a workday, but Nonna had demanded Chase bring Nichole to see her when he'd bailed from the family intervention yesterday. "Wesley had to go to school."

"That's unfortunate." His grandmother

scowled. "Being with family should always come first."

"Wesley was quite upset, Nonna." Nichole smiled. "He offered to do extra chores for three months if I let him skip school today."

"Sounds like a good boy." Delight lifted Nonna's paper-thin cheeks. "Now let's look at you. You're lovelier than ever, dear."

"You always were too kind, Nonna." Nichole gripped both of Nonna's hands as if she wanted to hang on and not let Nonna go.

Chase wanted Nichole to hold on to him the same way. As if she wanted him beside her and never intended to let him go. He picked up a fork, tested the potatoes and pierced his misdirected thoughts. One potential ski-moon had rewired everything. "Nonna wasn't always kind to me."

"You didn't need kindness." Nonna tucked Nichole's arm around hers. "Still don't."

His grandmother always minced garlic and never words. Chase concentrated on the pot and hid his smile. Arthritis had stolen the strength from his grandmother's grip but hadn't slowed the quickness of her wit. "What do I need?"

"You need a good reason to stop seeking thrills and quit avoiding home." Nonna guided Nichole into her apartment as if Nichole was the guest of honor at a society gala, not an old acquaintance. Nonna glanced at him. "But you just might have found a very good reason to come home."

His grandmother had been reciting a version of her accusation for over a year now. Despite the fact Chase lived less than ten minutes from her, fifteen minutes from his mom and both of his sisters. He was surrounded in every direction on the compass by his family and home. Family dinners belonged to Sundays and weekday visits happened at least twice a week. Avoidance would not be tolerated by the Jacobs family. Yet Nonna accused him of constantly being on the run. Chase stabbed at the potatoes. "Why are you boiling so many potatoes? You have at least two dozen in here."

"Haven't lost your ability to count. It's good to keep your mind sharp." Nonna led Nichole to the pair of kitchen barstools. "Your mind will be all you can count on if you reach my age."

Chase tapped the stainless-steel fork against the pot. "About the potatoes."

"Those are for the gnocchi we are going to make." More delight infused her voice. "Together."

Nonna stressed the word as if to underscore

she'd heard Chase earlier about needing assistance. It wasn't the last Chase would hear
about his impertinent reminder of her weaknesses. Still, she could've lost her hold on the
knife and cut herself. She had a scar on her
forearm from just such an accident and that
scar wasn't alone.

"I can't cook." Nichole gripped the wrought
iron back of the barstool.

"No one in our family cooked as good as
my own mother." Nonna patted Nichole's
shoulder. "We all have challenges we must
face."

"How were you going to overcome the
challenge of lifting this pot up to drain the
water?" Chase used the fork to point at the
oversize pot. Osteoporosis had weakened
each one of his grandmother's bones. A sign
outside her apartment door read Fall Risk.
Though she'd chopped potatoes and filled the
pot as if she'd intended to cook for the retirement home lunch rush.

"I wasn't going to lift it. You are." Nonna
gave two quick, irritated tugs on her blue-
striped apron. "My hands work a little slower
these days, but they still work. It'll do you
good to remember that."

"I was only trying to help, Nonna." Chase
added a dose of remorse to his words. "Mom

would scold me if I didn't remind you of the rules."

"Your mother needs to concentrate on her own rules and let me live like I'm used to." Nonna sniffed. "Now find yourself and Nichole some aprons."

His grandmother intended for them to cook together. Nichole included. But Nonna had always been selective about who she allowed in her kitchen. Who she shared her recipes with. The kitchen had always been reserved for those his grandmother considered family. Cooking was an event from the preparation to the cleanup. An intimate, private experience. Almost sacred. Nichole and Chase cooking together as if they were a real couple. "This was only supposed to be a quick catch-up visit. Nichole has to work on her business."

"Do you have any family traditions, Nichole?" Nonna shifted away from Chase to focus on Nichole.

Again, Nonna acted as if he hadn't spoken. Her typical default once she'd heard something that went contrary to her intentions. Chase crossed his arms over his chest, intending to stare his grandmother into cooperation.

"Not opening Christmas presents until

Christmas morning." Nichole's hands fluttered in front of her. "Homemade eggs Benedict. It's the one thing I can make."

"We'll make eggs Benedict together another time." Nonna nodded, pleasure spread into the creases fanning from her eyes beneath her round glasses. "Today we're making one of our family favorites."

No. No cooking. Chase cooked alone at his house. Never invited anyone he'd dated to cook with him. He couldn't recall cooking a meal for anyone he'd dated. That would've invited a woman into his house, granting her permission to critique his food and him. There were too many obstacles to surpass before they cooked together. Before he knew for certain they'd work well together. Neither Chase nor his past girlfriends had been interested in escalating their relationships beyond casual and informal.

His grandmother believed gardening and cooking opened the mind and the heart to love's true meaning. Chase already knew what love meant. Love meant exposure and rejection. No one wanted to face that. Besides, he'd avoided his heart for so long, there were too many weeds to find it anymore.

"This is our family tradition. Every new couple learns a family recipe from the current matriarch." Nonna shuffled into the kitchen beside Chase. "Your grandfather and I cooked with my grandmother. Chase's mother and father cooked with Chase's great-grandmother. Of course, Chase's father burnt the sausage and spilled the olive oil. We should've honored that unfortunate sign from Fate." Nonna nudged Chase aside and opened a drawer. Aprons burst forth like wishes on a shooting star. "Never underestimate the importance of signs, dear."

His grandmother always packed a lot of words into one breath as if worried she might be on her last breath. As if she might not get the chance to finish her thought and get her message across. There was always a message.

Nichole reached for the apron, her movements slow and hesitant.

But Nichole wasn't Chase's real wife. They weren't a real couple. Surely there was some kind of sign happening now. Something not to be overlooked. But all he saw was his petite grandmother, her shoulders stooped, her faith strong, and Nichole, welcoming and kind and all too appealing. Chase stumbled for an excuse to leave.

Nichole stepped into the kitchen, set the apron strap around her neck and turned her back toward Chase. "Can you tie this please?"

"You have work." Chase kept his hands at his sides and his gaze fixed away from the dangling apron straps. *I never promised this.*

"I can go back further in the family tree." Nonna pulled a stainless steel bowl from a cabinet. "Generations in our family have been honoring this particular tradition and proving that food brings you closer together and love bonds you. We had a rather impressive streak until Chase's father."

"I can call on vendors and businesses later." Nichole twisted and took Chase's hand, easy and effortless as if she'd been reaching for him always. She squeezed his fingers. "This is important to Nonna."

It was even more important not to act like a couple. Not to link his fingers with hers or notice how her hand fit inside his as if they belonged. Chase might start to believe in more than a business agreement between them. Chase might start to believe in walks down the aisle, vows and a different sort of future. But Chase only knew how to succeed one way: on his own.

"I wouldn't imagine you'd want to go out and about at all today." Nonna set the mixing bowl on the kitchen table next to the cutting board and cookie sheets.

Chase narrowed his eyes. All evidence of

crafts had been replaced by cooking supplies. Not a scrap of wreath ribbon or forgotten silk butterfly littered the table. Nonna had planned their cooking session. If he wasn't mistaken, she had help preparing. Now he had his mother and sisters to blame too.

Nonna added, "I'm sure the media will be tracking your every move."

"I work from home." Nichole released him and tugged several strands of hair from beneath the apron strap around her neck. The movement distracted Chase. He wanted her hand back inside his and he wanted to help her. "And nothing I do is all that interesting."

"But you're the headline, my dear, and that makes you interesting. The press announced your identity late this morning on the news." Nonna shuffled into the kitchen and picked up the salt container. "Nichole, if you're going to be tied to my grandson, you have to make the news part of your morning routine like brushing your teeth and eating breakfast. None of it can be skipped or you risk ruining your entire day."

"That's not possible." Chase had factored in one day, maybe two, before the media figured it out.

"The press knows my identity?" Nichole

smashed the front of her apron between her hands.

"Released your full name in the article." Nonna returned to the kitchen table and her makeshift prep station. "Marie is a lovely middle name, my dear. Is it a family name?"

"After my grandmother." Nichole fiddled with the apron, her tone distant.

"A touching tribute." Nonna checked over the table.

Releasing Nichole's name in the press was not touching or a tribute. "Nonna, why didn't you say anything earlier?"

"I told you I was preparing my statement for the press." Nonna waved toward her notepad; her focus remained on the table.

Chase summoned his patience. "You won't need to make a comment."

"One never knows." Nonna tucked her hands into the pockets on her apron and looked at Chase over the rims of her glasses. "Last week, Harold Mathis and Mary Lou Tanager spent the night together at a motel. Both of their families were contacted for comments as if we haven't earned the right to do as we please."

"I have an agent." Chase wiped his hands on his jeans as if that would remove his unease. "Travis fields these very things for me. To help protect my family."

"Where was Travis yesterday?" Nonna eyed him. "If you wanted to remain anonymous, why were you at the school yesterday out in the open together?"

He'd gotten out of the car to support Nichole. Panic had paled her cheeks; worry had drained the color from her lips. He'd wanted to help.

"I was quite certain your whole marriage was a farce." Nonna stepped over to the kitchen counter and shifted her notepad to face Nichole and Chase. "However, now that you made it simple for the press to identify you, dear, I believe there might be merit to your impulsive union. Such an emotional hug."

Chase edged closer to the counter, close enough to see the pictures displayed on Nonna's notepad. Yet not close enough to touch, as if he stood outside a rattlesnake's nest and feared an attack. The larger picture included Chase, Wesley and Nichole. Wesley had wrapped his thin arms around Chase and hung on. The boy had been enthusiastic and his embrace all-encompassing, as if Wesley had been more than thrilled to call him Dad.

As if Wesley had believed Chase could be his dad. *Dad.*

Chase's world tilted again. He'd never imagined being called Dad. Never considered the humbling power and overwhelming emotion in one word. He'd clung on to Wesley until his own feet had settled back on solid ground.

After all, Chase knew little about being a dad. Even less about how to be a good dad. But he knew one thing for sure. A good parent was never selfish. He had only to look at his mother, Nonna and Nichole. As for Chase, he owned the title on self-centered and hadn't earned the privilege of being called Dad.

"And your wedding gown, my dear. Wherever did you find it?" Nonna clasped her cheeks between her hands and shook her head. "I learned to sew at my grandmother's knee. That gown was not a hasty store purchase."

Nichole bumped Chase as they both leaned closer to the notepad. The second picture, although smaller, pulsed with energy. Nichole in Josie's wedding gown. Her hand, with her new ring, on Chase's lapel. Their gazes locked on each other as if it'd been their actual wedding day. His heart thumped in his chest and picked up its pace. The same as yesterday—it'd skipped at seeing Nichole in the gown. Raced with Nichole in his embrace. So reckless. So careless. And way too alluring.

"What does this mean?" Nichole's voice barely qualified for a whisper.

"You should leave for your ski-moon early." Nonna spun the notepad back around and tapped the screen. "That is if you want some privacy and to avoid the press and those pesky statements."

"Is that really necessary?" Nichole twisted toward Chase.

"Do you have your statement prepared?" Nonna peered at them both, her eyes wide and bold behind her glasses.

Nichole shook her head and swayed against Chase. "We haven't prepared one."

"Travis will handle that." Chase wanted to take Nichole into his arms and promise her everything would work out. Everything would be fine. He hadn't earned that right. Empty promises never sat well with him. He moved away from Nichole, a reminder they both needed to rely on themselves. He leaned back and gripped the counter, rather than reaching for Nichole. "What about Wesley?"

"He'll want to call Brad Harrington for a

personal bodyguard." A faint smile wafted over Nichole's stunned face.

Chase straightened. "I can protect him."

"As can I." Nichole tipped her chin up. "He'll still want the bodyguard."

"I can be one," Chase vowed. This was one thing he could do: protect Nichole and Wesley. After all, it was his fault the media had gotten involved.

"You can't be with him all the time." Nichole fussed with her apron. "It's fine. The school won't let unauthorized visitors inside. Dan is on car pool and soccer practice duty this afternoon."

"Then you can leave early for the ski-moon." Nonna beamed.

A notification pinged on Nichole's phone, lighting up the home screen. Nichole picked up her phone and gasped.

"Everything alright?" Understatement of the year. Chase flinched.

"My grandmother just texted." Nichole stared at her phone. Her voice distant and distracted. "One of my supposed high school friends just left their house. He works for the local newspaper. My grandmother thinks he's wonderful and their conversation so delight-ful, she has invited him back."

Nonna tsked. "The press will be waiting outside your house too, my dear."

"Seriously?" Nichole's phone dropped into the wide apron pocket.

Chase lowered the heat on the potato pot and the bleak edge in his voice. "It's their job."

"It was one wedding. People get married all the time." Nichole paced around the small kitchen; her hands waved in front of her. "At courthouses, churches and backyards every single day."

"But they don't marry Chase Jacobs, the city's favorite adventurer bachelor." Nonna tracked Nichole's restless circular path from the refrigerator to the sink and back again.

"I'm really sorry." Chase stepped in front of Nichole, suspending her pacing. Still her hands drifted from the back of her head to her chin to her waist and back up again. Chase moved closer, locked his gaze on her. Waited. Waited until she concentrated on him. Only him. "I am sorry. And we can stop all this. Right now."

Her hands settled between them, resting on his chest. Her bewildered gaze searched his face and cleared. "You're serious."

"I'll take the blame. All of it." Chase locked his elbows and kept his arms stiff at his sides.

If he took her hand, he'd forget. Forget this was his fault. Forget he'd exposed her private world to public scrutiny. Forget she wasn't his.

"What about the fallout?" Her fingers curled into his shirt. "Your reputation. Your contract."

Chase ignored the warmth from her touch. "I'll make sure the sale of your app is finalized."

"That was our agreement." A smile creased across her lips, only a shadow. She whispered, "I can't ski."

Chase blinked. Everything slow-rolled into a tumble and settled. "We're doing this? The ski-moon?" *The pretense. The everything.*

"We have an agreement." Nichole leaned forward, pressed a kiss against his cheek. "Last time I checked we hadn't signed our contracts."

Last time he'd checked, kissing Nichole Moore hadn't topped his priority list. His cheek tingled. "I'll teach you to ski."

Nichole stepped away from him and pulled out her cell phone. "I need to call Brooke and the school."

Chase gave in and curved his palm around his cheek. "I'll call my agent."

Nonna dashed around the kitchen, grinning

into her potato pot, humming into the flour container. "The potatoes are ready."

Chase slid his phone into his back pocket and picked up the pot from the stove.

"I like Nichole." Nonna adjusted the colander in the sink and nodded at Chase to empty the pot. "I like her a lot."

"I like Nichole too." And he did. More than he wanted to admit.

"You can't treat her like the others, Chase." Nonna picked up the potato ricer and handed it to Chase. "Her heart is good. She's not used to your lifestyle."

"What others?" Chase grabbed another mixing bowl and the potato ricer. He'd dated other women. Nothing serious. Nothing lasting. He wouldn't have asked any of his past girlfriends to act as his pretend wife. One would've misinterpreted the pretend part. Two would've reminded him that marriage wasn't part of their five- or ten-year career plans.

"The ones you kept at a distance and used for the occasional photo opportunity." Nonna scooped steaming potatoes into the ricer. "Those others. Nichole isn't like them, Chase."

Nonna's wisdom set Chase back at times.

She was no ordinary grandmother. And Nichole was no ordinary single mom either. She was a longtime friend. Nothing more. "I know who Nichole is."

"I don't suspect that you do." Nonna waited for Chase to squeeze the potatoes into the bowl and added more. "But you'll see what I'm talking about soon enough. Time brings insight. Look at me, at my age, I've gained more wisdom and clarity than a library."

He knew all he needed to know about Nichole. He didn't need more time. He wasn't interested in learning more or discovering secrets she'd never shared with anyone.

Nichole returned to the kitchen. Chase wondered about her secrets. Wondered about the intriguing woman she'd become. "Everything good?"

"Brooke and Dan will take Wesley the next two nights and meet us in Tahoe on Friday afternoon. The school is on notice." Nichole rocked onto the balls of her feet and back down, rubbing her hands together.

Exhaustion tinted the skin beneath her eyes. Or perhaps that was the doubt and uncertainty. Uncertainty that they were doing the right thing. Chase had never second-guessed his decisions so much. He had to commit. If only committing to Nichole sounded as simple as accepting a drone flight dare. Chase pushed more potato through the ricer and pushed confidence into his tone. "Travis is finding us a rental home."

"What now?" Nichole asked.

"We make gnocchi." Nonna thrust the flour container at Nichole. "Together."

CHAPTER TWELVE

YOUR GETAWAY CAR has arrived.

Nichole sent a thumbs-up reply to Brooke's text, stuffed her phone in her jacket pocket, grabbed a pair of boots from her entryway and peeked into the front yard one last time. Still inaccessible. Thanks to the news van parked in her driveway and the two news vans crammed in front of her neighbor's house. Another news van crawled along the street, marking the latest addition in the last fifteen minutes.

On the sidewalk, a dark-haired reporter smoothed her blouse down, adjusted her wireless microphone and spoke to the cameraman as if Nichole and Chase's marriage required live coverage. A hysterical laugh crawled into Nichole's throat. Nonna hadn't exaggerated about the press.

Forty-five minutes ago, Chase had tried to drop Nichole off after they'd set the last tray of gnocchi in Nonna's freezer. Nichole and Chase had surveyed the news crews gathered around her house, then decided to take Nonna's advice and leave that afternoon for their so-called ski-moon. Worried Chase's truck would be identified, Nichole had gotten out two blocks from her house and sneaked into her backyard through a forgotten side gate. She'd crammed clothes in a suitcase and waited on her backup.

Brooke and Dan had finally arrived. Nichole picked up her suitcase, scanned her backyard for lurking reporters and raced to the side gate. Thankful for once she hadn't had the funds or inclination to tackle her overgrown backyard. She tugged ivy and weeds out of her face and squeezed through the rusted gate into an alley wide enough for skateboarders to ride in single file.

Two blocks later, she spotted Dan's truck, opened the back door and climbed onto the back seat. "I owe you guys."

Dan started his truck and frowned. "I still don't know why I couldn't have parked in Nichole's driveway and yelled 'no comment,' then 'go away.'"

"That would've incited the reporters." Brooke shifted in her seat and touched Dan's knee. "And that's not the low profile that Chase and Nichole want to maintain right now."

"That's why you're meeting me in an alley blocks away from my house." The truck rolled away from the curb. Nichole scooted lower on the bench seat. "So, we can get out of the city without the press knowing."

"So, you really are married to Chase Jacobs." Dan looked at Nichole in the rearview mirror.

She held Dan's gaze, refusing to blink and forcing herself to nod. Was it less of a lie without words spoken?

Brooke supplied the words for her. "Of course, she is married to Chase."

"The news gets it wrong sometimes." Dan let the truck idle at a stop sign and drummed his fingers on the steering wheel as if debating which direction to turn. They'd arranged to meet Chase at a grocery store on the way out of the city, then Brooke and Dan would pick up Ben and Wesley from school.

"But best friends don't get it wrong," Brooke argued. Certainty and complete faith thickened her tone. "Nichole knows if she got married or not."

Nichole knew alright. But Brooke's loyalty deflated her. Nichole was the worst type of friend. Her mounting guilt pressed her into a slouch against the bench seat.

Worse, she'd lost track of time inside Nonna's place this afternoon, working beside Chase. Lost a bit of herself after she'd kissed Chase's cheek. After Chase had offered to reveal the truth and accept the full blame to protect her. He'd even vowed to ensure *In A Pinch* sold. But Nichole had given her word too. They hadn't made a one-sided deal. So, the ruse continued.

"Besides, no one gets a ring like that for no reason." Brooke peered over the seat at Nichole's hand.

There was a reason: to bolster the farce. The diamonds captured the daylight and the deception, splintering it across the seat in a brilliant display of sparkles. There was nothing flawed about the ring, only Nichole's continuous dishonesty. Would her friends ever forgive her? Would she ever forgive herself? A chill swept through her. She rubbed her cold palm against her leg.

"And Nichole cooked with Chase and his grandmother earlier today." Brooke grabbed Dan's hand and laced their fingers together.

Their connection was effortless. Sincere. So very genuine. Once Nichole sold *In A Pinch*, she'd have something real too. Nichole glanced out the window, away from diamonds that hugged her finger as if custom-made for her and vintage wishes.

"That is a big thing." Dan nodded and slanted a soft smile at Brooke.

"It's no big deal really." But Nonna had wanted to meet her first great-grandson. That was a *big* deal. Now Wesley had a supposed stepdad and another very interested great-grandmother. That chill burrowed into her bones. But the time for cold feet had long since passed. Now Nichole worried only regret waited at the end of the aisle.

Dan shook his head. "Cooking with family matters."

"Wait." Nichole straightened and leaned forward. "You were skeptical of the marriage until Brooke told you that I cooked with Chase and his grandmother. How does that work?"

"Chase Jacobs is protective of his family. He's admitted it in interviews." Dan shrugged. "He'd do anything for them. A guy like that doesn't just invite anyone into his home to meet his family."

"We've known each other since high school." *You were the only girl I ever invited home.* Nichole tugged on her sweater, pulling the too tight collar away from her neck. Still, she struggled to swallow around the lump lodged in her throat. "It's different."

"If you say so," Dan said.

She'd said it, but she knew the truth. She'd skewed their business arrangement into something more personal. Trespassed across family boundaries that should've remained intact. She never should've put on that apron. Or kissed Chase. She never should've started any of this.

Chase had moved around Nonna's kitchen as if he'd always belonged. As if cracking eggs into flour mounds on the table came as naturally as throwing a thirty-five-yard pass downfield. From Nonna's approving squeezes on her grandson's arm to Chase's awareness of his grandmother and her tired hands, the blend of love and joy had elevated the morning into an experience.

Nichole had wanted to linger until she'd figured out the recipe and the right combination to belong. But Nichole was frozen pizza, takeout and microwave savvy. Chase was fresh herbs, gourmet and five-star polished.

Brooke leaned forward in her seat and pointed out the window at a navy sedan driving in the opposite direction. "I think we just passed another car with a cameraman lurking in the back seat. Surely that's the last of them. We're out of your neighborhood."

Nichole tried for upbeat. "You're a brilliant getaway driver, Dan."

"I had to be." Dan's easy laughter flowed around the truck. "I was afraid you'd take back your invite for us to crash your Tahoe ski-moon."

"Dan hasn't stopped talking about spending an entire weekend with Chase Jacobs," Brooke said.

Dan grinned. "This is like bucket wish–list big."

Never had Chase appeared on any of Nichole's wish lists. Until now. Chase and she had to remain friends. Friends were rarely replaced and forgotten. Not like love. Love was temporary, easily set aside and too often one-sided.

"But this ski trip might be an even bigger deal for Ben and Wesley," Brooke said.

Wesley. Nichole needed caution tape to mark off all the boundaries she couldn't risk being crossed. Wesley required his own set of boundaries. The ski-moon was simply a getaway with friends. It could not become something more. Something meaningful that involved more than a business partnership. Nichole pressed her palms against her eyes, trying to hold on to her conviction.

Ten minutes later, Dan parked his truck at the back of the grocery store parking lot beside Chase's truck. He jumped out, left his door open and hurried to shake Chase's hand.

Brooke opened her door and peered back at Nichole, laughter in her gaze. "I got everything on your shopping list and added something extra, in case you want to celebrate tonight."

Nichole wanted to turn back the clock. Reverse time and start over before she'd called Chase her husband. Before boundaries got blurred.

Chase walked over, brushed his fingers across her shoulder. His touch and his gaze gentle. "You're still covered in flour."

And Nichole's heart tumbled right back into the game.

The iced-down cooler with the perishables and the shopping bags loaded with snacks and fruit stashed behind their seats, Nichole climbed into the passenger seat of Chase's truck. She waved goodbye to her friends, wrapped that caution tape around her heart and committed to keeping her distance to business appropriate.

"Any problems with the press?" Chase buckled his seat belt and started his truck.

"As far as I know, no one saw me enter or leave my house." Nichole slipped on her sunglasses, adding another barrier between her and Chase.

"Travis will issue a statement requesting our privacy."

"Will that work?"

"Not for the more aggressive reporters." Chase frowned.

"But you're used to this." How many interviews had she read about Chase? How many news reports had she watched featuring Chase?

"Doesn't mean I like it." Chase adjusted his sunglasses. "Usually it's just me I have to worry about."

"That's what you prefer, isn't it?" *To be alone.* One more reason Nichole must keep Chase in the friend zone. He only looked out for himself.

He nodded. Tension tightened his jaw, his stiff shoulders and his grip on the steering wheel as if he guarded himself from her and any more probing questions.

Nichole preferred to be alone too. Yet Chase's loneliness drew her in and became impossible to overlook. *Not my business.*

"Sorry about Nonna's ambush today." Chase rested his right hand on his thigh, his fingers curled into a weak fist. The edges of his grin tensed. "I really had no idea."

"I had fun." That was a suitable answer. Coworkers were allowed to have fun together.

"Me too." He glanced at her, surprise on his face.

"We need to go over our stories about the wedding." And she needed to pretend she never noticed his wince of pain with every shift of position. *Not my business*. She had to focus her concern on the practical things.

"I told Elliot and my agent we got married in Vegas," Chase said.

"I told Brooke and Josie we went to Reno," she said. "It's closer to drive."

"I figured we'd taken a private plane."

Nichole latched on to their differences like a scientist gathering evidence to prove a theory. Clearly Chase and she were too opposite to attract. "I also told them we got married in a chapel and I had a rose bouquet."

"Really?" He glanced at her. "But lilies are your favorite flower."

"You remembered that?" *No big deal*. She remembered minor details about him too. They were even. That her heart flipped over in one of those forbidden cartwheels was not relevant.

"I also remember that you had questionable music taste in high school," he teased.

"I was in a soundtrack phase." Nichole

shifted in her seat, opting to keep the conversation in the easygoing lane. "And Broadway musicals would've definitely been playing in the Hearts Forever Chapel in Reno."

"What music would you play at your real wedding reception?" Curiosity lightened his tone. His fist relaxed, his fingers flattened against his leg.

Had she distracted him from his pain? Nichole leaned into the back seat and rummaged through a shopping bag. "Jazz band. What about you?"

"Live cover band." His eyebrows arched above his sunglasses. "Is that red licorice?"

The hope in his tone reminded her of a younger Chase. The one who'd started every tutoring session with the same impractical question: *Don't suppose we can skip today and have fun instead?* Nichole had quickly discovered food represented fun for Chase. She opened the bag of licorice and pulled out a candy rope. "Is it still your favorite?"

"Haven't had it in too long." Chase reached across the console, wiggling his fingers. For the moment, his face masked in happiness. "But yeah. It is."

"Good thing I bought several packages." Fact: food still distracted Chase. Fact: she hadn't forgotten his favorite things. Fact: he kept his guard up and she wasn't interested in breaching his defenses. She knew all she needed to about Chase: he was a bachelor and wanted to remain one.

He waved the licorice at her. "Destination wedding. Where do you go?"

"Vineyard in Napa." She settled back into the seat and prepared to tally more differences to prove they didn't belong together. "You?"

"Island." He smiled and bit into his licorice. "Add in a private yacht equipped with all the toys—Jet Skis, speedboat for waterskiing and tubing."

Nichole wanted a beach chair under a shady palm tree and a good book. "Guest count at the reception?"

"Island-wide, open invitation." He laughed and added, "It'd be a week-long celebration. What about your guest list?"

"Friends and family only." Quaint and intimate versus rowdy and crowded. How much more proof did she need? "Your wedding sounds exhausting."

"Let's head back to your vineyard." His chuckle released his grin. "What else is happening? An insider tour. Wine-making classes. Horseback rides."

"Strolls through the vineyard. Simple wine tastings. Long, casual dinners." She straightened, added a defensive edge to her tone. "What? When do we get to relax and enjoy each other's company at your wedding festival?"

"Simple. At night under the stars on the yacht deck," he said. "No other guests allowed."

She liked that image. Too much. Nichole curled her fingers around the licorice package. The plastic crinkled into the silence.

Chase changed his grip on the steering wheel and remained quiet as if he too lost himself in the idea.

Annoyed his words made her consider more than she ever should, she yanked out another licorice rope, intending to distract him. She waved the licorice around. "These are not my favorite."

"Don't waste it." Chase snatched the candy rope from her. "You must have chocolate truffles or a chocolate bar back there too. You were never without chocolate in high school."

"I've upgraded to dark chocolate now that I'm an adult." And she'd upgraded her standards. Recalling her favorite things would not make her heart tumble.

Nichole pulled out a package of sea salt truffles, her vendor call list and concentrated on the practical.

CHAPTER THIRTEEN

THREE HOURS AND too many licorice ropes later, Chase opened the front door to the main level of the secluded three-story château Travis had secured for Nichole and Chase's ski-moon. A blast of cold air greeted them like a harsh hug from winter. "It feels colder inside the house than outside."

"We need to get the heat on quick." Nichole's breath stalled in the air beside him, suspended as if encased in ice. She stuffed her hands into her pockets. "I'll find the thermostat, if you unload the car."

"Deal." Chase rubbed his hands together and headed to his truck. It wasn't long before he had moved the last suitcase and the cooler inside. Every step farther into the house, the air cooled another degree. And Chase second-guessed Travis's choice of rental homes and his own ski-moon inspiration.

Nichole held her hand over the in-floor heat vent and scowled. "It just keeps blowing cold air."

"I'll call Travis." Chase pulled out his cell phone, left Travis a voice mail and pressed buttons on the thermostat as if searching for proof he'd made the right choice coming to Tahoe.

He was alone with Nichole, cold and entirely too curious to know what else she remembered about him. Even more, he wanted to learn her story, not review game footage, study play charts or discuss offensive strategy. All because he'd been sidetracked by red licorice and Nichole's consideration. She'd thought about him as she'd packed for their fake honeymoon. He'd forgotten the gnocchi Nonna had put together for their dinner. He'd only ever had one commitment: *football.* He belonged in one place: *the football stadium.* But with Nichole, he started to consider...

His cell phone vibrated in his hand, ruptured his thoughts and realigned his priorities. Working heat, first. Contract renewal, second. Chase disconnected his phone call and walked into the kitchen. "Good news. Travis got us a service appointment with a local heating company."

Nichole closed the refrigerator and rubbed her hands together. "Bad news?"

"The tech won't be here until tomorrow morning." Chase motioned toward the door.

"We can head into town and find a hotel room for the night."

"Or make our own heat." Nichole motioned to the wide stone fireplace. A stack of freshly cut wood waited beside the fireplace.

"Not sure we can warm this room up." Chase stared at the log ceiling, more than two stories above his head. The right choice: leave and find a hotel. But another choice tempted him. "Let's check out the rest of the house."

Nichole headed upstairs. Chase searched the master bedroom suite on the opposite side of the main level. Five minutes later, Nichole called his name.

"Found an electric blanket in the guest room up here." She leaned over the upstairs railing.

"Nice." Chase locked his gaze on her, willing her to make the right choice. "Found a fireplace in the master bedroom with wood piled in the grate. I opened the flue and lit the fire."

Now she'd tell him to extinguish it. Tell him to start the truck and head to a suitable hotel with individual hotel rooms.

"You know how to work a real fireplace?" She clutched the blanket.

"Come on down." He turned around and

headed toward the master bedroom suite. "See for yourself." Then they would leave.

Nichole warmed her hands by the fire. "There are two more bedrooms, both suites, upstairs."

"We both have to stay in here tonight." Chase poked at the logs in the fire and his ir- rational suggestion. He added another log and waited for Nichole to walk out. She scooted closer to the fireplace, keeping her back to- ward the door.

Chase closed the wire mesh fire screen and opened his mouth. Now he'd tell her they should head to a hotel. If they stayed in the house, he'd forget. He'd forget he'd vowed not to learn more about her. He'd forget this was all pretend. "I can stretch out on the love seat."

"You're twice the size of the couch." Nich- ole shook her head. "We'll build a pillow wall and share the electric blanket on the bed."

"A pillow wall?" Chase followed her to the four-poster bed, paused on the other side and scratched his chin. A cement wall dividing the bed wouldn't cut off his awareness of her.

"It's a barrier down the center of the bed. Made with pillows." She quickly divided the bed into two halves.

"You've done this before?" Chase crossed

his arms over his chest. She couldn't seriously be constructing a pillow wall. He couldn't seriously be agreeing.

"Wesley claims he's too old to sleep with his mom." Nichole fluffed a pillow. "During renovations at my grandparents' house last summer, we shared a room. This was his solution."

"And if I cross the barrier?" *Wrong question.* He didn't want to know.

"I get to wake you up, then steal all the covers for myself." She laughed and adjusted the electric blanket over the bed. "Wesley's terms."

Chase could have terms, too. If he wanted more with Nichole. "I accept."

She fumbled with the cord on the electric blanket. "It's a big bed. We'll both have plenty of room."

"Now that sleeping arrangements are solved..." The fire worked too well. Heat spread through him as if he'd wrapped himself in the electric blanket and set it on scalding. Chase dropped his jacket on the chair. "Let's concentrate on dinner."

"I vote grilled cheese, soup and hot chocolate for dessert." Nichole walked to the door and glanced back at Chase. "And yes, we have everything we need, even marshmallows."

Chase rushed after her, escaping the warmth and welcoming the slap of cold air. "I'll take the grilled cheese. You heat the soup."

She opened drawers until she located the can opener.

"This is going to be a grilled cheese experience, courtesy of Nonna's recipe." He pulled a cutting board from a cabinet and cut thick slices of bread. "One you'll want to repeat again and again."

Nichole looked at him, her gaze searching. Chase resisted the urge to pat himself down to make sure he hadn't removed his shirt too. The more her gaze probed, the more exposed he felt.

Finally, she blinked. "I'll be the judge of the grilled cheese experience."

After the dishes had been washed and their hot chocolate mugs emptied, Nichole declared Chase's grilled cheese the best she'd ever tasted. Nichole decided she'd ask Nonna for her recipe after Chase had claimed for the fifth time he couldn't reveal family secrets.

Chase added more logs to the fire, waited for the flames to build. The night pushed in against the windows. The pain in his shoulder pushed against his nerves, pulsing deeper. He stacked several pillows, restacked and repositioned them again.

Nichole curled under the blankets and stared at the fire. The quiet would've soothed if not for the escalating throbbing in Chase's shoulder. His gaze fell on Nichole. Her light brown hair fanned across the pillow, one strand curved across her cheek. He wanted to curl his fingers through her hair, absorb the softness. The ache in his shoulder eased. "Can I ask about Wesley's real dad?" His curiosity had gotten the better of him.

Nichole rolled onto her side and studied him. "Only if you'll tell me about your shoulder injury."

"I'm good." He hadn't really wanted to know about Wesley's father. Chase stretched his shoulders, clenched his teeth and stifled his wince. "There's nothing to tell."

"You're right-handed yet you rarely used your right hand to drive today. You wince before your other hand even touches your right shoulder. Every so often, you reach toward your shoulder as if you want to test the pain." She scooted over and set her cheek on top of the pillow wall. Her gaze landed on him, concern in the hazel depths. "I watched the game, saw the tackle."

"Then you know it wasn't that bad of a hit."

Chase folded his left arm behind his head as if to prove he could relax through the discomfort.

Nichole's gaze drifted to the fire and away from him. In that moment, Chase lost something. Something he wanted back. But he was fine alone. Better. He didn't want her pity. If he wasn't a football player, what could he offer her? Certainly not a heart too afraid to ever trust in love.

"Wesley's biological father is nothing more in our lives than that—a sperm donor." She slipped her hand underneath her cheek to prop herself up.

Perhaps the guy was no one in Wesley's world. But Chase heard the anguish in her low tone. Like his shoulder, there was much more beneath the surface.

But Nichole blocked him out. As it should be. He'd stonewalled her too. Their arrangement was only temporary. "The hit to my shoulder was not bad. Or it wouldn't have been bad if I hadn't already had multiple surgeries on it."

Her gaze drifted back to him. Again, that compassion and concern settled on him as if he deserved the kindness. As if she truly cared about him. Like he suddenly wanted her to.

"What does Mallory think?" she asked.

Chase blinked. "My sister?"

"Of course. Mallory. Who else?" Nichole pushed on his leg and sat up. Her hands waved around her as if she wanted to catch the words spilling out. "Don't tell me you stopped asking Mallory's opinion now that she's an actual licensed doctor. Because that never stopped you in high school or college. Every time you got injured, you'd tell me, 'Well, Mallory thinks... Mallory believes...' You never once mentioned what the doctors told you."

Chase leaned into the pillows and his memories. Mallory had a first aid kit in elementary school. By middle school, his sister had known she wanted to be a doctor. By high school, she'd started volunteering in a local physician's office. Chase had always gone to his sister. First for Band-Aids and ice packs. Then to ask if he needed stitches and to try to convince Mallory to do the job herself. He still relied on his sister's opinion.

Until recently. After Mallory had insisted that he have another surgery. Would Nichole take Mallory's side or his? "Physical therapy got me through the season and the playoffs. After the last hit, I increased my physical therapy to every day and added extra rest to the regimen."

Nichole assessed his shoulder as if determined to make her own diagnosis. "How do you plan to do your therapy here?"

He hadn't planned. He'd canceled his physical therapy sessions against JT's advice. JT had asked to join the ski-moon party, but then Chase risked Nichole and the others learning the true depth of his injury. "I have exercises I can do."

"I can help," Nichole offered. "Maybe a massage?"

Not from her. Chase usually ignored boundary lines, however, that was one he'd heed like a fully charged electric fence. "Why?"

"You're in obvious pain, Chase." Nichole pressed her palms on the pillow wall, smashing the feathers down and demanding his full attention. "You're struggling to get comfortable right now. You keep moving, small shifts to the left, then the right. Small bend forward, then back. Your eyes narrow with every move. You're in more than a little pain."

"It hurts." He'd give her that much. He kept his arm behind his head, refused to flinch. "It's nothing that won't heal." If he kept reciting those words, it would come true.

"Well, I can also fix a mean ice pack. You just have to let me know if you prefer frozen peas or frozen steak." Nichole flopped onto her side of the divide. "As you know I've had some experience with physical therapy routines."

"That's right." Chase flipped through his memories and moved away from his shoulder. "You tripped on the bleachers, broke two toes and ended up in that bootie for over a month."

"Don't remind me." But she laughed. The sound low and beguiling as if her disbelief still made the whole thing hard to process. "It was on the auditorium stairs during the regional debate finals. Three toes broke, not two."

She'd shown up at his house in the walking boot. He'd wished he'd been there to help her. "Break anything recently?"

"Only my heart." She flattened her lips together. The truth was already settling on the pillows between them. "But it wasn't recent. I've healed."

The fire snapped and crackled. The warmth expanded into the corners of the room. Everywhere except Nicole's bronze gaze. Her heart may have been broken years ago, but she hadn't forgotten the anguish. He said, "Wesley's father broke your heart, didn't he?"

"Professor Myles Dillon, PhD, is Wesley's biological father." Her voice was remote, as if distance, not time, healed pain. "I took his business econ and economic theory classes. Then I became his teacher's assistant and a cliché."

He disliked Professor Dillon for hurting Nichole. Still, Wesley's real father had earned a PhD and was a college professor. A professor was the right kind of guy for Nichole. Not a football player, facing the possible end of his career, who knew more about being alone than being a couple. Chase cleared his throat. "If you loved each other, how was it a cliché?"

"I loved him, hence the broken heart." Nichole traced her finger over the snowflake design on the pillowcase. "I don't think his heart was even bruised after things ended."

"You were having his child." Chase wanted to believe he'd act differently. Wanted to believe he'd welcome the news. Be a good father. But his own father had failed on the good part. On doing the right thing. Chase had never wanted to test if he'd inherited more than his green eyes from his own dad.

"Not all fathers are created equal." Nichole's frown deepened.

Chase knew those words quite well. Chase's father had left long before Chase had met Nichole. But she'd witnessed Chase's father's return. Days before the football draft, his father had walked back into Chase's life and asked to be a permanent part of Chase's world again. Seemed Chase was finally worthy enough of his father's attention.

Nichole had argued his father deserved a second chance for simply being Chase's dad. Chase had replied: *not all fathers are created equal*.

He'd never wanted Nichole to gain that kind of clarity, especially at Wesley's expense. A different ache settled into his chest. One for a young boy who'd deserved so much more. So much better. He wanted to find Professor Dillon and lecture him. Right now, he wanted to pull Nichole into his arms and hold her until she forgot her pain. "Wesley is a really terrific kid."

"I know." A bitterness constricted her voice, squeezing her words together. "His biological father wasn't interested in knowing anything about his own child."

"He never met Wesley." Even Chase's father had a few years with his own children. He at least knew their names. Chase's lecture for the professor intensified. That ache in his chest—the same one he knew Wesley felt—

worsened, and he wanted to take care of a boy he hardly knew but understood.

"Myles doesn't even know if he has a son or daughter." The bitterness seized control of her words. "That was entirely his choice."

Chase's mother had glowed in the early photographs of her pregnancy with Ivy, framed by his father and a young Mallory. Nichole would've glowed too. Chase had seen her love for Wesley at the school. That same love would've already lit her from the inside at the very first news of her pregnancy. How could Professor Dillon not have been captivated by an excited Nichole? "You told the professor you were pregnant, and he walked away?"

"I told him I was pregnant." Nichole focused on Chase. Strength in tone. "Then I walked away."

"He never came after you." Chase would've gone after Nichole. If he loved her. If he loved her, he'd have to show her his true self. But Chase's love hadn't been enough for his father to stick around.

"We wanted different things," Nichole said. "It's much better this way. Wesley doesn't have to deal with the disappointment of a disinterested father."

Chase had finally stopped dealing with his

own disappointment one year after his father had left. He'd forced himself to concentrate on football. On the field, the physical pain was real. Every tackle, sack and collision strengthened him. "What did you tell Wesley?"

"I told him the truth. His biological father never wanted to be a dad." Her voice sounded waterlogged. She'd accepted her own broken heart, but not Wesley's. She'd found strength for her son. She added, "I didn't want him to have illusions about his father."

Chase understood. He'd spent his entire first grade believing his own dad would realize everything—everyone—he'd left behind was worth fighting for and come home.

Now Wesley had been forced to learn his own lessons from a father who'd never wanted to know him. Chase ground his teeth at the pitch of grief for an innocent boy. "My mom had wanted my dad to be better for us, but she'd known. Even warned me a few times not to get my hopes up."

"Did you?" Nichole asked.

"Of course." Chase stretched both arms out in front of him as if that proved he no longer hurt. "Each time my dad failed, it hurt a little less. Until finally it didn't hurt at all."

Nichole nodded. "Then you'll understand when I ask you not to get Wesley's hopes up."

He understood but didn't want to listen. "Get his hopes up?"

"He's a huge fan of yours," Nichole stressed. "But he doesn't know you."

"What does that mean?" Chase crossed his arms over his chest, blocking the jab of her words. His fans, even the kids, wanted his autograph on their jerseys, footballs, hats. Wanted pictures. People wanted to know him everywhere he went. "Are you saying I'm not worth getting to know?"

"That's not it." Nichole covered her face with both hands. Inhaled. Exhaled. "Let me start over."

Chase waited. He might not be worth falling in love with. What was wrong with getting to know him?

"Wesley believes in the image of you. The superstar athlete with the superstar lifestyle." Nichole rushed on. "You're the guy all the kids want to grow up to be."

That was much better than wanting to be like his own disinterested father or even Wesley's negligent biological dad. "And that's a bad thing, to want to be me?"

"Your reputation does need some polishing." Nichole tied her hair up as if settling into her topic.

Everyone close to Chase talked about his reputation. Yet the public adored him. Chase scowled.

Nichole lowered her hands. "But that's not my point."

"What is?" His voice sounded sour as if he'd sipped Nichole's bitter tonic from earlier. "That I'm not good enough to get to know Wesley." Good enough for Wesley. Or even Nichole. He locked his jaw against the discomfort of the truth.

"I don't want him to get hurt." Nichole motioned between them. The movement quick and concise like her words. "This is not a family bonding weekend. This whatever it is between us isn't permanent. It's temporary."

"Until our contracts are signed and official," Chase clarified, restating their terms and disengaging from any sentiment.

"Exactly." Nichole lay down and tugged the blanket to her chin as if they'd reached an understanding. "When this is over, I don't want Wesley hoping you'll continue to be in his life."

Nichole didn't want her son waiting at the front door for Chase to arrive. Checking voice mails and text messages every ten minutes for a message. A message that would never come. Chase had done that and more during first grade. He'd hoped and wished and waited for his father. His father had never returned. That old hurt tangled his distress for Wesley. "I can be his friend."

"He won't understand." Nichole straightened her arms on top of the blankets. "He'll want more. He'll want the illusion. We cannot create an illusion this weekend."

Chase stared at the bed. Divided and separated. But walls and defenses could be breached. He should agree with her. She was right. Wesley had to be protected. And he didn't really want anything more between himself and Nicole. Even if the illusion tempted him. "What do you want me to do?"

"Keep your distance." Nichole curled under the blankets, away from Chase.

Chase jammed his elbow into the pillows, searching for a comfortable position.

"Wesley will be busy with Ben," Nichole added. "Those two are inseparable. They can enjoy the snow and their weekend together. And we can…"

"Watch from the sidelines," Chase finished for her.

He'd never been any good at standing on the sidelines. But for Nichole, he'd try. After all, what did he really know about being a father or a good friend? He'd forgotten the gnocchi. She'd remembered licorice. All he really knew about fatherhood was the kind of father he wished his own dad had been and never was. But he'd stopped wishing in grade school. "I'll keep my distance."

He reached over, turned off the light and scooted to the edge of the bed, away from Nichole and her ridiculous pillow wall, as well as his absurd urge to prove to her that what was between them was more than an illusion.

CHAPTER FOURTEEN

NICHOLE CURLED HER hands around her mug and paced in front of the fireplace. She'd woken up alone, the covers straightened and the pillow cold on Chase's side of the bed. He'd kept the fire burning and the bedroom door closed to keep the heat inside and Nichole suitably separated from him. Like she'd asked. Like she wanted. She scowled into the steam streaming from her coffee.

Her phone lit up on the fireplace mantel. Congratulations and well-wishes from former coworkers and distant friends filled her text alerts. Two names weren't on her missed call list or unopened texts: her mom or dad. Perhaps her parents would return home now. Her mother would love the media attention and the subterfuge. Certainly, her father would want to write a script to capture the storyline. At the very least, Nichole's news of marrying a celebrity of sorts was worthy of a phone call, wasn't it?

Nichole scrolled through her contact list

and selected the one person who'd always understood Nichole's long-standing wish for her parents to act like typical parents, even just one time. Nichole's grandmother answered on the second ring. Nichole waited for her grandfather to pick up the other phone, launched into her apology and veered into an explanation. One her grandmother quickly and efficiently ended with: *I always liked Chase. Such a darling boy.*

Nichole started her explanation again.

Her grandfather interrupted with: *About time.*

Followed by a deep hum of approval. Nichole stared at her phone. Where was the disappointment about her secret wedding? About not being included.

Her grandmother jumped into the silence and insisted Chase join Nichole and Wesley the following week for Wesley's weekend visit. And wished Nichole a memorable skimoon as if she used that term regularly.

Nichole managed a stunned and awkward thank-you.

Her grandmother promised Nichole once her parents learned about their daughter's marriage, they'd certainly be in touch. After all, they hadn't missed important milestones in Nichole's life growing up. Cards and presents had arrived early for Christmases and birthdays. *I love yous* exchanged, the call ended.

Nichole flopped onto the bed face-first and replayed the conversation. Chase was darling. Their wedding overdue. And Nichole's parents suddenly reliable. Even though her parents' visits had been less consistent and all too often unreliable. Chase and Nichole's wedding a fake. And Chase…

The doorbell chimed throughout the house. Laughter rolled against the closed bedroom door like an invitation to join the merriment and ditch her self-imposed distance.

Nichole hopped off the bed, opened the door and stopped in the doorway. Chase stood near the massive stone fireplace. A lanky, tall technician in pressed jeans, a pin-striped blue work shirt and steel-toed work boots moved closer to Chase's side. Both men tilted their heads up to look at the camera on the technician's phone. The one he held at an angle high above their heads. Several selfies later, the pair broke apart and checked the photographs.

The technician—his name, Alden, embroidered above his shirt pocket—greeted her. His blond curls covered his forehead, brushed over his brown eyes as if reaching for his twin dimples. "The heat is not quite fixed yet, but it will be. I promise."

"It'll be warmer if you shut the bedroom door," Chase said. His jacket hung on the back of a kitchen chair. A pair of gloves and a hat rested on the table. He appeared more than immune to the walk-in-refrigerator-level cold in the house.

Nichole leaned against the doorframe and crossed her arms over her chest. Her toes curled inside her thick socks, willing her to retreat into the bedroom and the welcoming warmth. But Chase gripped Nichole's attention as firmly as Chase's hold on his permanent marker. Chase signed everything Alden set on the counter.

"I think we've covered all my family." Alden dug through his tool bag on the floor. The sheer joy on Alden's face saturated his voice. "Could you sign these gloves for my cousin and a pair for his brother-in-law? They never miss a game."

Chase appeared in no hurry to stop signing. His excitement rivaled Alden's. He appreciated Alden's reenactment of specific plays, added his own version, then steered the conversation back to Alden's family. Always he brought the conversation back to Alden. Chase was kind, thoughtful and engaging.

"I really appreciate this, Mr. Jacobs." Alden gathered his items like a kid collecting his winning prizes at the midway in the State Fair.

"Chase." He grinned and swirled the marker across a work glove. "How long have you been working as a technician?"

"Little over two years." Alden tucked his autographed merchandise away as if he'd never take it out. He brushed his hair out of his eyes, his voice timid. "I'm saving up to buy my girl a ring."

"That's special." Chase handed the gloves to Alden. His smile genuine, his voice sincere. "She's really lucky to have you."

Nichole watched Chase. Surely Chase would advise the young guy to wait longer to get married. Have more fun before tying himself down. Surely the city's favorite adventurer bachelor would dissuade Alden, discourage marriage and laugh off love.

"Could you sign something for her parents?" Alden scanned the living room as if the chateau was his personal Pioneers' fan store. "They're big fans too."

"Absolutely." Chase held up his hand, interrupting Alden's search. "I'm pretty sure I have an extra jersey in my suitcase."

Chase carried extra jerseys to give out to

his fans? Had the sweatshirt Chase loaned Nichole been intended for a fan? And then she understood, his star power came from his ability to center his full attention on someone. To make that person feel valued and important, not a bother or an intrusion. He made her feel recognized. He made her feel noticed and appreciated. Nichole held her position in the doorway.

Chase slowed, squeezed around Nichole. Only his arm brushed against her shoulder.

For a breath, she wanted more of his undivided attention too. She turned and tracked his movements around the bedroom. "You enjoy this?"

"He's a good guy." Chase dug through his suitcase and held up a Pioneers jersey. "If this will help Alden win over his in-laws, then it's time well spent."

Would he consider their time together, time well spent too? "You're a good guy too."

"Don't forget to shut the door to keep warm until the heat is fixed." He slipped around her and glanced back. His gaze warm, thoughtful. "Did you make your calls to potential vendors like you wanted?"

Nichole pointed at her phone on the mantel, reminding herself more of Chase's attention wasn't what she needed. "Doing that right now."

Chase handed Alden the signed jersey and followed him upstairs. He asked Alden a series of questions as if he intended to become a technician after his football career ended. Nichole returned to the master suite and her business.

Four phone calls concluded, heat poured through the in-floor vent, warming the master bedroom into sauna-level hot. Nichole rose, stretched her legs and walked out to the kitchen.

Chase and Alden headed toward the front door. Chase carried Alden's tool bag as if it belonged to him, not the young technician. Alden lifted his 10-foot ladder.

"Thanks, Alden." Nichole called out. "You've saved our vacation."

Alden's grin split across his face, his dimples anchoring it into place. "My pleasure, Mrs. Jacobs."

Mrs. Jacobs. Nichole blinked, tried to cut off the swirl of delight curling through her. She was a fraud. An imposter. Her heart stretched against that caution tape and refused to listen.

Chase closed the front door, moved around the large island and opened the refrigerator.

"We've got lunch and dinner to plan. Any ideas?"

Banning the use of *Mrs. Jacobs* would be a good start. Nichole swiped across her phone screen, pulled herself together and restored those boundaries. A new text from Brooke flashed on her phone, distracting her. "Brooke and Dan are coming up early. Wesley and Ben convinced them nothing was happening in school tomorrow since it's the day before spring break. They'll be here in about an hour. And everyone is hungry."

Chase clapped his hands together. "What should we cook?"

We. No, they were definitely not a *we.* Couldn't be. They had a business arrangement. Yet everything was starting to feel normal. Too natural. As if they always planned meals together. Always vacationed together. She had to break their connection. Remind herself they were opposites. And opposites could not attract. "I brought boxed mac and cheese and hot dogs just for times like this."

"You're serious?" He frowned at her.

"It's a family favorite." Nichole lifted her chin. "It's one of Wesley's favorites."

He stepped closer to her. "Let's make a deal."

Deal? Nichole moved toward him and

tipped her head to lock her gaze on his. The last deal she'd made with Chase had her married to him. How much worse could it get? "What do you have in mind?"

"You make your food." He grimaced and recovered. His gaze warmed and searched her face. "I'll make my version and we see which one everyone prefers."

"What are you making exactly?" Nichole eyed him. He reached forward, brushed her hair off her shoulder. His touch light and swift. But the effect left her restless and wishful. She cleared her throat. "It has to be healthy, no ice cream or brownies to sway the vote." No more tugs on her heart to sway her resolve.

"It'll be something simple. Kid-friendly." He opened the refrigerator and peered inside. Then turned toward her. His gaze lit up. "Baked ziti with fresh tomatoes, spinach and broccoli."

"You might want to reconsider so many vegetables." And she'd reconsider her urge to move closer to him. "It also doesn't sound so simple."

"Don't underestimate a kid's palate. I'll add sausage too." He held out his hand. "Do we have a deal?"

Chase could cook. Very well. Nichole

hardly knew her way around the kitchen. She kept her hands in her pockets. "What happens when you lose?"

"The loser has to cook breakfast for everyone for the rest of the weekend." He grinned at her.

"Done." No way would she lose this. She knew both the boys too well. Spinach would stop the conversation before it started. Nichole set her hand inside Chase's.

A jolt of awareness bounced between their palms and vaulted toward her chest. And she wondered if she'd made a different sort of bargain. One that had nothing to do with cooking and everything to do with distance. And not keeping hers.

Chase filled a pan with water, turned on the front burner, then adjusted the oven to preheat. Vegetables and several cheeses shared space on the large island with mixing bowls and cutting boards. "Don't you want to prep anything?"

"I have time." Nichole poured herself another cup of coffee and slid onto the barstool to give herself a good view of Chase's prep station. In minutes he had sausage cooking and a red sauce simmering. The scent of spices and good food filled the air. But she still had the advantage—comfort food was a family standby. "I need to boil water and open a box."

Chase laughed and chopped broccoli like a trained chef, at ease and confident. He worked without a recipe. Relied on taste and patience.

Nichole preferred exact measurements and directions more specific than *Mix a little. Add a dash.* Their cooking styles hardly meshed. She motioned toward the dishes gathering in the sink. "If I cook the hot dogs in the pasta water, I only need one pan."

"This is part of the joy in cooking." Chase added the cooked sausage, noodles and chopped vegetables to his sauce. Then inhaled the steam from the pot. "Creating is fun."

Watching Chase cook was fun. More than fun. He made her want to take more risks like asking if she could help. Like testing the boundaries of that *we.* Opposites could balance each other.

She remembered his favorite things. He'd loaned her his sweatshirt and kept the fire going all night. He'd also respected her wishes about Wesley. That hardly made him right for her. Even if her heart tumbled more than once, tugging her ever closer to the pillow wall and Chase last night. And tempting her even now. "You don't really think eleven-year-old boys are going to willingly eat spinach and broccoli, do you?"

"I do. It's all in the preparation." He waved his hand over the casserole dish he'd started to assemble and smiled at her. "Want to taste a sample?"

She wanted... Her mouth dried. "I'll wait."

"Probably for the best." He nodded. Grated more cheese, sprinkled it over the casserole, then slid the dish into the oven. "One taste and you'd probably be tempted to cheat later."

Nichole sputtered on the coffee she sipped. "I'll have you know that's the bestselling mac and cheese in the nation for a reason."

He drew a spoon around the empty pot, scraping up the last of the sauce and held it up. "And this is the best-tasting baked ziti sauce for a reason too."

"Why's that?"

"It's made from the heart." He stuck the spoon in his mouth and grinned. "Just like Nonna's."

"Now you're cheating." Nichole jumped off the stool and rounded the island, closing the distance between them.

"How am I cheating?" He tossed the spoon on the island counter and locked his gaze on her.

She had his full attention now. All she'd wanted the entire day. She charged forward, straight through every caution sign. "You're using Nonna's recipe."

He held up his hands. "Those are all I know."

And all she knew was that she'd displaced her common sense. All she knew was the heat from Chase's gaze encouraged her to cross all kinds of boundaries, pillow walls and defenses. Nichole stepped into his space, placed her hands on his chest and forgot to be practical. She leaned forward. Chase met her halfway. Their lips came together.

And their kiss intensified into something beyond strangers. Beyond friends. Something meaningful and lasting. That lingered and searched and learned. Both gave and received. Something that sent hearts soaring above the clouds.

Nichole surrendered completely.

A pounding echoed on the front door. The doorbell chimed as if set on repeat.

Nichole jumped back, flattened her hand over her racing heart. "They're early." And she was caught.

Chase held on to her waist and her gaze. "You have to get the door."

And catch her breath. Her gaze dropped

to his mouth—only a quick dip—and kick-started her heart again. "That was…"

"Something we'll definitely be discussing later." Chase gripped her shoulders, turned her toward the door before she could finish her thought. He whispered, "We might need to add new options to our agreement."

Or not. And kissing definitely could not be repeated. No matter how much she wanted to. Nichole opened the door to two excited boys and Brooke, holding twin grocery bags.

The boys asked to pick out their bedroom first, tossed their snow boots on the deck and raced upstairs. Nichole led Brooke into the kitchen.

Chase dried his hands on a towel and greeted Brooke. "I'll go help Dan with the rest of your stuff."

Brooke hefted the bags onto the counter and nudged her elbow into Nichole's side. Her eyebrows raised. "Did you celebrate last night?"

"No." Nichole shook her head. Not last night. And right now, she'd lost track of their business arrangement and broken her own rules. She'd warned Chase to keep his distance. He'd listened. Now she had to heed her own demands. "We had no heat."

"Sounds like the perfect time to make your own together." Brooke laughed.

Dan wrapped his arm around Brooke's waist, Brooke leaned her head against his shoulder. Both nodded in unison and worked to keep their own grins restrained. They were a couple—united and in love. Chase and Nichole were united in their business arrangement.

"Make your own what?" Chase stood in the doorway leading to the laundry room, snow in his hair and a one-sided grin on his face.

"Never mind." Nichole filled a pot with water, turned the burner on high and blamed the warmth in her cheeks on Alden. He'd fixed the heater too well. "I need to make the mac and cheese."

Wesley slid across the hardwood floors in his socks and grabbed an apple off the counter. "Don't forget the hot dogs."

"Already on it." Nichole smoothed out her smile, squashed the triumph in her voice. "We have two options for dinner. Mac and cheese with hot dogs. Or…"

"Baked pasta with a meat sauce," Chase said.

With her next words, Nichole would wipe away Chase's expanding grin. "With broccoli and spinach."

Wesley scowled as if his apple suddenly turned rotten. "There's spinach in the pasta?"

"And broccoli?" Ben stepped beside Wesley and wrinkled his nose.

"Vegetables are good for you," Chase offered. "And you won't even know they're in there."

Wesley bit into his apple, chewed slowly. His gaze remained fixed on Chase as if he'd suddenly turned into one of his puzzles. "How do you know?"

"You'll have to trust me." Chase closed the distance and held out his fist. "At least try it and if you don't like it, your mom will finish it."

"Cool." Wesley fist-bumped Chase. Both wore matching grins as if they were suddenly united.

She wasn't helping Chase win. Nichole pressed her hand over her stomach. "I don't know. I'm going to be pretty full after eating all that yummy mac and cheese."

"What's going on?" Dan looked at Nichole, then Chase and back to Nichole. Suspicion wove through his voice. "What are we missing?"

Brooke tapped her finger on her mouth. "We're definitely missing something."

"Nothing is going on." Nichole spread her

arms wide and added a more lighthearted note to her words. "We just have options for dinner. Everyone likes options."

"Like at a restaurant," Ben added.

"Only at this one, you can eat all you want." Chase fist-bumped both boys, then opened the oven to peer inside. "How's that mac and cheese coming, Nichole? Baked ziti is just about ready."

"Only need seven minutes and the feast can begin." She poured the noodles and hot dogs into her pot and grinned at Chase. "Funny. I'm already considering what sounds good for breakfast tomorrow."

"Who's cooking?" Wesley asked. "'Cause if it's Mom, you can have toast or cereal. Those are her specialties."

Chase swiped his hands over his mouth as if catching his laugh.

Ben stuffed his hands in his back pockets. His toes wiggled inside his socks. "My dad's specialty is funny-shaped pancakes."

"With chocolate chips," Dan added. "Those are the best part."

Nichole drained the noodles and prepared the mac and cheese according to the directions on the side of the box.

Chase pulled his casserole out of the oven

and set it on the counter. "We haven't determined who's cooking breakfast tomorrow."

"We'll know soon enough." If cooking breakfast meant another stolen kiss, Nichole might not object. But kisses and cooking together had never been part of their original agreement. And amendments had to be avoided. Other options need not be discussed. After all, Nichole's heart had no veto on their agreement.

Brooke handed out plates to the boys. Dan located the silverware and napkins.

"Remember, it's all you can eat. Don't stop until you're full." Nichole pulled a serving spoon out of a drawer and waved it over the dinner options like a wand. But there was nothing magic in her and Chase cooking together or their kiss.

How many lies could she tell?

CHAPTER FIFTEEN

"TEN MINUTES LEFT," Dan yelled from a ladder and set the head on their towering snowman. "Better get those finishing touches done. Losers have to clean up the breakfast dishes and that syrup has been hardening on the plates all morning."

A snowball bounced off Nichole's shoulder. She glanced over at Brooke, her snowman-building teammate, and brushed the snow off her jacket. "Hey. What was that for?"

"We aren't going to win if you keep sighing and daydreaming about your new husband." Brooke sorted through a pile of clothes they'd grabbed from a closet inside the house.

"I'm not sighing." Nichole knotted a scarf a little too tight around her snowman's neck. "I'm simply checking out the competition. I already cooked breakfast this morning. I don't want to clean up too."

"It's okay if you are daydreaming about him." Brooke leaned around her snowman and lifted her eyebrows up and down. "He is your husband."

Except he wasn't. Nichole smashed a carrot into her snowman's head and glanced over at Wesley and Chase, their competition in the snowmen challenge. Wesley and Chase had laughed, plotted and planned the past hour. Then laughed even more. Heads always together and sharing more high fives than she could count. The only break Wesley took was to rub his glove under his nose. Chase never tired. Never lost his patience. Never stopped listening to Wesley.

But Nichole was Wesley's team. Chase was only temporary. Their arrangement short-term. If she started relying on Chase, then expectations developed that Chase could be something more permanent in their lives. Her heart would start to believe again, and there'd be no going back. Then Wesley would get hurt. Chase had to remain on his own team.

"Time," Dan shouted. "Hands off the snowmen."

And Nichole had to keep her mind off Chase, off repeating stolen kisses, and off imagining that something more real existed between them. Something that could last past contract notarizations and app sales. The head on her snowman listed to the side as if doubting her resolve.

Dan called the teams together. Wesley spread his arms wide and shouted, "May we present Zombie Snowland."

More than a half dozen snowmen covered their Zombie Snowland in various stages of formation from full bodies to heads only. Broken twigs served as arms. Their rock eyes drooped into their half-formed mouths. They'd added a sports drink to stain the snow of their zombies' bodies bloodred. And even wrapped one poor normal-looking snowman up in a rope, held by a zombie. Nichole granted them high points for creativity, despite wanting to split up their team.

"It's an infestation of zombie snowmen." Chase grinned and high-fived Wesley. Their rapport natural, genuine and growing stronger. "It was all Wesley's idea and it was awesome."

Wesley nudged closer into Chase's side. Chase's praise straightened his thin shoulders. Nichole frowned into her scarf. She complimented her son often. But next to Chase, Wesley looked even more confident. Even more sure of himself.

"Cool." Ben's awestruck mouth dropped open. "You guys totally win."

"But you guys have the tallest snowmen ever." Wesley smiled and pointed at Ben's snowmen.

Ben and Dan had built two extra-wide bases and then kept stacking more snow mounds one on top of the other. Dan had retrieved a ladder at the halfway mark and tapped in Chase for assistance. The effect was two massive, towering snowmen that looked ready to stomp all over Zombie Snowland.

Wesley continued, "They're giants and almost reach the sky. That's even more awesome."

Complimenting the rival team. Had Wesley learned that from Nichole or Chase? It shouldn't matter. But those pesky connections that could turn into deep bonds kept interfering. She had to be responsible for Wesley's life lessons. Chase had to be responsible for keeping his distance.

"What about ours?" Nichole set her hands on her hips. "If the giants and the zombies take each other out, our snowmen are the last ones standing."

"Clearly we should win just for outlasting everyone else." Brooke nudged a carrot nose back into her snowman's face.

Wesley shrugged. "But yours are just plain snowmen."

Ben's eyebrows drew together, and he nodded. "Yeah. They're really plain."

Dan stepped beside Chase. The pair made an effort to pretend to consider Brooke's and Nichole's snowmen. Then they nodded in unison, their expression as grim as the boys'. The foursome completely united.

"That was the challenge," Nichole argued. It was a snowman challenge, not a team building exercise. "To make snowmen. We did that."

"Ours even have hats and sweaters." Brooke buttoned the sweater on Nichole's snowman. "And we absolutely met the challenge to build the best-looking snowmen."

Brooke and she were also a great team. Brooke had even helped Nichole make breakfast that morning. Chase had kept his distance and played video games with the boys. And she hadn't been the least bit disappointed. Nichole frowned; tallying her lies was becoming harder and harder. "The challenge wasn't to build the best zombie attack."

"You think it's the best zombie attack." Chase grinned.

"She did say the best," Dan pointed out.

"Boys win." Ben and Wesley high-fived. "Can we go explore before lunch?"

"We should've expected this." Brooke

groaned beside Nichole. "We know they like to gang up on us for every challenge."

"We have to come up with a better plan before game night this evening," Nichole whispered. She'd lost her bet last night with Chase. The boys had eaten most of Chase's casserole themselves, especially after Chase had helped himself to a huge portion of the baked pasta and finished every bite. Nichole had clearly underestimated the Chase factor in more ways than one.

"Not so fast." Dan caught the boys by their jackets before they sprinted off to explore. "I'm coming with you and you won't argue about it."

The boys rounded on Dan and listed off the places on the property they wanted to check. Dan finally raised his hands and said, "Just lead the way. I'll follow."

The trio bounded off toward the back of the château.

"I'll go in and start washing the dishes." Brook headed for the stairs.

Nichole gathered the extra clothing they hadn't used for their snowmen.

Chase picked up a scarf, shook off the snow and set it gently on the pile she held. He asked, "Want some help with lunch?"

She wanted help remembering their kiss

had been a mistake. She wanted help putting a wedge between him and her son. She wanted help reminding herself this was all pretend. "We've got it. Don't you want to go explore with the boys?"

He tugged her hat over her forehead. "We never talked about that kiss. Or our options."

There were no other options. But she'd lain awake thinking about their kiss most of the night, until she finally decided she'd created a simple memory for later. For the nights she couldn't sleep, and the loneliness joined her. Nothing wrong with that. "It was a late night after we finished dinner and playing cards."

"We have time now and no one to hear us besides the snowmen." He tipped his head toward the snowmen. One corner of his mouth tipped up, offering a different sort of suggestion.

No one would see if she kissed him again. *No.* She already had enough memories of kissing Chase. Two to be exact. More than enough. Nichole hugged the clothes pile tighter and locked her hands together to keep from reaching for him. "I should really go help Brooke. She's worse than me in the kitchen."

"Then you do need my help." Chase set his hand on her lower back and walked with her up the stairs. He held the door open for her, but set his hand on her elbow and stopped her just inside the doorway. He leaned in and whispered, "I know you don't want to talk about that kiss. But at least tell me I'm not the only who can't stop thinking about it."

Nichole closed her eyes, willed that shiver to recede. Ordered her heart to stand down. And opted for one of her son's favorite defaults when he wanted to avoid getting in trouble.

Deny. Deny. Deny.

CHAPTER SIXTEEN

"HEY, YOU GUYS!" Wesley barreled through the back door. Snowflakes dusted the floor around him, jarred free by his unrestrained shout of glee. "Guess what we found?"

Chase slid the pancake griddle into the lower cabinet on the island and closed the door, removing an obstacle from Wesley's erratic path. Chase remembered running into Nonna's back porch or his mom's kitchen, yelling *guess what I discovered*. The discoveries had ranged from snails, slugs and snakes to wild mushrooms; bird feathers and bird eggs to turtles, possums and earthworms. Every discovery, down to a broken piece of colored glass had always been better than the last. He considered the boys and the mountains outside and decided the options were endless. And seriously intriguing.

Nichole set the last of the sandwiches they'd assembled for lunch on a platter and leaned her hip against the marble counter. Her voice unhurried as if to temper Wesley's energy. "You found a snow fort for your snow zombies to hide out in."

Ben bumped into Wesley, unable to contain his own squeal. He threw his hands up, flinging out more delight. "Better than that."

Brooke added honey to her teacup and held up the plastic jar shaped like a bear. "You found bear tracks."

"Bears are hibernating." Ben's dry tone indicated his displeasure with her guess. "It's winter."

"We know that." Nichole wrapped her arm around Brooke's shoulders and motioned between them. "We wanted to make sure you were paying attention."

"It's way better than bears." Wesley stretched out his joy into several hops in place, knocking more snow free from his snow pants.

Chase channeled his inner boy and joined the game like he'd been doing since their arrival yesterday. Despite his promise to keep his distance. Last night, they'd needed him to round out the teams for cards. Then again, this morning for the snowmen challenge. He hadn't wanted to disappoint the boys. And he really liked being included. "You're telling me that you found something better than a snow fort and bear tracks right outside."

Both boys nodded repeatedly. Each head bob notched their grins wider.

Chase rubbed his chin and considered the pair. Exhilaration radiated from their red cheeks to their owlish round eyes. They looked about to burst. "It must be really good then."

"It's awesome," Wesley shouted.

"So awesome." Ben's holler lifted into the loft.

"I can't take the suspense anymore." Chase stuck his hands in his hair and clutched his head in an exaggerated stance. "Just tell me already."

The boys rushed him. Wesley gripped Chase's arm with both of his hands. Together the pair erupted with their find. "There are snowmobiles in the garage."

"Two." Ben held two fingers over his head.

Nichole set another platter on the island. The hard thunk on the marble countertop drew their attention. "They might not work."

Ben shook his head, sweeping his copper bangs across his forehead. "Dad already turned them on."

Not the news Nichole wanted to hear. Her scowl tightened around her eyes.

Wesley's grip on Chase's arm flexed, then

locked tighter. "It's the best day ever. First snow zombies and now this."

Chase looked at Nichole. Her gaze fastened on Wesley's hold on Chase, her scowl fixed deeper on her face. He wanted to spend time with Wesley, but he refused to hurt Nichole. "There might not be enough helmets for everyone."

Her shoulders released. She picked up her tea mug and eyed him over the rim. Gratitude in the barely noticeable dip of her chin and her muted eyes.

Wesley shook his head. "I counted nine helmets on the shelf."

Ben bumped into Chase like a pinball stuck between the high point bumpers. "Dad says they'll fit us fine."

"Perfect," Chase replied. *Or not*. Nichole wanted Chase to keep his distance, after all, not encourage a snowmobile jaunt, no matter how much he wanted to join them. "What if your mom has something planned for you already this afternoon?"

Nichole added several heaping teaspoons of sugar to her mug as if sweetening her drink might soften Wesley's disappointment. How could she possibly top snowmobiles?

"Did you make plans, Mom?" A challenge

dropped into Wesley's voice as if he dared Nichole to ruin his day.

Chase disliked the idea of spoiling Wesley's day too. Besides, moms were always forgiven. Eventually.

Worry drifted over Wesley's face, softening his hold on Chase's arm. "Chase, you haven't forgotten how to drive a snowmobile, have you?"

That would be like asking if Chase had forgotten how to drive a motorcycle, ride a mountain bike or throw a football. Had he forgotten how to drive a snowmobile? Not likely. He slid a glance at Nichole, waiting for her to step in.

"He couldn't have forgotten that fast." Ben held up both hands as if preparing to recite one of Chase's adventures. "It was just last winter when Chase raced on a special snowmobile track."

Snowcross. Chase had taken part in a snowcross race thanks to several friends who had participated in the X Games and invited him to their training site. Nichole grimaced. Chase rubbed the back of his neck and kept those particular details to himself.

"That's when Mom told me boys would be boys." Wesley looked at Chase through his eyelashes. More color shaded his face and highlighted his voice. "Then you know what, Chase? Mom told me that I wasn't allowed to be that kind of boy. What kind of boy are you anyway?"

The completely wrong kind for Nichole. She deserved someone who put her first. Someone who avoided risks and embraced responsibilities. He shouldn't be pleased Nichole followed him during the off-season too. If he was a better guy, he'd take the blame now and ruin the boy's day. He clenched his teeth together instead.

Ben giggled. "My dad said he wanted to be one of those boys."

Brooke spun around, slapped the faucet on in the sink and picked up the soap dispenser. Suddenly determined to clean her coffee mug in record-breaking time, she let the water wash away her laughter.

Nichole picked up a dish towel and twisted it around her hands. Chase concentrated on the boys, controlling his own laughter.

"So, you can still drive a snowmobile, can't you?" Wesley pressed.

"Yes, I can." Chase gained control of his grin. "But we need to get your mom's permission to go riding on one." There, he'd given her another out.

Wesley sighed and faced his mom again.

"Mom, if we promise not to be those kinds of boys, can we please go on the snowmobiles? Please." Hope extended his plea into one long drawn-out exhale.

Nichole opened her mouth, but the back door swung open and banged against the wall.

"We've got gas for the snowmobiles." Dan stepped inside, shook the snow from his hair. His smile as contagious as the kids'. Every inch of his wide frame broadcast his inner child. "Now we can have an afternoon adventure."

The boys cheered and leaned around Chase to high-five each other. Clearly, they'd deemed one parent's approval more than enough.

Ben hugged his dad. "When are we leaving?"

Dan rubbed his hand in Ben's hair. "Remember what I told you."

"After we eat a good lunch and then after I check my numbers." Ben peeked at his dad as if making sure no other conditions remained.

Chase watched the pair. A twinge twisted in his chest. His inner kid craved adventure, accepted every challenge, yet never quite accepted his dad's abandonment. He still craved a bond like Dan and Ben shared.

Chase stuffed his hands in his pockets and slammed the door on past hurts.

"Then we really get to go?" Wesley chewed on his bottom lip. His gaze skipped over the adults, unable or unwilling to settle.

"Why don't you change out of your snow clothes and search the house for a trail map," Dan suggested. "It'll make lunch time arrive quicker."

The boys scrambled out of the kitchen. Hats, gloves and jackets dropped like a bread crumb trail on the floor and up the stairs. Ideas about which direction to ride, what they would find in the mountains and what they could take home filled the rest of the space.

Dan grinned at Chase. "Suddenly I'm anxious for lunch to be over."

Chase's smile was barely there. Nichole hadn't agreed. Wesley escaped, avoiding her verdict. But Chase remained and disliked seeing her upset. Disliked even more that he'd caused her unhappiness. Wariness lowered Chase's enthusiasm into a simmer. He glanced at Dan. "Maybe we should get more gas before we head out."

"That's a really good idea." Brooke dried her hands on Nichole's towel and snatched her jacket from the kitchen chair. Her words tumbled out as swiftly as her sprint to the back door. "Dan and I can do that now. Right now, in fact."

Brooke grabbed Dan's hand, pulling him along with her to the back door in one fluid motion. Dan called out, "Text us if you need anything else—like a referee." The door clicking shut cut off Brooke's reprimand.

Nichole paced the kitchen, one arm crossed over her stomach, her other hand propped under her chin. Her fingers tapped a quick beat against her cheek. This was not his fault, yet guilt raced through him. Of course, he wanted to go. That was a given. Boys like him craved afternoons like this. The man in him—the one way too aware of Nichole—hesitated, wanting Nichole's consent. Otherwise he feared he might not enjoy the afternoon. He narrowed his gaze on Nichole. What was it about her? "I won't go."

"Of course, you have to go." Nichole paused, then refilled the coffeepot, as if she intended to restart the entire morning. "Did you see how excited Wesley was?"

Chase had seen. He'd experienced the same rush of excitement as the boys and even Dan. Except his joy dimmed as Nichole's distress increased. "You could take him."

"No. He wants you to go with him." She rubbed her forehead, her voice bleak, her gaze sad. "I've already ruined too many other adventure-like moments over the years."

"I'm sure that's not true." Chase walked to her. He wanted to hold her until her usual happiness returned. Hold her as if he could make her happy.

"I'm good at the dual parent thing. Really good." Her gaze slipped away from him, sweeping her voice along with it. "But I'm not always enough. Or the right fit for some things."

Chase ached. The catch in her voice caught in his chest and hooked deep. Chase took her hands, guided her closer and then fell back on all he knew: humor, light and easy. "Action adventures aren't always much fun."

"Tell that to Wesley." Nichole laced her fingers around his and held on. The faintest of smiles drifted over her face. There and gone like the last spark of a sunset.

"We can tell the boys only one snowmobile works." Chase tightened his hold and searched for an option she'd approve. "Dan can take them for a ride individually after lunch."

Nichole squeezed his hands. "Promise me you won't make any steep jumps or race over any moguls."

"There aren't any moguls out here."

Nichole arched an eyebrow at him, revealing her no-nonsense mom expression. The one that moms for centuries had perfected to ensure obedience and respect. He had received the same look from his mom and Nonna growing up.

"I was kidding." Chase drew her to him and locked his gaze on hers. His voice solemn like a pledge. "There won't be any moguls or jumps or races. We won't go over the speed limit. We'll leave our helmets on at all times and stay on the trail only."

"And you'll be careful." Nichole set her hands on his chest. "Very careful."

"Absolutely." Chase tucked a strand of her hair behind her ear. Tipped her chin up to capture her full attention. "I promise I'll watch over Wesley."

"Who's going to watch over you?"

"I'll be fine." Her concern for him was sweet. Welcome and familiar. But he took care of himself now. "Don't worry. This won't be like a bonding thing between Wesley and me."

"You already connected over your zombie land." She dropped her forehead on his shoulder. "It's too late." Her voice sounded hopeless.

"We won't connect anymore." Same as

he wouldn't kiss Nichole anymore either. Or learn any more of her secrets.

She straightened and frowned at him. "How do you intend to do that?"

"We can't talk much with helmets on." Chase pulled her against him and wrapped his arms around her waist. "It'll be about the ride."

The same as their relationship. He'd pretend he hadn't forgotten this was all fake. A sham. He'd pretend being with Nichole and Wesley was nothing he wanted. "Besides, tomorrow they'll discover something even cooler than snowmobiles. Then today will be forgotten."

"You believe that?" she asked.

"Absolutely," he said. "For boys like them every day is about outdoing yesterday." He knew because he was one of those boys. Except when it came to Nichole. He just wanted to be with Nichole every day. That would be more than enough.

Chase released her and stepped back. He needed to walk away and remember what Nichole wanted. And that wasn't him long-term. "I'm going to go change and put on dry clothes."

And he'd keep adding layers until he'd buried everything he truly wanted.

CHAPTER SEVENTEEN

CHASE PARKED THE SNOWMOBILE, slid off his helmet and checked his cell phone. Still no bars or signal reception. He ran his gloved hand through his hair and frowned at the sky. Every tree looked the same: barren, snow covered and dreary. Every trail turn appeared the same as the last. The clouds seemed to have stalled in the sky, offering the same view in all directions. Nature wasn't to blame for their situation. Rather, the fault belonged to Chase's poor map reading skills. He'd convinced himself he'd conquered maps. Clearly, he'd lied to himself. "I think we should've turned left, not right, back there."

"So, this isn't a shortcut?" Wesley slipped off the back of the snowmobile and scooped up a handful of snow.

"Definitely not a shortcut." Chase set his helmet on the handlebars and stretched his legs.

"Then we should've turned left three turns back, then made two rights." Wesley rubbed his gloved hand under his nose and launched his snowball across the trail. "I thought you knew a shortcut so we could beat Dan and Ben back to the house."

At this rate, they'd be lucky to beat the sunset home. Dan and Ben were most likely already off the mountain, sipping hot chocolate and relishing their win. The foursome had bet on which of two trails back to the château was faster. The winner got to pick the movie to watch later that night. The losers were on dinner cleanup duty and required to make sure the popcorn bowl never went empty. "I shouldn't be trusted with a map."

"That's okay." Wesley formed another snowball. "Mom says I shouldn't be trusted with white clothes or nice new things."

Chase watched Wesley. The kid tossed his snowball aside, stripped off his glove and stuck his bare finger into the snowdrift as if testing the bath water temperature. No distress wrinkled his face. No fear shadowed him. Chase asked, "You're really okay that we're lost on this mountain?"

"Not lost. Just turned around." Wesley crammed his hand back inside his glove and took the map from Chase. "We just need to backtrack our steps to get to the original trail."

"You're sure it's that easy?" Chase willed it to be that easy. But he'd gotten lost before and had spent hours fixing his mistakes. But he'd never been lost with a child. One he'd vowed to protect.

"Sure." Wesley shrugged. "I do it all the time to find whatever I've lost."

"Do you lose things often?" Chase formed a snowball. He liked Wesley—liked his honesty and openness.

"I lose things more than Mom likes." Wesley studied the map, glanced at the trees and then the trail. "She's always telling me to pay more attention." He paused and pitched his voice higher. "'Respect your things, Wesley. Take more pride in your appearance, Wesley. Use a napkin, not your jeans, Wesley.'"

"My mom still tells me to sit up straight," Chase said, and earned a laugh from Wesley. "And my nonna tells me to eat more vegetables and get off my phone at least once a week."

"My great-gramma just cooks lots of cookies and pies for me." Wesley laughed louder. "My great-gramma never gives me any lectures. She tells me that's my mom's job."

Wesley was better behaved than Chase had ever been. "I started cooking with my nonna when I was your age. She taught me how to garden too."

"Cool." Wesley smiled over the map, and his eyes sparked. "Can she teach me to cook too? Mom's great at everything except cooking."

Chase rolled his snowball away and rubbed his chest. He'd never considered having a child who Nonna could teach to cook too. He liked the idea a lot. "We'd have to ask her. But first we need to get home." Before Nichole sent out a search party and banned him from ever taking Wesley on another outing again.

Wesley traced his finger over the map. Chase suggested hand signals for when Wesley needed to tell him which way to turn. Hand signals learned and memorized, Wesley slapped his helmet over his head and climbed on the snowmobile behind Chase. Two miles and several turns later, Chase stopped the snowmobile in a small clearing and willed his panic to stand down. "Anything look familiar?"

"Those are the tracks we made earlier." Wesley pointed toward the tree line.

Chase squinted at the trail, unsure if those were the tracks they'd made on the wrong trail. He leaned forward, followed the direction Wesley pointed and noticed the second set of tracks. "You're good at this."

"I've had years of practice." Wesley's tone sounded wisdom-aged as if he'd lived eight decades, not one.

Chase laughed and checked his phone for service. Barely half a bar lit the top corner of his phone screen. Every mile should take them closer to a cell tower and service. Then he'd open his map app and let the satellites guide them home.

Wesley set his hand on Chase's arm, drawing his attention away from his phone. He whispered, "Do you hear that?"

"The bears are sleeping," Chase murmured, and glanced around the clearing. "Are they snoring?"

Wesley giggled and slid off the snowmobile. "Not bears. It sounds like crying."

Chase followed Wesley across the clearing toward several fallen tree stumps and branches. A small gray fur ball darted from beneath a thick branch. Chase stepped forward and stopped. Another silver-streaked fur ball raced in the same direction. "Is that…"

"Kittens," Wesley shouted, and slapped his gloves over his mouth. His eyes round, he pulled his hands away and lowered his voice.

"We have to rescue them. They'll freeze out here."

Chase checked the time on his phone and the angle of the sun. He'd promised Nichole they'd be back long before sunset. "But they're most likely wild cats and know how to survive out here."

"We can't leave them, Chase." Wesley watched him, worry and fear on his face. "We can't. They're only babies. Babies should never be left behind. Ever."

Neither should pregnant moms or young sons. Chase swallowed around the lump in his throat. He couldn't refuse Wesley. Even Chase wouldn't sleep well knowing they hadn't tried to help the kittens. He checked the time again. "Okay. We have fifteen minutes to try and get those kittens. Then we need to leave."

"We can do this." Wesley set his hands on his hips and pointed at a fallen tree, the kitten's current hiding place. "How should we do this?"

"We need a plan." Chase glanced around the clearing. "And something to trap them in."

The first trap consisting of a thin branch and pinecones failed. Clumps of snow dropped onto their heads, covering them in snowflakes and laughter. The kittens skittered away.

Wesley guided Chase on the second trap made of four snow walls and a tree branch roof. Chase managed to swipe his gloves across the silver-and-black kitten's back. Then the trap fell apart and the kittens escaped again. And the fifteen minutes quickly shifted into thirty. Chase rubbed his hands together. The temperature dropped along with the sun. The kittens would be hard-pressed to survive the night. They had to succeed.

Together, Chase and Wesley used the best parts of their earlier traps and constructed a new one. Wesley captured the gray kitten. Chase bent down and scooped up the silver-and-black sibling.

"It worked." Wesley snuggled the kitten closer, then sneezed. "I'm not allergic. Just cold."

Chase unzipped his jacket and motioned toward Wesley. "The kittens will be warm inside my coat."

"Are you sure?" Wesley peeled the kitten's claws out of his jacket sleeve.

No. But they had few options. Wesley needed his hands free to hang on to Chase and use his hand signals to guide Chase in the right direction. A kitten would distract the boy. "I'm the best they've got."

Wesley settled his kitten inside Chase's jacket. "What about their mom?"

Chase had already considered the kitten's mother and whether she had more in her litter. He checked the time on his phone and noted the last of the setting sun. "We can do a ten-minute search. Then we leave. Remember she's wild too and has been surviving out here longer than us."

"Okay. We should start at the log where we first found them."

Chase unwrapped his scarf and wound it around Wesley's neck. "Lead the way."

At the twelve-minute mark, Chase called a halt to the search. He tugged off his gloves and tied them to a high branch. "We have to leave, or your mother is going to be really mad."

Wesley kicked at the snow and frowned into Chase's scarf. "Fine."

"Look, my gloves will be here as a marker." Chase pointed at the tree branch. "We can come back tomorrow during the day and search for their mom."

Wesley straightened and grinned. "Promise?"

"Promise." What was it about the Moore family that caused Chase to keep making promises?

CHAPTER EIGHTEEN

THE SOUND OF a snowmobile drew Nichole outside. She rushed onto the balcony, wrapped Wesley in a tight hug. She pulled away, touched his cold checks, examined his face, ran her hands over his arms. No visible injuries. The frantic worry hammering inside her chest dulled to a steady pounding. Wesley was safe. Her son was fine. But there was another someone and that worry persisted. Her hands still shook. One more hug for Wesley then she released him. "Get inside and warm up."

"But…" Wesley started.

Nichole pointed inside. "Not now."

Wesley frowned, ran inside and shouted for Ben, Brooke and Dan. Nichole never waited to find out what Wesley wanted to tell them. She raced down the stairs and sprinted toward the garage. Anger and fear knotted inside her, pushing her faster. She wanted to yell at Chase for scaring her to her core and hold on to him and not ever let go.

Chase walked out of the garage, closed the door and stopped.

Nichole surveyed him from his uncovered head to his boots and back up. No bruises. No scrapes. Only wind-chafed cheeks. He was fine. She'd been worried. Scared. So very frightened for Wesley. For him. *Him.*

But she was never supposed to worry. To care. Not this much. Not this deep. Not this fast. Nichole bent, packed snow between her hands and launched her attack. "How dare you." *How dare you make me feel again.*

Better yet, how dare she. How dare she let herself get so attached. She knew better. Hadn't she learned the first time? Frustration rolled through her, at herself. At him. At the situation. She released another snowball. It smashed against the garage door behind Chase. He never flinched. Never moved.

"You promised." *A business arrangement only.* The next volley she aimed at his head, hit his good shoulder and she formed another snowball. And she'd promised herself. Not to ever let herself fall again. Not to open her heart again.

He tucked his hands into the pockets of his jacket and waited.

"I was so worried." *Frantic. Frightened.* For Wesley. For Chase. She lived inside her comfort zone for a reason. It had never let her down. But Chase made her feel a different kind of alive. Even now inside her anger and frustration, a warm affection stirred, steady and growing stronger. But it was only an illusion. How could something that started on a lie, began as a sham, become real? Become mutual?

Her snowball splattered against his left arm. Nichole widened her stance, firming her balance to improve her aim, but the fight inside her dwindled. Still, she drew her arm back and paused midstrike. Waited. She tilted her head and frowned. "Your jacket is wiggling."

Chase unzipped his jacket and revealed one of the tiniest kittens Nichole had ever seen. He cradled the gray fuzz ball in his arm and looked at her. "We couldn't leave them out there."

"You rescued a kitten?" Nichole sputtered and wanted to shout *foul*.

Chase unzipped his jacket farther, revealing a second silver-and-black-striped head. His smile grew. "Two, actually. We tried to find the mother, but it was getting too dark."

"You also looked for the mother?" Nichole brushed the snow off her hands and touched her forehead. Chase held two baby kittens.

Kittens that he and her son had rescued on the mountain. She'd feared the worst. And they'd been saving two little lives. The last of her anger melted like the snow beneath the full sun.

"Wesley made a good point about there possibly being more kittens and a worried mother cat." Chase held the gray kitten in his palm, gentle and attentive. "Wesley was worried about the mom being even more stressed once her kittens came home with us."

"This was Wesley's idea?" Her son never wanted anyone left behind. He would've insisted on searching for the mom and any more siblings. Chase had listened and helped rather than dismissing Wesley's concerns.

"Wesley heard the kittens crying first." Chase held up the gray fuzz ball until the kitten sniffed his nose. "Then I saw this one peeking out from under a tree stump. Its blue eyes are larger than its face."

"And you decided to save them?" Nichole set her hands on her hips. This was the same man who'd told her earlier how he liked being on his own and worrying only about himself. Yet he had stopped to save kittens and had extended the search for their mom. She'd called him a good guy earlier and he'd proven it again. Good guy or not, she had to stop noticing. The sigh inside her heart slipped out before she could snatch it. "Where are your gloves?"

"I tied them to the tree so we could go back in the morning and look again for their mom." Chase tucked the kitten inside his jacket.

"And your scarf?" She'd seen him leave with the bulky fleece scarf wrapped around his neck. She reached up, searching for her scarf to wrap around him. She'd raced outside without a scarf or jacket on.

He touched his bare neck. "I gave it to Wesley."

Nichole pursed her lips and searched for the man Chase tried to convince her he was. The selfish, only in it for himself, confirmed bachelor. The one she needed him to be to keep her heart from getting any more involved.

"We made a plan to capture them." His soft laughter spilled from his small smile. "Okay, we made three different traps and even more plans. It wasn't as easy as simply picking them up. Even half-frozen, they're quite quick and crafty."

Footsteps thumped across the deck and down the stairs. Nichole turned to watch Ben and Wesley scramble off the last step and hurry toward them.

Wesley looped around Nichole and bee-lined for Chase. "Can we bring the kittens inside now?"

"Brooke is putting together a spot for them. She's using a laundry basket and towels." Ben rushed to Chase's other side. "She told me to tell you guys that Nichole and her need to go to the store for supplies."

Nichole tugged her sweater up under her chin. "We should all go inside. I need a better coat." And Chase needed to release the kittens, thaw himself out and return to the man she'd made her original agreement with. The unavailable bachelor, not the cat rescuer who protected her son from the cold and made her feel… He made her feel too much. That had to stop. Otherwise she feared the fall would shatter more than her heart.

Chase glanced at the boys. "Looks like you two are on kitten duty while the men make dinner and the women head to the pet store."

"Can we keep them in our room?" Wesley asked.

"Let's get them inside first." Nichole headed up the stairs, away from Chase and her urge to cuddle closer to him and the kittens. Once indoors, she grabbed her jacket and gloves, anxious to leave for the pet store. Distance would reset her focus and realign her thoughts. Then she'd only need to enjoy dinner with her friends and keep her hands to herself. Reaching for Chase was not a risk she intended to take.

CHASE PRESSED THE lid on the leftover cacio e pepe and set the small container in the refrigerator. The boys had eaten three servings of the simple cheese and pepper noodles. Then they'd devoured the Chicken Francese and even sampled the green beans. Everyone at the table had declared the meal a grand success. Chase had skipped over the praise and been more interested in postponing the cleanup and continuing their lively conversation.

A conversation that had wandered from favorite superheroes to favorite holidays to *would you rather* challenges. So much like the Jacobses' kitchen table growing up and yet different, but equally inviting.

Chase couldn't recall preparing a meal for friends and enjoying himself quite so much. Not that he planned a repeat. This was a one-time, spontaneous thing to make up for being late and causing Nichole to worry. Cooking dinner was something he could easily do for Nichole and her friends.

He intended to do something else for Nichole, but it wasn't easy. He hadn't found any information on Fund Infusion or its senior partners to suggest Vick and Glenn were anything more than interested investors. Still that kink in his gut expanded, refusing to let him give up. Chase tapped his phone screen as if it held the truth about Fund Infusion in some hidden code.

"Problem?" Dan tipped his chin toward Chase's phone.

"Sort of." Chase looked toward the family room. Brooke and Nichole talked and played with the kittens. Satisfied that Nichole wasn't listening, Chase asked, "Do you know how to research a business? Not the name and public information, but the backside of a business."

"No idea." Dan poured soap into a large frying pan. "But we know someone who can."

"We do?" Chase picked up the drying towel and one of the mixing bowls Dan already washed.

"You married into an eclectic family tree." Dan chuckled and grinned at him. "Bet you had no idea."

None. Chase had only ever met Nichole's grandparents. Knew she was an only child and her parents traveled in a theater group. But from Dan's expression, Nichole's family was much larger and way more interesting than that. "I have my grandmother, mom and two sisters on my family tree."

"Now you have a paramedic, physician's assistant, pet shop owner, private investigator, animal rescuer, photographer, wedding dress designer, lifestyle expert, ER doctor and inventor." Dan laughed and rinsed the frying pan. "Don't even get me started on the retired in-laws and extended family of siblings. They are all yours too now."

"Just like that?" Chase had an entire fifty-two-man team behind him. But he'd had to earn their respect and loyalty over several seasons. Chase stacked the mixing bowl inside the others. Now he'd gained Nichole's supposed family tree by marrying Nichole. Could it be that easy? Perhaps if it'd been true and not one big scam. That ever-present guilt warred inside him.

"Pretty much. Nichole is our family. You are too," Dan stretched out his words. "Until you aren't."

Chase straightened, searched Dan's face, wondering if he'd misheard the warning. "What does that mean?"

"Exactly like it sounds." Dan scrubbed a small sauté pan and never elaborated. "Now what is this about wanting to research a business? You looking for a good investment?"

"It's not research per se." Chase leaned against the counter in order to face the family room. He kept his gaze fixed on Nichole to ensure she wasn't paying attention to them. The gray kitten climbed onto her shoulder and swatted at her hair, and she laughed. Her smile encouraged his own. "I want to find out the bad stuff."

"Now, that's way more interesting." Dan looked over his shoulder.

"Not to Nichole, it isn't." Chase lowered his voice and lost his smile. "It's about her potential buyers, Fund Infusion."

Dan shut off the water and addressed Chase in the same low voice Chase had used. "She likes them. They're the answer to her dreams."

"Until they aren't." Chase held Dan's gaze one extra beat.

Dan leaned his hip against the counter and crossed his arms over his chest. "What do you mean?"

"I don't trust them." That sounded lame. Like he had indigestion and no antacids. Chase wadded up the towel and tossed it on the island. "But I'm not enough to sway Nichole. She never relies on her gut instinct."

"You do know her." Approval deepened Dan's tone.

"Since high school," Chase admitted.

"She never mentioned she knew you. Ever." Dan frowned. "Not once during any Pioneers game or during any event at school. And she had plenty of opportunities to mention she knows you."

"We'd known each other in high school and college." A long time ago, yet the more time Chase spent with her, the more he felt like she'd always been right there. Right beside him. Right where she belonged. "People change and move on. I don't think she ever thought she'd see me again."

"Or marry you." Dan tapped his fist against Chase's shoulder.

She definitely never considered that. "I'm worried she's making a mistake selling to the Fund Infusion guys."

The same sort of mistake he made convincing her to continue their ruse. Then sharing a bedroom with her. Then letting himself get to know her. He was becoming used to being with Nichole again. Though it was only temporary. Her app wasn't. That was her future, and he intended to make sure she didn't make a mistake for her future.

"Have you talked to her?" Dan asked.

"I tried," Chase admitted. "She defended their request for her full app code and the entire business plan that she put together herself. I'm probably overreacting." Most likely due to learning about his new and very large extended family. A family he'd let down once the truth came out about the fake marriage.

"I've watched a lot of Pioneers games." Dan's fingers tapped against his forearms. His gaze centered on Chase like an opposing team's defensive coach determined to call the right play to stop him. "I can't recall a time where you overreacted on the field or off."

"Could you tell that to my mom?" Chase slipped a hint of humor into his voice and grinned at Nichole. She'd glanced back as if to check on their progress. "My mom would disagree with you."

"Moms earn the right to be our biggest critics. They put up with us all those years growing up." Dan dried his hands on a towel. "Still, you've called some of your best plays a gut reaction on the field. I wouldn't discount those instincts now."

If Dan knew the full truth, he might discount Chase completely. "What do you think?"

Dan rubbed his chin. "You need a professional to talk to her."

"My thoughts exactly," Chase said. "Or

even proof that the Fund Infusion guys might not be all they claim to be."

Dan snapped his fingers. "You need the Harringtons."

"As in Ella's grandmother, Mayor Harrington." Wesley had mentioned Ella's connection to a well-known person the first day Chase had met him.

Dan nodded. "You need her sons, Brad and Drew."

"Brad Harrington has bodyguards," Chase said, recalling Nichole's earlier claim about Wesley requesting his own personal bodyguard.

"Among other things. Brad runs a security and private investigation firm." Dan opened and closed several drawers in the island. He pulled out a pen and notepad from the last drawer. "Drew Harrington is the former DA who recently entered the private law sector. He'll know a good contract from a bad one."

"And the Harrington brothers will take my call because..." Chase took the paper from Dan. Chase was a pro football player and well-known athlete, yet that wasn't always enough to grant him carte blanche to anyone he wanted to meet.

"Besides them both being huge Pioneers' fans—" Dan clicked the pen closed as if everything was settled "—they're also part of your family now. Brad married Ella's mom, Sophie. She runs the pet store where Brooke and Nichole work with the fosters and rescues."

"Then we'll have a place to bring the kittens." Chase sounded less than indifferent and almost disappointed. But they'd only brought home the kittens several hours earlier. He couldn't be attached that quickly. He wasn't one to get attached.

Dan nodded. "Nichole's landlords changed to a no pet policy at the beginning of the year. So those kittens aren't going home with her and Wesley. What about your house?"

"Uh…" Could Chase even have animals at his place? He'd never inquired about the owner's pet policy at his rental house. Never considered adding more things to take care of in his house other than his herb plants.

"We already have two dogs and two cats." Dan's affectionate tone matched his bemused expression. "And we're about to get three more fosters later this week."

"I can't take kittens to my house." Beyond the animal policy Chase didn't know of, he had absolutely no idea how to care for baby kittens.

"Don't worry. They'll be safe there until

you can get them to Sophie's shop." Dan's hand landed on Chase's shoulder, solid and reassuring. "Brooke will teach you every-thing you need to know about proper kitten care. And in case you do keep them, Sophie will set you up with every kitten item you could possibly ever need."

"But…"

"You rescued them," Dan said. "You can't abandon them now."

Chase followed Dan into the family room. The kittens weren't the only ones he was con-sidering inviting into his home and not aban-doning.

CHAPTER NINETEEN

"You're bonding." *And so am I.* Nichole stood in the bathroom doorway of the master bedroom and glowered at Chase.

He'd cooked her favorite chicken in a delicate parmesan white wine sauce for dinner, added chocolate chip cannoli—another one of her weaknesses—for dessert. And blended the evening together with consideration and the attentive skill of a seasoned, executive chef. During the meal, he'd looked after Wesley, refilled her glass before it emptied, delivered second helpings as if on cue. He cleared plates, shared stories and fit in among everyone as if he'd always cooked for them. Always cared for them.

"I'm not trying to bond." Chase rebuilt the pillow wall, fluffing and restacking each pillow. "Wesley is a great kid. I can't just ignore him."

"Maybe you could be more like you're supposed to be." Nichole waved her toothbrush at the newspaper on the end table. If he'd act

CARI LYNN WEBB   283

like she expected, she wouldn't be standing in the bathroom, searching for all the reasons that opposites were not supposed to attract.

Chase released a pillow and glanced at Nichole. "What does that mean?"

"You could be like the Chase Jacobs who makes headlines." She pointed at the newspaper, her arm stiff, the toothbrush aimed like an arrow. Panic shuddered through her, weakening her resolve.

"I am him," Chase argued.

"No." Nichole tossed her toothbrush on the counter, charged into the bedroom and crashed through their self-imposed distance. She'd make him understand and force her own heart to stand down. "That Chase Jacobs wouldn't rescue kittens. He wouldn't leave his gloves as markers and risk frostbite, then make plans to continue searching for the kitten's mother the following day."

"Media Chase" would've ordered takeout, signed Pioneers' gear and entertained his guests with football facts and stats. That Chase would've been bored, searching for an excuse to leave and discover a nighttime thrill on a closed ski slope. He definitely would not share mishaps from his childhood, inquire about Wesley's likes and dislikes or agree to play cards using colored marshmallows for bets.

Chase scratched his chin and considered her. The slow motion of his fingers curving around his cheek drew her gaze like a misguided moth to a flame. The curious interest in his eyes collided with awareness. She remained silent and tried to wrangle her own mixed-up feelings.

"Actually, he would." Chase leaned forward, his gaze locked onto her face. "Don't you remember my junior year when I made you quiz me while I searched the woods for the injured squirrel I'd seen?"

"We walked miles that afternoon while I went through my stack of note cards. And you carried water and a hand-tossed salad you made out of a squirrel's favorite foods." The memory warmed Nichole better than a fleece blanket. She slashed a hand through the air as if cutting the memory in half. "That's not the same. That was high school."

"I can give you something more current." Chase walked to the fireplace and poked at the logs.

Currently Nichole watched Chase too closely, every movement, every expression. She'd never paid attention in high school, never tracked his swagger down the crowded hallways. Now she feared she could locate him in a sold-out stadium. She focused on him so completely. *Totally. Not. Good. Really not good.* She blamed the fireplace. Who installed a storybook fireplace in their bedroom? The fireplace created an illusion and made her believe in happily-ever-afters.

"The reason we got caught on the snowmobile race last winter was because I made the guys reroute the course." Chase added a log to the fire and turned toward her. "I made them change the route because of the snowy owls."

"Snowy owls. Never mind." Nichole shook her head as if unplugging her sudden interest. "I don't want to know."

"Snowy owls are ground nesters and hunt during the day, not at night like most owls." Chase stretched out on the bed, crossed his legs at the ankles and looked entirely too comfortable. He stacked his hand behind his head as if content to recite owl facts into the night.

Nichole was entirely too ready to curl into his side, content to listen to him all night. She turned off the bathroom light, cutting her connection to Chase. But her gaze latched on to him as if she'd developed enhanced night vision.

"I saw the snowy owls and knew we had

to change the course. The snowmobiles would've disturbed and stressed them too much." Chase's voice stretched through the room, tugging her toward him. "If we'd raced on the original trail, the park rangers would not have caught us."

"That's not true." Nichole sat on the bed and tucked her feet under the blankets.

"Scouts' honor." Chase shifted, rolling on his good shoulder to face her.

"You were never a Boy Scout."

"I should've been." Chase reached across the pillow wall, grabbed her hand and flattened their palms and fingers together. He stared at their joined hands. A rasp scored his voice, etching the temptation deeper in his tone. "I clearly missed my calling."

The glow of the fire fell across the bed like an invitation. She laced her fingers between his. His other hand reached out, curved around her cheek. His thumb brushed across her bottom lip. Just one slow caress. Nichole held her breath. Even the heat from the fire stalled as if the room itself remembered their most recent kiss.

But that was all there could be. No more kisses. No more memory-making moments. She turned slightly, pressed her lips against his palm. Too brief. Too fleeting. But all she could offer.

Tomorrow they left Tahoe. The ski-moon ended, along with the fantasy her heart wanted to believe in. Tomorrow, she'd return to the city and plant her feet firmly back on the cement.

Tonight, she fell asleep, her hand tucked firmly in Chase's.

CHAPTER TWENTY

"HERE'S YOUR MICROPHONE." A woman handed a wireless mic to Chase. Her gray-tinged brown hair poked out around her headset as if she'd stuck her finger, not the headpiece into an electrical outlet. Her frazzled voice matched her erratic hand motions. "The teleprompter is there."

Chase clasped his hands behind his back and eyed the wireless microphone like a writhing snake. Beside him, Wesley gaped at the harried woman. Wesley and Chase had only just arrived at the Pioneers' week-long Spring Break Camp for Kids. They'd returned late from Tahoe, but not late enough to miss Travis's reminder that Chase had committed to helping at the camp. Nichole had scheduled vendor meetings that morning, and conveniently Wesley declared he wasn't allowed to remain home alone. Chase had offered to bring Wesley with him, grateful for the company. Nichole hadn't been as pleased, but she'd finally agreed.

Chase kept his expression contained, not wanting to rattle the headset-wearing woman any further. "I think you have the wrong person."

"You are Chase Jacobs, correct?" The woman rapped a metal clipboard against her leg.

Chase nodded, his chin dipping by gradual degrees.

The same hesitation never seized Wesley. The boy planted his hands on his hips and even widened his stance as if he'd suddenly signed on as Chase's bodyguard. "Of course, he's Chase Jacobs and my new dad."

Dad. Chase stuttered, lost his focus. There it was again. That one word that shuffled his insides and rearranged his equilibrium.

"Then he's the emcee for the morning sessions all week." The woman clutched her clipboard under her arm and thrust the microphone at Chase's chest. "Travis Shaw volunteered you."

This was not the kind of help Chase had planned to offer. He gripped the microphone but missed the tackle on his sudden panic. "When do we start?"

"Fifteen minutes we go live for the welcome." The woman already moved on to the next item on her clipboard. "Then you head to the field to cover the day's activities."

"Any chance I could share the duties with Wesley?" Chase set his hand on Wesley's shoulder. He slowed his words into calm and collected to cover his unease. "It's a kids' event. So, getting a kid's perspective on the morning might be entertaining."

"We need waivers and release forms signed by a parent or guardian then approval from legal." She gave Wesley an absent glance. "I can get those forms to you. We could possibly work your son in for a short guest spot late this week."

His son. Those two words slammed everything into another level. *Dad and son.* He'd always wanted that bond. Wesley was so much more than just a kid. They'd built zombie snowmen, rescued kittens, discovered an easy rapport. Laughed and bonded like a team. *Dad and son.* Chase coughed. A guest spot for Wesley did nothing for Chase now. *Nothing.* Chase's sweaty palm captured the microphone.

"But can I stay with my dad?" Wesley asked. "I promise I won't go on camera."

"Sure." The woman stilled long enough to touch Wesley's shoulder and motioned to someone behind them. "I'll get you a headset and you can watch on the camera and listen in."

"Cool." Wesley grinned as if delighted with his role on the team.

"Wait here." The woman rushed across the makeshift studio that had been built near the visitors' end zone.

Chase wanted to run into the locker room. Wesley couldn't help Chase read the teleprompter. Or read the teleprompter for him. He faced a disaster. He should've worn glasses off the field for the past few seasons. Added glasses to every press appearance. Then he could've claimed he'd forgotten his glasses and couldn't possibly emcee. Chase touched his forehead.

"You okay?" Wesley's hand dropped on Chase's arm. "You look sweaty and weird."

Chase walked into an empty corner and leaned toward Wesley. His voice hushed. "I don't like speaking on microphones."

"But you do it all the time after games." Wesley's gaze narrowed on Chase's forehead. "Are you sick? My head gets wet when I get sick too."

Could he claim a sudden attack of food poisoning? Clutch his stomach and rush to the restroom. Tempting, but cowardly. Nonna and his mother hadn't taught him to retreat like a quitter. He refused to teach the same lesson to Wesley. "I'm not sick. But remember when I said your mom tutored me?"

Wesley nodded and edged closer as if he understood the gravity of the situation from Chase's subdued manner alone.

"Well, your mom helped me read," Chase confessed. Tossing his weakness into the space between them like a coach's challenge flag. Except Wesley never picked up the flag. Never paused to demand a replay. Chase added, "I mix up the letters and get words wrong a lot."

Wesley brushed his bangs off his forehead and looked at Chase. Understanding shifted across his face. "Ella uses braille to read because her eyes don't work like mine. Mom is like your braille."

Nichole was more like his best half. If he wanted another half. Needed another half. Teleprompter panic had jumbled more than his focus.

Wesley stuffed his hands in his front sweat-shirt pocket. Worry pinched his face. "How are you going to read that screen now without Mom?"

He appreciated smart kids; even more, he adored Wesley in this moment. Though he knew the boy would eventually think less of him for his weakness. How could he not—Chase's own father had. Chase shrugged. "I have no idea. Got any good ones?"

Wesley straightened his shoulders as if pleased he could assist Chase. "I can read for you."

Great minds. Chase had already tried that option. "Except you can't go on camera."

Wesley's concentration was clear. "We could put one of those little microphones in your ear. I could sit over here and read the lines to you. Like the spies do in the movies."

If only he had an earpiece, Chase would channel every spy-action hero he'd ever watched on the big screen. "We don't have the right equipment."

Wesley nodded and stepped right into Chase's side. He tugged Chase down to whisper into his ear. "Then you have to distract them."

Chase leaned back and eyed Wesley. "What do you mean?"

"Mom always says I'm distracting her when I get in trouble." Wesley ground his shoe into the turf.

Chase understood distractions. Nichole was one all by herself.

"One time I broke a window on the porch." Wesley's hands dropped out of his pockets as he stepped into his story. "So, I made Mom coffee and her favorite sandwich. It's pickles and peanut butter by the way." He made a gagging motion before continuing. "I did all that before she got home. Then I hugged her and hugged her and hugged her when she came inside the house. Then kept on hugging her when she finally saw the window."

"And…" Chase pressed. He'd gotten stuck on the image of hugging Nichole. How much he liked being in her embrace. How much he would've liked her here now with them.

"And she was really mad." Wesley clutched both Chase's shoulders, moved their faces together until their noses almost touched and grinned. "But she wasn't really *really* mad because I distracted her first. Get it?"

Chase nodded.

No. No, you don't want to do this. Nichole's insistent voice slipped through Chase as if she stood right beside them. How many times had she tried to dissuade him from some idea or another? How many times had he disregarded her advice?

Wesley squeezed Chase's shoulders as if he were pumping him up before a game. "You just need one super good distraction. Then they'll forget you were supposed to read the monitor. It really works."

Chase scanned the studio, searching for a distraction. His gaze landed on the teleprompter. "Can you tell me what it says on that screen?"

Wesley rose up onto the balls of his feet and read the opening message out loud. Chase closed his eyes, asked Wesley to repeat the same paragraph. Wesley reread the message a half-dozen times. Then Chase repeated back the welcome.

Wesley scratched his cheek. "You missed the middle and last lines."

"But it's close," Chase said.

"Definitely." Wesley lifted his eyebrows. His voice an urgent murmur. "Now you need the really good distraction."

"Still working on that." *Still working on ignoring Nichole's voice inside his head.* Chase waved to the headset woman, calming the producer's frantic search. Her shoulders dropped and she rushed toward him. She handed Wesley a headset, pointed at a chair, then grabbed Chase, guiding him to his marker in front of the camera.

Chase rolled his shoulder and stretched his neck. He could do this. Movement at the entrance of the tent caught his attention. A familiar player, his curly hair and smile in place, stepped inside the tent. Confidence erased Chase's distress. He muted Nichole's voice and locked on to his distraction. Surely, she'd understand once he explained.

Chase finished his welcome remarks, stepped closer to the camera and spoke as if imparting a very good secret. "I'm going off script, but I think you'll really enjoy this part of the program."

He motioned for the cameraman to follow him, turned his back on the teleprompter and the foreboding sensation twisting around his spine. He worked his way toward Beau Bradford—the cornerstone of his distraction. A firm handshake brought Beau in front of the camera. A quick question about the best part of the obstacle course outside granted Beau a reason to stay. And revealed unexpected information, including Beau's involvement in designing the individual obstacles.

"If you designed the obstacles, you must have tried each one already." Chase's smile widened. Now he'd maneuver them both into the perfect distraction. And his reading disability would remain hidden like always. "Which one is the hardest?"

Beau scrubbed his hand over the back of his hair, disrupting the curls. "I haven't tried the course yet."

"Perhaps we could change that this morning." Chase lifted his shoulders and spoke into the camera, adding interest and speculation to his voice. "A trial run before the course opens to the teenagers."

"Yeah." Beau's fingers stilled on the back of his head and his arm lowered. Laughter and anticipation flashed into his gaze. "You know, it's meant to be a race. The obstacle course has two sides."

"I'd heard there is some good competition out there warming up now." *Don't.* That word echoed inside his head. Another silent order from Nichole. But Nichole understood him like no one else. She'd recognize the difficult position he'd been put in.

Beau grinned. "But if I'm going to do a trial run, I'd like to choose my competition."

"Anyone you'd like to compete against?" Chase looked at the camera as if requesting suggestions from the audience. Inside, his inner competitor raised his hand and jumped up and down. "I'm sure we can find someone willing."

"You." Beau pointed at Chase.

Chase wanted to point at Wesley and celebrate. Operation Distraction worked. He shook his head. "Unfortunately, I'm on emcee duty."

"Surely we have a stand-in." Beau looked around the studio. "It's just one race."

The onlookers and crew cheered. The frazzled producer woman gave Chase a thumbs-up. Chase faced the camera. "I'm getting the all clear. Looks like Beau and I are heading to the obstacle course. Stay tuned."

Chase turned off the microphone and handed it to the cameraman. Wesley raced to his side, shook hands with Beau and the trio walked out onto the field. Cheers sounded from the participants and camp attendees. Teammates called out odds and favorites, Beau or Chase for each of the different obstacles.

"Want a rundown of the course?" Beau asked.

"Can't hurt." Chase lifted his foot, grabbed his ankle and stretched his thigh, then his other leg. Beau described the course. The high-level details gave enough information for Chase to build a contingency plan for his shoulder. He'd rather dislocate his shoulder than divulge his dyslexia to the public. In a perfect world, his shoulder would hold up, his distraction would capture the good kind of attention and his image would remain fully intact.

The world wasn't perfect.

Four obstacles into the course, Chase's shoulder cursed him and his so-called ideal distraction. He'd finished the balance beams without jarring his shoulder. The abrasive landings on the dozen jumps from one solid wooden leap pad to another had trembled along his nerves. He'd relied on his good arm and legs for the wall climb and the rope swing. Now he caught his breath and glared at the long mud crawl under a set of heavy, thick ropes. A ball pit, tire run and net climb still waited on the other side. Beside him, Beau gained ground after faltering on the wall climb. Around the stadium, spectators shouted advice and encouragement.

Chase dropped onto all fours, sank into the mud and army crawled under the first rope. His shoulder throbbed. He tightened his core, transferred more weight to his legs. He'd always preferred physical pain over the frustration of reading. And reading to an audience would've been a new level of torture. Chase gritted his teeth and pushed forward. He cleared the last rope and shoved himself out of the mud.

Wesley jumped up and down, cheering near the end of the ball pit. His shout splintered above the others. "You got this, Dad."

Chase concentrated on Wesley and the

pride on the boy's face. Letting down Wesley became unacceptable. Being called Dad in front of an audience energized him like nothing he'd experienced before. Chase launched into the ball pit and sprinted through the tire run. Wesley paced him on the edge of the course, shouting his praise and approval. Chase filled his lungs at the net climb and willed his shoulder to cooperate for one more obstacle. Adrenaline and Beau's presence propelled Chase up the rope wall. At the top, he collapsed onto the slide, slid to victory at the bottom of the fifteen-foot drop and accepted an enthusiastic hug from Wesley.

"I've been challenged." Preston Park, Chase's stand-in emcee, thrust the microphone at Chase and beamed. "Your turn to commentate."

Preston ran off to join Elliot at the starting line. Behind the duo, more retired and current players paired off to run the course. Volunteers wove camp attendees between the players, making introductions and allowing the players and teens to strategize together.

Chase rubbed the mud from his face and rallied past the intense ache in his shoulder. Later, after the adrenaline rush and inside the privacy of his own home, he'd give in and call JT for an emergency physical therapy session. And remind himself he wasn't qualified to be a dad.

But on the field, inside the Pioneers' stadium, he had to be the version of Chase Jacobs that everyone expected. They'd settle for nothing less. He turned on the microphone, grinned at Wesley and continued the rest of the morning off script.

CHAPTER TWENTY-ONE

"WHAT ARE YOU DOING?" Nichole walked into their small kitchen, crossed her arms over her chest and eyed her son. Mud coated his running shoes, splattered up his shins and covered the knees of his sweatpants. More mud flaked through his hair and smeared across one cheek.

Wesley closed the freezer door and concentrated on closing the large plastic bag filled with ice cubes. "Making an ice pack."

"I can see that." Nichole picked up a stray ice cube from the floor and tossed it in the sink. "Why? Did you hurt your knee at the Pioneers Camp?" She'd met with the owners of Tally's Corner Market and secured them as a vendor for her app. Chase had offered to take Wesley to the camp. They both had convinced her nothing would happen. Nothing other than fun with the other kids. Worry sheared through her.

"It's not for me." Wesley bent his left knee

and his right as if to prove he remained in perfect health. "Chase needs it."

"Chase?" Nichole touched her hair as if she suddenly cared what he thought about her appearance. "He's here?" He was only supposed to drop Wesley off. They hadn't planned anything else. Not like a date or dinner. She glanced at the ice pack. "And Chase asked you to get him an ice pack." Another worry sliced through her. What had happened?

"He'd never do that." Wesley shook his head and wrapped a kitchen towel around the bag of ice. "But he really needs it."

"How do you know that?" Nichole blocked Wesley's exit.

"I just do." He avoided looking at her and fiddled with the edge of the towel.

"What happened?"

"You can't tell anyone." Wesley looked around as if making certain no one else stood in the kitchen. His voice was tense and determined. "You have to promise, Mom. You can't even tell Chase that you know."

"I promise."

Wesley eyed her and shook his head. "You need to promise on Great-gramma's favorite glass pie dish."

"It's that serious?" she pressed. They only

reserved Great-gramma's favorite pie pan for unbreakable vows. Things like promising to only hit the snooze button twice in the morning. Or to do one kind thing for a stranger each day. Or never leaving anyone behind.

His nod was too solemn, his gaze too somber.

"Then I promise on Great-gramma's favorite pie dish." Nichole took the ice pack and sealed the top of the bag tightly.

"Chase hurt his shoulder at Pioneers Camp, but he doesn't want anyone to know." Wesley grabbed the bag from Nichole and hugged the ice pack as if the cold would cancel his confession.

"But you know," she said.

Wesley arched one eyebrow. "Because I was right there beside him when it happened."

"Were you involved?" Neither Wesley nor Chase would have talked each other out of any fun at the camp.

Wesley shook his bangs out of his eyes. "Sort of. But it wasn't my fault or Chase's."

Nichole tilted her head at him and waited. Wesley relied on the very same argument quite often, as did Ben, when the boys wanted to protect each other. Now Wesley wanted to protect Chase. Made Chase an ice pack and made Nichole swear on Great-gramma's cherished pie dish not to tell anyone about Chase's injury. Her son had bonded with Chase. And she had done nothing to stop it. She'd done little to stop herself. Nichole concentrated on Wesley. She'd deal with breaking bonds later.

"Beau Bradford challenged Chase to the obstacle course." Wesley wiped his hand underneath his nose. "Chase accepted and won."

"If he won, then he couldn't have gotten that hurt," Nichole argued, and cautioned her concern to back off. What could've happened on a kids' obstacle course? Between the tire race and balance beams she'd once seen in the school gym, she couldn't imagine Chase could've put much strain on his shoulder.

"Mom." Disbelief amplified his round eyes and his stunned tone. "Chase never used his right arm the rest of the morning. Not once."

"How do you know that?"

"I stood beside him the whole time," Wesley said. "On his right side."

Wesley had never left Chase's injured side the rest of the morning. No doubt he'd been guarding Chase. That was Wesley's way—to always look after the ones in need. Nichole grabbed the ice bag. "Where is he?"

Wesley pointed behind her. "On the back porch."

Nichole spun around and hurried onto the

porch. Chase sat on the couch, head back, eyes closed. He braced his right arm in his lap. His entire face pinched together and held. An ache punched through her core and she hurt for him.

Wesley tripped over the door ledge. Chase's gaze landed on Nichole and the shadows returned, locking her out. He straightened, started to push himself off the couch.

Nichole rushed over to his side and pressed the ice bag toward him. "You need to sit back and put this on your shoulder."

"It's…" Chase dropped back against the couch.

"Totally not fine." Nichole sat next to him and handed him the ice.

"Sorry, Chase." Wesley shuffled his feet and muttered at the ground. "Mom figured out you were hurt."

"That's a mom's job." Weariness, not irritation or anger, coated his words. "It's what makes your mom the best, and you, too. Thanks for getting me an ice pack."

Wesley perked up and pointed at the ice bag. "I even wrapped it in Mom's special towel. Whenever she makes me an ice pack, she tells me that towel is the secret healer, even though it has so many hearts and flowers all over it." Wesley grimaced as if hearts and flowers ruined his taste buds.

"I need all the secret healing I can get." Chase set his hand on the flowery towel as if wanting to absorb every flower, heart and any good energy.

"Wesley, go jump in the shower and then get everything you need for the farm." Nichole watched him race toward the door, then she called out, "And make sure you wash all the mud off your face, hair and body."

"I got this, Mom." Wesley's footsteps pounded up the stairs to the second floor.

"Wesley gave me his version. Now I want yours." Nichole dropped onto the couch beside Chase. "What exactly did you do?"

"I didn't do anything." Chase pushed himself off the couch, away from Nichole and the ice pack. He paced the small room. "I couldn't read the teleprompter."

"What?" Nichole followed his restless path across the porch and back.

"They wouldn't let Wesley on camera. Something about waivers and release forms needing to be signed by a guardian or parent, then legal needed to get involved." He picked up one of Wesley's baseball caps from the side table and traced his finger over the faded Pioneers' emblem. His voice as worn as the rim on the hat. "Wesley called me his new dad. I couldn't disappoint him."

That sealed the bond. It was mutual between Wesley and Chase. Nichole sidestepped that disaster and concentrated on Chase's version of the morning. She said, "But…"

"But I couldn't read the script on the teleprompter. It was scrolling way too fast and I didn't want to ask them to slow it down so I could read it." Anger and frustration tinged his admission. He tossed the baseball cap on the table and continued his restless movements. "So, I went off script."

"And ran the obstacle course." He'd always chosen physical pain. Nichole wanted to reach for him, hold him until he lowered his guard. Until he let her in. Then promise he'd always be safe with her. But she was afraid she wouldn't be enough. She was only one woman in his world—a world filled with spotlights and so many adoring fans.

"It was my shoulder or my reading. You know I hate reading out loud." A bleakness outlined Chase like a second shadow, exposing his inner fear and turmoil. "I chose the shoulder."

Nichole wanted him to choose her. She wanted to choose him. *Impossible*. She'd decided in the beginning no amendments would be accepted to their arrangement. She couldn't change the terms now. Couldn't allow hearts and emotions to undermine their deal. She also couldn't leave him. Not like this: in pain and alone.

Upstairs, she heard the shower turn off and Wesley thumping around his bedroom.

"Let's go." Nichole grabbed the ice pack, opened the screened door and motioned into the backyard. Chase followed her around the side of the house and into the driveway. She opened the passenger door of Chase's truck. "Get in and give me the keys."

"Why?" He eyed her, then the front seat of his truck, but never moved.

"Because I'm driving." She held out her hand.

"Where?" He clutched his keys.

"You should just give her the keys, Chase." Wesley dragged his suitcase across the gravel driveway and paused beside Chase.

"I should?" Chase widened his stance as if joining forces with Wesley.

"She always wins." Wesley wheeled his suitcase into his leg as if he intended to use his luggage for a chair to observe their stand-off. "Especially when she gets like this."

"We're going to my grandparents and you're coming along." Nichole picked up

Wesley's suitcase and tossed it into the back seat of the truck. "Your truck fits tall people better than my car."

"Cool." Wesley climbed into the back seat. "Chase, you get to have Great-gramma's apple pie and meet Great-granddad's horses."

Nichole held her palm out and stared at him.

"I can stay here." Dark circles filled in his skin underneath his eyes. He'd hate that she noticed.

She disliked his misplaced pride. She shifted into her authoritative mom stance. "You'll get in the car and put the ice pack Wesley got you on your shoulder."

Chase obeyed.

"She's only like this with the people she cares about." Wesley accepted the ice pack from Nichole and scooted between the front seats to continue his counsel. "At least, that's what she always tells me."

She often told Wesley she only bossed around the people she loved. She cared about Chase, but love... Nichole climbed into the driver's seat, adjusted the mirrors and her feelings. "I've always liked trucks." Had she always liked Chase, too?

"You can drop me off at home and still take

my truck." His voice lacked his usual persuasive edge. His tone drifted into uncertain.

"Not happening." Nichole reversed out of the driveway. "If you're at home, you might find yourself accepting another challenge from your teammates or friends. I won't be there to stop you."

Wesley giggled in the back seat.

A faint smile slipped across Chase's face. And Nichole grinned, even more certain she'd done the right thing.

Chase adjusted the ice pack and leaned the seat back, dropped his head on the headrest and promptly fell asleep. Wesley stretched out on the bench seat, propped his pillow on the door and copied Chase, quickly falling asleep, too. The only difference—Chase slept with a grimace on his face, Wesley a grin. Wesley had always been hers to protect. She shouldn't want to protect Chase now. She had the rest of the drive to get over her wants and focus on her priorities.

Over an hour later, the ice pack leaked down the front of Chase's shirt yet hadn't woken him up. However, the bumps on the dirt road leading to her grandparent's farm jarred him wide-awake.

Served him right. Accepting an obstacle course challenge to keep from disappointing

Wesley. Exhaustion paled his skin and pooled under his eyes even after his nap. He spent too much time running around, being everything to everyone and forgot to take care of himself along the way.

The truck bounced over two more dirt holes and bounced frustration and awareness through Nichole. Chase was a grown man. He should know how to take care of himself. He wasn't her responsibility.

Nichole glanced over at Chase. "Sorry. I've been trying to miss the potholes, but it's impossible." Almost as impossible as not noticing every detail about Chase. Or not wanting to take care of him, too.

"Thanks for looking out for me." Chase reached over and grabbed her hand. "The ice and nap helped."

Still, pain lingered at the edges of his eyes and his voice. Nichole twisted her fingers around his, telling herself she'd let go soon enough. She looked in the rearview mirror. "Wesley, you awake back there?"

Wesley leaned on the center console between Chase and Nichole. "I can't believe we're here already. We need to take Chase's truck more often. It's faster than your car, Mom."

But if they took Chase's truck, they'd have

to take Chase. She'd only brought him now to keep an eye on him. Nichole parked the truck and waved to her grandparents, who were stepping off the porch that wrapped around their ranch-style home.

Wesley launched himself out of the car and raced to hug his great-grandparents. "Great-granddad, I promised Chase he could meet Buckeye."

"I don't believe I ever met Buckeye." Chase reached out to shake her Grandpa Harland's hand.

"Clover's foal. You'll remember her." Her grandfather slapped his hand on Chase's back in an open hug he only ever reserved for those he liked. "Good to see you, son."

Grandma Marie embraced Chase, then Nichole. "The boys can check on Buckeye while we put out supper."

Supper? Nichole had only planned to drop off Wesley, stay long enough for a glass of fresh lemonade and maybe a cookie or two. She hadn't mentioned supper to Chase. Supper had long been her grandparents' main and longest meal of the day. Supper was an occasion, inviting family and guests to settle in around the dining room table, reminisce and bond. Nichole released her grandmother. "We can't…"

"We can't eat too much at supper or we won't have room for apple pie." Chase set his hand on Nichole's lower back. His voice, dynamic and excited, overrode any pain he might be feeling. "I heard a rumor about apple pie."

Wesley laughed. "It's not a rumor."

"If this apple pie has two scoops of home-made vanilla ice cream on each slice, then it sure is real." Grandpa Harland high-fived Wesley.

"The pie is already in the oven." Her grandmother brushed at the water stain on Chase's shirt. "We've got warmer clothes inside the house. I'll get you a dry shirt."

"You always did look after me." Chase pressed a kiss to her grandmother's sun-stained forehead. "Any chance we can have dessert before supper?"

"The answer is still no." Her grandmother touched Chase's cheek and shook her head, loosening several pure white curls from her bun. "You always did like to live in reverse."

Chase laughed, released her and walked to the stables with Grandpa Harland and Wesley.

Nichole wrapped her arm around her grandmother's waist, both for comfort and support. The pair strolled back to the house.

"What did you mean that Chase likes to live in reverse?"

"Your grandfather always said Chase jumped first, then looked for a good place to land."

"Unlike me." Nichole opened the front door for her grandmother.

Her grandmother chuckled and patted Nichole's shoulder. "You always looked and looked. Then you'd look again. You spent so much time looking, you never jumped."

"Until the one day I jumped." And ended up pregnant, alone and heartbroken. She followed her grandmother into the open kitchen and stared at the feast spread over every counter. Nichole hadn't confirmed Chase would be coming. "This looks like Thanksgiving." For the neighbors and their families.

"I knew you'd bring Chase." Her grandmother checked a pot on the stove.

Nichole hadn't known until right before they'd left. And she'd only forced Chase to ride along to rest his injured shoulder. At least she hadn't jumped yet with Chase. Hadn't let her heart float too long in those deceptive clouds.

Her grandmother tapped a spoon against a saucepan. "You do know you ended up with the best gift ever—your son—when you took that leap."

Nichole opened the silverware drawer, took out forks and knives and stepped into the routine as familiar and comfortable as a worn pair of jeans. She'd always set the table while her grandmother cooked and her grandfather finished in the barn. Normal bolstered her. There was strength in the typical. In the known. "I want Wesley to be proud of me."

"We all are." Her grandmother squeezed Nichole's arm, her warm gaze full of sunshine and love.

"I feel like I'm getting this parent thing wrong most days. And making it up the other days." Now she'd allowed Wesley and Chase to bond. Surely that was a mistake. She should've dropped Chase at his house like he'd requested. But she'd sensed the loneliness inside him and only wanted him not to hurt anymore.

"You're too busy second-guessing yourself. You're missing all you've done right." Her grandmother retied her apron as if to support her insight.

"Wesley is a great kid." Nichole added plates and napkins to the table. "He's funny, smart and works hard."

"You've taught him that." Her grandmother handed her a serving bowl of creamed corn.

"I want to protect him." From Chase. From getting hurt. From suffering. And she wanted to protect herself. But she worried she might already be too late.

Her grandmother shuffled back to the stove. "Sometimes the best we can do is love them with all we've got."

"And when they get hurt?" Nichole picked up the salad bowl.

"We love them that much harder."

Nichole clutched the stainless steel bowl against her stomach. "Is that enough?"

"Love is always enough." Her grandmother smiled and tipped her head toward the wide windows.

Her love hadn't been enough before. Nichole watched the trio crossing the yard from the stables. Wesley chattered between her grandfather and Chase. Both men laughed and added their own commentary to Wesley's story. Three generations together. Wesley could learn from both her grandfather and Chase. Things she couldn't teach her son. "Love is also a big risk."

"Some risks are worth taking." Her grandmother opened the stove and poked at her apple pie.

Nichole turned her back on the window and everything she was too scared to want. "But if I risk and take the leap, I might land wrong."

"Or you might land exactly where you're meant to be." Her grandmother carried a large roasted turkey to the table.

How could she trust that? She'd landed wrong before.

Wesley burst through the back door and announced, "Grandpa Harland says we can ride tomorrow."

"In the corral only," Nichole cautioned.

"He's ready for more." Her grandfather pressed a kiss to her cheek.

Nichole shared a look with her grandmother and admitted, "I'm not."

CHAPTER TWENTY-TWO

"I DON'T NEED to eat again until Friday." Chase tugged the seat belt away from his too-full stomach.

"It's only Monday," Nichole said.

"I had three helpings of turkey, too many scoops of mashed potatoes and an extra piece of apple pie." And way too much fun with Wesley, Nichole and her grandparents. Time was forgotten like it always was with his own family and he'd enjoyed every minute as if he was a part of Nichole's family too. Chase motioned to the back seat. "And Grandma Marie sent me home with an oversize to-go carrier with leftovers."

"She's worried I won't feed you." Nichole stopped at a red light and glanced at him. A smile in her voice. "After all, she knows I don't cook."

"But she's going to teach me how to make her piecrust." Chase pulled off his sunglasses and tucked them inside the case. Supper had extended into the early evening and now the sunset hovered. "That recipe has only been handed down from mother to daughter each generation, you know."

Nichole's nose scrunched up. "I can't believe she's willing to alter a family tradition for you."

"I promised her I'd teach her how to make pasta." And he'd promised both her grandparents that he'd watch over Nichole. *Always*. That vow had been rather simple to give as he wanted to protect Nichole. Even if he wasn't with her, he wanted to know she and Wesley were safe. Still, more and more he preferred being right beside her.

If he stayed too long, he might start listening to his heart. Might be tempted to believe his heart—his love—could be valuable to her. But his love had never been worthwhile. Not even for his own father. Love required too many conditions. He'd find better ways to keep his promise and watch over Nichole and Wesley. "Grandma Marie and I made an even trade. And we both agreed to let you taste-test our creations."

"You had no choice." Nichole laughed.

The whimsical sound soothed Chase like the balm Mallory always encouraged him to use. He was full, not only from Grandma Marie's feast, but also from the day itself. A day spent with those he cared about. He adjusted the seat belt around his shoulder and watched the sun dip lower. Now he'd return to his house and only hope he was full enough to displace the emptiness that waited for him.

"How's your shoulder?" Nichole asked.

"Ready for ice and JT's acupuncture needles." Although his therapy session would need to wait until tomorrow morning. It was going to be a long, long night. "Any chance you might be willing to put together one of your infamous ice packs? My freezer is empty."

"I've got an array of frozen foods at my house." Nichole glanced at him with concern on her face. Worry coated her words. "How bad is it really?"

"Let's just say the rope wall and mud crawl were two of the worst decisions I've ever made." Chase grimaced at the reminder of the obstacle course.

"Even worse than paragliding off the cliff?" Nichole added, "Or cave diving?"

Chase nodded. At least in cave diving he hadn't gotten injured and only suffered a mild case of the bends. And in paragliding he'd been lucky, and the wind hadn't swept him back into the cliffs, only farther out over the ocean.

"Say no more." She pulled into the parking lot of a grocery store and parked the truck.

"What are we doing?" Chase unbuckled his seat belt.

"You're waiting here. I'm getting ice pack supplies." Nichole opened the door and leaned back inside. Her smile brightened the dim cab. "Still like cookie dough ice cream and popcorn?"

"Definitely." Chase wondered how he'd get used to not seeing her smile every day. "Why?"

"We're having a movie night at my house." She shut the door before he could protest.

Not that he would have. At least not much. He wasn't ready to return to his house with only the pain in his shoulder for company. Besides, he couldn't recall the last time he'd indulged in a movie and ice cream night. He definitely hadn't spent an evening at home with his past dates. But something about Nichole made him want to settle into the evening with only her beside him.

His phone rang, disrupting his unusual thoughts. He'd never wanted to sit at home. *Never.* He answered the call and greeted Drew Harrington. Outside, he watched Nichole work her way around several cars and head toward the truck. He relayed the information Drew requested, thanked him for his assistance. He ended the call before Nichole opened the back door and dropped the grocery bags on the seat.

Nichole bounced into the front seat, her eager words tumbled across the console. "Vick just called. They want to know if we can meet them in an hour at Sapphire Cellar to discuss the next steps and some contract details."

Chase willed the dull ache in the back of his skull to recede. Drew had just requested Chase give him a day or two to look into Fund Infusion. Then he'd asked Chase not to entertain any meetings with Fund Infusion until Chase had heard back from him. Chase had agreed, thrilled Drew hadn't brushed him off and had taken Chase's concerns seriously. Meeting Vick and Glenn in an hour would certainly be considered the kind of meeting Drew wanted Nichole and him to avoid. Chase rubbed his forehead as if the motion would conjure a good explanation for Nichole.

"Chase." Nichole's hand landed on his thigh.

Chase closed his eyes. Tried to ignore the warmth and kindness in her touch. He should tell her about his phone call with Drew Harrington. He should tell her about his wariness of Fund Infusion. He should admit how much he really cared about her. He curled his fingers around hers. "Sorry."

"It's your shoulder, isn't it?" Nichole clenched his hand. "We need to get home."

As if they shared a home. As if they had taken vows to protect, love and cherish. To put each other first. "What about Glenn and Vick?"

"It was last-minute," Nichole said. "Vick mentioned they'd understand if we couldn't make it."

"But…" Uncertain how to finish his sentence, Chase let his voice drop away. He should tell her to go without him. It was her deal—her dream—after all. Yet Drew might find something. Something that would change her mind. What if she signed tonight and Chase wasn't there to caution her to wait?

"It's fine." Nichole started the truck. "I don't want to go without you anyway."

Neither do I. But they were both going to have to go on without the other one soon. That had always been the plan. "Maybe we can reschedule for later this week."

"They'll be out of town until Friday." Nichole chewed on her bottom lip.

"Friday we've been invited to dinner at Travis's house." Chase opened the invite in his email. "He wants to go over our statement and some publicity things."

"Then I'll schedule Vick and Glenn for early next week." Nichole nodded. A grin relaxed across her face. "That gives me more time to work on a few coding errors in the app before I show the full program to them."

"Then movie night is back on."

"Absolutely," Nichole said. "I call first pick."

And Chase called one more night to pretend. A few more hours to pretend they could be a real couple. That movie night was their own weekly tradition. That what they shared could be enough.

CHAPTER TWENTY-THREE

Two MORE MOVIE nights rounded out the week. One had been a given after both Chase and Nichole had agreed they couldn't leave the fantasy trilogy unfinished. The second night had resulted from Chase's confession that he hadn't seen *The Maltese Falcon* and Nichole's determination to resolve that oversight.

Between therapy sessions, visiting Nonna and Nichole's work on her app, it had been go, go, go. Chase had even stepped in as a test user on *In A Pinch*. He'd also introduced Nichole to one of his local sponsors who wanted to become a vendor on her app. More than one kiss had been shared. But it was holding her hand, sitting beside her and simply being with Nichole that had enriched every day.

Chase parked his truck in Travis's horseshoe-shaped driveway, grabbed Nichole's hand and pressed a kiss against her knuckles. "If I failed to tell you before, you look terrific."

"Thanks." Nichole squeezed his fingers. "Why am I nervous? It's only dinner."

"With the man who negotiates my career." Chase opened his door and laughed. "He's no big deal."

"That's not helping." Nichole shut her door and scowled at him.

Chase wrapped his arm around her waist. A motion that was becoming more and more natural. If Nichole was in a room, he wanted to be right beside her. Letting her go was quickly becoming less and less appealing. "Travis likes details as much as you. You'll like him."

Nichole stopped on the doorstep and turned to Chase. "Will he like me? Will he believe we're married?"

"Of course." Chase almost believed they were married. He should eject himself from the game. He'd stepped out of the neutral zone. And yet he kept running toward Nichole. He tipped her chin up and pressed a soft kiss to her mouth. "He'll like you because I like you." *A lot*.

But his feelings were nothing he couldn't handle. Nothing he couldn't control just as he controlled the plays on the field to help earn a win for his team. Besides, liking Nichole *a lot* was far from confessing to something stronger. Something deeper and terrifying, like loving Nichole.

Nichole set her hand on his chest, her voice confession soft. "I like you too."

Time-out. Offside. Too many men on the field. Chase searched for a penalty flag. All he saw was Nichole. All he felt was her hand resting over his heart. She said the word *like* delicately and carefully as if the word deserved special handling. As if the word possessed more meaning. His pulse raced, loud enough for his own ears to listen. She *liked* him too. But they hadn't agreed on that.

The front door swung open and Travis flung his arms wide. "Security cameras are a thing of beauty. Welcome and get in here. You've had more than enough private time. We can't start the festivities without you both."

"Festivities?" Chase frowned at Nichole and linked his fingers with hers. His pulse tripped over his sudden unease.

Travis greeted Nichole and ushered them through the foyer and massive great room. An expansive outdoor living area spread from the patio doors toward an infinity edge pool. The view would've been spectacular if not for the crowd gathered outside.

Nichole's hand clenched his. Chase's steps

slowed. His words came out measured and deliberate. "Travis? What's going on?"

Travis nudged them onto the patio and shouted, "They're here. Mr. and Mrs. Jacobs have finally arrived!"

The one hundred or more guests cheered and yelled, "Surprise!"

Nichole gasped. Chase swallowed and searched for his smile.

At the front of the crowd, Mallory and Brooke high-fived each other. Mallory pointed at them. "We did it. We surprised you both."

Brooke pressed champagne glasses into their hands and announced, "Happy wedding reception."

Wedding reception. This was only supposed to be a simple dinner to discuss publicity and appearances as a couple. Later, Nichole and Chase would've added their own private discussion: their breakup plans to the conversation. Chase lifted his glass, greeting Elliot and his teammates, several offensive coaches. He anchored his smile into place and willed his cheeks to relax. The Pioneers' owners, Charles and Claire Faulkner, and the team's general manager, Keith Romero, waved from the opposite side of the pool.

Nichole's friends descended from the outdoor bar and kitchen area, wrapping Nichole and Chase in enthusiastic hugs. For the first time ever, Chase had no interest in being the life of the party. He wanted to tug Nichole through the side gate and disappear. Before he could anchor Nichole to his side and plot their escape, his sisters swept her away.

"Before you follow your new bride, and I don't blame you, can I have a word?" The amused voice stalled Chase's own retreat.

He turned and took in the linebacker-sized man eyeing him, his thick hand outstretched. Except he wasn't any player Chase had ever faced on the field. "Have we met? I'd remember you."

"I get that a lot." The man shook Chase's hand. "We spoke on the phone. I'm Drew Harrington."

"I should've known." Chase grinned and enjoyed having to tilt his head to look into Drew's eyes. It was rare he encountered someone taller than him who wasn't playing for the opposing team. "The press hasn't exaggerated your presence. And I'm suddenly glad we never met on the football field."

Drew laughed. The sound, genuine and natural, transformed his entire face from imposing to teddy-bear approachable. "I have to agree."

Chase followed Drew away from the crowd. Drew rubbed his hand over his short beard and glanced at Chase. "I would've called sooner, but I'm waiting on one more contact to get back to me."

Chase scanned the crowd, spotted Nichole surrounded by his family and her friends on the far end of the patio. "Is Fund Infusion legit?"

"It's a real, functioning company." Drew frowned and studied the deck as if he'd stepped in a red ant hill. "If Nichole had any other product, I'd let her sign a contract with them."

Chase straightened, suddenly more alert, and eyed the former DA. "What's wrong with her app?"

"Fund Infusion already represents Nichole's biggest competitor in the market." Drew lifted both eyebrows and allowed Chase to fill in the rest.

Like a serious conflict of interest. Glenn and Vick wanted *In A Pinch* but most likely not to launch it nationwide. "She could still take the deal and the money. Build a different app."

"She could." Drew accepted a glass of champagne from a passing waiter. His voice remained noncommittal.

"Except she's already worked years on this program. It's personal to her. She believes in her product." Chase scrubbed his hand through his hair. "Killing it would be like destroying a part of herself."

"We're looking too serious and drawing attention." Drew tapped his glass against Chase's and smiled. "I'll put together my findings and you can tell Nichole."

"Why me?" Chase forced his smile wider. Nichole and Chase's deal had been until both contracts were signed. Now he was going to ruin her deal with Fund Infusion and there'd be no contract to finalize. He'd have his contract signed, his life reclaimed on the football field and his freedom. Nichole would have bad press from their sudden fake divorce and an app that never launched. The last of his optimism deflated inside him, lowering his shoulders. Regret seeped in.

"I don't envy you." Drew drank his champagne and shuddered. "I never could handle disappointing a woman. Something about their tears always gets to me."

This was about much more than tears. This was Nichole's future. And Chase had promised to protect her. He had given his word to her grandparents. His gut clenched as if wanting to be wrong. "Thanks, Drew. Wish

I could say it was good to know my intuition was still sharp."

"Hey, at least she'll have you to lean on." Drew set his palm on Chase's shoulder, supportive and encouraging. "Bad news is always better with someone you love beside you."

Love. The word lodged in Chase's throat like an elbow thrust to his windpipe. If he'd loved Nichole, he'd never have fake married her. Never have convinced her of the brilliance of his plan. Never have entwined her in his world of schemes and slanted press. If he'd loved her, he would've walked away.

"Looks like you're wanted." Drew angled his chin toward the tables situated near the beach entrance of the pool.

Nonna sat at one of the rectangular tables and motioned to him. The Pioneers' general manager, Keith Romero, and Travis talked to her. From her position at the head of the table and her regal bearing, Nonna appeared to control the conversation and every decision being made. Perhaps he should've requested she join Travis for his contract negotiations. His grandmother could be a formidable opponent or valuable ally. Chase shook Drew's hand, thanked him again and headed toward his grandmother.

Nonna removed her glasses—something she only ever did when she wanted to see a situation clearly, or so she always claimed. A thread of apprehension trailed through Chase. He intercepted Nichole on his route, wrapped his arm around her waist, suddenly needing her by his side. "Having fun?"

"Would you be surprised if I said yes?" Her arm curved around his waist and she leaned into him.

He'd miss that connection—simple yet so very settling. He said, "I like your friends."

"Your teammates are funny and kind." Nichole grinned; delight colored her voice. "Your sisters and I already have lunch scheduled for next week."

"If your schedule is open, you can join Nonna and me for lunch." Chase leaned over and kissed his grandmother's cheek. The tension creasing around her eyes wrenched Chase's calm, knocking his composure askew. He shook Keith's hand, worked the kinks of worry out of his words. "My grandmother and I haven't missed our weekly lunch in over two years."

"It's quite the streak." Nonna patted the seat beside her and smiled at Nichole. "Sit, my dear."

Chase dropped into the chair beside Nichole, noted Nonna's slight toward him and pushed his shoulders down against the unease.

"But it seems all streaks must be broken." Nonna touched her ear as if signaling Chase to listen well. Her mild tone rendered her voice all the more grim. "The surgery on your shoulder and neck will certainly disrupt our weekly lunch plans."

Surgery. Chase froze in the chair, wouldn't have been surprised to watch his body wilt onto the deck. Now he understood that phrase, *world crumbling.* Understood how it felt: numbing and disorienting. And him: powerless.

"So, it's true." Travis rocked back in his chair, betrayal thick in his voice.

Keith shook his head. Anger lit his dark gaze.

"Chase." Alarm rattled Nichole's voice.

He locked onto her and stumbled over the pieces of his broken future. Guilt paled her skin. "Who…who told you?" *Who did she tell?*

"Mallory and I were talking…" She wavered, became soundless. She cleared her throat. "Mallory assumed you'd told me."

"You never corrected her." Bitterness seeped into his tone.

"You should've told me," she countered brusquely, as if she were the injured party. As if she had the right.

"Why? So, you could tell my agent, my coach, the rest of my family? Ruin my life." His anger rolled toward fury. "Wait. You already did that."

She flinched. Her voice never trembled. "I was only trying to protect you."

"Why?" He lashed out. "You aren't even my real wife."

Their audience gasped. Or perhaps that was the shocked cry of his mom. Or Mallory's sharp inhale. Anything decent left inside Chase shriveled and faded. His career was most likely over and he'd exposed their deceit. Thrust Nichole into the lion's den without protection. He really was a bad guy—selfish and cruel. She deserved so much better than him.

"You're right. I'm not your real wife." She shot up and out of the chair, rigid and proud. Her gaze uncompromising and resolute. "I'm only the woman who loved you before all this. And the woman who loves you now, faults and everything included."

She couldn't love him. He barely even liked himself. A chill rooted into his core; ice-coated vines extended the incessant cold to every part of his body. His voice, even to his own ears, sounded frigid and detached. "This was all a farce. One elaborate lie."

Elliot's deep curse rumbled through Chase. Travis closed his eyes, his hand curled into a fist on the table. Ivy pressed her hand over her mouth; her gaze skidded away from him. Disappointment, so much disappointment, flowed from his family and friends. Betrayal, not warmth, poured from the outdoor propane heaters around the patio. And Chase flatlined to a new low. A new rock bottom. He'd betrayed them all. Betrayed those he'd loved the most.

The handful of reporters Chase had noted mingling within the crowd swooped in, alert for the unfolding drama.

"Was it?" Nichole's gaze never wavered.

Chase rose and kept his focus on her. Only her. *Don't love me. Please. Don't. Love. Me.* "Yes. One big publicity stunt like I always do. It was only ever about me."

But it could've been about us. If he was any other man. A better man. The kind of man she deserved.

His words aimed true. The illusion shattered. Sadness cracked through her gaze. Her shoulders stiffened. Her chin tilted up. She turned, set her diamond ring on the table.

"My sincere apologies, gentlemen." She shifted again. "Nonna."

Only then did her voice crack. Only then did something splinter inside his own chest. If he recognized his heart, he'd have considered it broken. But that would've meant he'd fallen in love too. *Impossible.*

Nichole walked away, linked her arm through Brooke's and never looked back.

Chase sidelined his own pain. Sidelined his concern for Nichole and his regret. They'd always planned to break up. Their plan was never supposed to be long-term. That chill overtook him. He'd been cold after his father had left. Empty and cold. Now the chill was sharper. More biting. The emptiness even more stark. Chase was more like his father than even he could've ever imagined. And it appeared the son had become the father after all.

He buried his heart and embraced the incessant cold and the man he'd always feared he was. Then he faced the table and focused on the only thing he knew: *damage control to save himself.*

CHAPTER TWENTY-FOUR

CHASE AND NICHOLE'S pretense had been exposed, along with her heart.

Nichole turned her cell phone to silent and dropped it on her kitchen counter. Calls from reporters requesting a statement now outpaced calls from her friends and family. Several calls had come in from Vick and Glenn, no doubt requesting a meeting to cancel their agreement. After all, what company wanted to invest in a known liar?

Last night, she'd mentioned Chase's shoulder injury to Mallory, wanting only to ask Mallory about other methods to ease his constant pain. Something else for Chase to try beyond physical therapy to help his shoulder heal. Nichole grimaced and replayed the conversation:

Mallory had scowled into her wineglass. "Chase will heal only after surgery, as you probably already know."

She hadn't known. He hadn't trusted her

enough with that particular piece of infor-mation. "I don't know when the surgery is."

"Neither do we." Mallory had directed her scowl at Chase across the pool, who'd been laughing and joking around with his team-mates. "He keeps putting it off."

Nichole had stammered, "W...why?"

"Why else?" Mallory had flung her hand out. "For football. It's always about football."

"But he can't play injured."

Mallory's gaze had dimmed, a grim shadow had crossed her face.

"What aren't you telling me?"

"He might not be able to play even after surgery."

Nichole had pressed on. "But what if he plays anyway?"

"Then he risks permanent damage. Dam-age that can't be repaired by a surgeon's scal-pel."

Nichole had blanched. Her arrangement with Chase concluded upon their finaliz-ing their individual contracts. Once Chase signed his extension with the Pioneers, Nich-ole would no longer be useful. No longer be with him. That had been the terms of their agreement—an amicable split to pursue their own goals.

She'd panicked, not wanting Chase to risk a

more devastating injury on the football field. She'd only wanted to protect Chase. Only wanted to find someone to reason with him.

She'd located Travis and Elliot. Thanked the sports agent for his hospitality and Elliot for his friendship. Travis had expressed his hope to have good news for them both the following week regarding Chase's contract extension, giving the happy couple another reason to celebrate. Nichole had requested the celebration wait until after Chase's surgery and stunned both men into silence. From there, an undercurrent of tension had washed across the outdoor patio.

Nichole had accepted Chase's anger, but not his dismissal. Or his firm declaration that everything between them had only ever been a lie.

She'd always protected those she loved. She wouldn't apologize.

Movement in her backyard caught her attention. A familiar figure closed the side gate and walked across the small lawn. *Chase Jacobs—her newly minted pretend ex.* Except there was nothing pretend about the tears that had dampened her pillow last night. The catch in her chest now. Or the dull thud of her heart in her ears.

Nichole stepped onto the back porch and

stood in the doorway. Surely there was nothing more to be said. He'd confessed his truths last night for the world to know. She crossed her arms over her chest, blocking him from taking another aim at her heart. "What are you doing?"

"There are reporters out front." He pointed at the back gate and tugged the rim of his baseball cap over his forehead. "I didn't want to be seen so I came in the back way."

And he could turn around and leave the same way. *Now.* Before she noticed his unkempt appearance and the misery in his tone. Or searched for regret in the shadows under his eyes. Nicole flattened her lips together and remained silent.

"I'm sorry about last night." He ground his foot into an anthill as if defending himself from her silent attack. "Football is my career. My entire life."

"There's more to you than football." Surely, he understood that. Recognized he was more than a football player. So much more.

"Nothing special." He scratched his fingers through his beard and grimaced as if surprised to realize he hadn't shaved that morning. "I wanted to give you something."

"I don't want it." Unless it was his...

He reached into his pocket. For a brief moment, Nichole's breath hitched. The silly hope that refused to shrivel up swelled inside her. Had he recognized his error? Acknowledged his heart.

His hand reappeared, holding an envelope. And that hope finally withered. As it should. Love had no place between them.

"I wanted to give you this." He held out the envelope. "It's for damage control."

Nichole glared at the envelope. She'd been given a similar one more than a decade ago. Still remembered the stunned ache inside her chest. She'd revealed her surprise pregnancy and had received a payoff to go away quickly and quietly.

Last night, she'd confessed her love and now stood ready to collect another payout. Once again, her love wasn't enough. She braced herself in the doorway. Her heart crumbled around her feet, tiny unrecognizable pieces, and still she refused to collapse. "I can handle the fallout. I've survived much worse than this."

"Take it." He clenched the envelope, thrust it toward her. Desperation punched through his words. "You can finish your app. Fund the launch yourself and secure your own future."

Funny, she'd started to imagine a future that included Chase. Beside her. With her.

She'd started to imagine more than she'd ever dared before. The cries of her shattered heart became silent. Soundless. She should ache. A full body splintering ache that dropped her to her knees. But she was too hollow. Too empty. "I don't want a free ride." Or his handouts. Or his pity.

"I want you to have this." He adjusted his baseball cap, revealed his tired eyes. Still, he held her gaze. "It doesn't make up for what I've done. But it can protect your future."

Ironic. That was all she'd ever really wanted. To feel protected and secure. "What about our future?"

"This is the best I can offer." His voice was flat and muted.

"You're more than a quarterback. More than a touchdown pass or an autograph." He rescued kittens. Took care of his family. Believed in her. Nichole pointed at the envelope in his tense grip. "You're more than the size of your bank account."

"Are we?" He stuffed the envelope back inside his pocket and set his hands on his hips. "You've been so busy chasing the sale of your app, you ignored the warning signs. And for what? To increase the size of your bank account and have a couple of strangers believe in you?"

"That's not fair." Nichole charged off the porch onto the staircase. The door slammed behind her, blasting force into her words. "Is that what this has become? A comparison of bank balances to determine who can claim to have a more fulfilling life?"

"Look around, Nichole." He gestured toward her home, the movement a rigid snap. "You already have that life. With or without your app sale, you win."

She clutched the wooden railing and searched his face. Where was the Chase she knew? "Why can't we both win?"

His smile was dark. Bitter, as if coated in contempt and dipped in cynicism. "That's not how real life works."

But what about love? "So, you claim defeat, pay me off and walk away."

"I messed up your world." That contempt scored his face. "The money can help fix that."

"You can stick around and fix it yourself." She launched her challenge. He'd always accepted before.

He shook his head. "I don't belong here."

"Why not?" She disliked the callous man standing before her. Despised the defeat in his gaze. Her heart was already broken. Still, she fought. "Because we don't ask for your autograph enough. Don't quote your football stats and recite your best plays."

"People want the football star. Not a has-been. Not a former." He stabbed his arms out to either side, punching the air.

Not me. She only ever wanted him. Just Chase. "I'm not everyone. But then again, I'm not enough, am I?"

"You're everything." He yanked off his baseball hat and scrubbed his hand through his hair. That bitterness fell from his words like fat raindrops. "You can't love me."

"Why not?" The air chilled. Or perhaps that was only the void inside her. "Why is my love so hard to accept?"

"I've always been damaged goods." His arms crossed over his chest, bodyguard intense. "Except on the football field. Even my dad returned for the football player."

But his dad had never returned for the boy. Never just Chase—his son who battled dyslexia and only ever wanted his dad's approval. Chase had accepted her no-bonding terms in Tahoe because he'd been the boy she'd feared Wesley would become. The child waiting for the phone call from his dad or the surprise visit or the quick show of affection. He'd been that child waiting for a father who never returned and yet he'd hoped. Always hoped.

She discovered more tears—these ones for the lonely, hurt child still inside Chase. She wanted to seize his pain and hurtle the burden back onto his careless father. She pushed her words through her anger and the tears she swallowed. "Your father was the broken one, Chase. Not you."

"Do you believe the same about your parents?" He eyed her, his voice guarded and restrained. "That it was their shortcomings, their inability to give you the stability you needed as a child. That's why they sent you to live on the farm."

Nichole blinked. She'd never considered that. Her grandmother always claimed her parents loved her in their own spirited fashion. But they were free spirits, wanderers, travelers. Always content to let the wind carry them away like dandelion fluff on the breeze. Whereas Nichole was like an oak, according to her grandmother. And the best thing for a tree was to plant it and let the roots grow. "I suppose it's time I do. I suppose it's past time we both do."

"I can't be the man you want me to be." His shoulders fell, his voice deflated.

"I only want you to be Chase Baron Jacobs." The man she loved.

"I don't know who he is." He tugged his

cap lower on his forehead as if hiding from himself already. "Or if I even like him."

Then how would he ever love? An all-consuming numbness seized her. She reached behind her, rapped her knuckles on the railing and left the pieces of her heart scattered on the grass. She worked her way up the stairs backward, away from Chase and everything she'd ever wanted. Her love would never be enough until he learned to love himself. She pressed against the porch door. "Then I guess we're done here."

He stepped forward, then caught himself. "What about launching *In A Pinch*?"

"It was always a long shot." Just like his love.

ONE HOUR LATER, too restless to remain inside her empty house, Nichole slipped out her backyard gate, walked several blocks and jumped on the city bus. Brooke had invited her over for dinner. Dan and Ben had gone to Nichole's grandparents' farm. Wesley had asked Ben to come and learn to ride with him and the great-grandparents had promised Dan hot cherry pie after dinner.

Nichole had skipped lunch and her appetite had dwindled after Chase's unannounced visit. Food held little appeal but being alone held even less.

Brooke opened her front door, wrapped Nichole in a long hug and ushered her inside the house she shared with Dan and Ben. No questions asked. No reprimands for being very early. No demands for an apology. Nichole leaned on her friend and walked into the kitchen.

"Nichole." Josie rose from the kitchen table and enfolded Nichole in another warm hug. "You don't have to talk, but we'll listen."

"And offer our advice." Mia stood and walked around to expand the hug into a group one. "We always have opinions. It's not fair to tell you that we'll only listen."

"I'm so sorry. So very sorry." Nichole clung to her friends, grateful for their support. She needed them more than she'd realized. "I never should've lied to you guys."

Her friends simply held on to her. Offered more support and their forgiveness, unconditional and absolute.

Nichole wiped at her damp eyes and glanced at the table. Brooke gathered photographs into a pile. Nichole asked, "What are you guys doing?"

Her friends glanced at each other, their gazes skipping from one to the other as if waiting for the other to field Nichole's question. Nichole stepped toward the table, caught a glimpse of a crystal and beaded wedding gown and familiar lily bouquet. The same bouquet Nichole had held for the photo shoot. Those were the photographs of Nichole, pretending to be a bride. Believing in the fantasy. But fantasies were only illusions. And illusions were always shattered. Certainly, the truth had been captured in those photographs, and the lies. "Are they…"

"Stunning." Josie squeezed Nichole's hand. "Yes, they are."

"And magical." Brooke paused on a photograph and sighed. "There's magic in every shot."

Chase had called her stunning that day. And standing inside his embrace, she'd started to believe again in magic. *It was all a lie. One big publicity stunt.*

"You missed your calling, Nichole." Mia returned to the table and picked up another 8x10 photograph. "You should've been a professional model."

Models received paychecks for playing a part on camera. Chase had tried to pay Nichole, too, for the part she'd played in his publicity stunt. But the cameras hadn't been there in Tahoe. Hadn't recorded their conversations in front of the fire or the kitten rescue. He'd listened and shared. Held her hand with affection, kissed her with emotion. Nichole stepped to the table, clutched the back of a chair and held on to something real. "Thanks for trying to make me feel better. Now you can all stop exaggerating."

"It's the truth," Brooke argued.

Josie shrugged. "And we haven't even started trying to make you feel better. That happens later with lasagna from Mia's mother-in-law and homemade red velvet cheesecake."

"There's always cheesecake and extra whipped cream for times like this." Mia rubbed Nichole's shoulder.

"Give me a picture." *And I'll prove you are all wrong.* Nichole held out her hand. "The stunning one. Or the magical one. Doesn't matter." She'd point out the truth inside each photograph and highlight the deception.

A dozen pictures later, Nichole slumped into a kitchen chair and studied a picture of Chase and her outside the cathedral. She struggled to find the deceit on his face. Or to recall the dishonesty in his embrace. She examined another one. Chase had picked her up and twirled her around. Again, only joy radiated from his face, delight widened his smile. Bliss highlighted his open gaze that was fixed completely on her.

Looking at the pictures, she forgot. Forgot he'd only been acting. Forgot he couldn't love her. "How can we look so real? So authentic?"

"Because your feelings are real." Mia eased the photograph out from under Nichole's fingers. "And in this moment, so were Chase's."

Nichole cradled her face in her hands. "You heard him yesterday. He'd claimed it was all one big hoax."

Then that morning he'd tried to pay her off like her ex. Claimed it was all he could offer. Ordered her not to love him. As if he could dictate her heart. Even she struggled to command her heart to withdraw. To let him go. She shoved the pictures and the memories away from her.

"I was at the pet store this morning helping Sophie with more rescues." Brooke slid a sealed large folder-sized envelope across the table toward her. "Sophie asked me to give this to you."

"What is it?" Nichole turned the envelope over and noted the unfamiliar law firm name in the corner.

"It's from Drew Harrington." Brooke hesitated as if she was working to regain her voice. "Chase asked him to look into Fund

Infusion. Drew wanted you to know what he'd found."

"Solid financials and fair business practices, I'm sure." Nichole fingered the envelope and willed her sudden disquiet to retreat. Surely Vick and Glenn hadn't deceived her too. Played for a fool twice in one day would be something of a new low.

"Want us to open it?" Brooke chewed on her bottom lip.

Nichole shook her head and slipped her finger under the sealed flap. The folder inside contained detailed financials. Nothing fraudulent or illegal was on the profit and loss statements. Fund Infusion was legitimate like she'd told Chase. Nichole skimmed through several pages before stopping abruptly. Everything about Fund Infusion was genuine. Everything except the company's intentions for *In A Pinch*.

"What's wrong?" Josie scooted closer to Nichole.

Brooke reached across the table and touched Nichole's arm. "If it's bad, we can fix it together."

"We can't fix this." The same as Chase's money couldn't fix her broken heart. Nichole swallowed. Nothing removed the distaste.

The bitter sting. "The investors want to buy my app to kill it."

Mia gasped. "That's not fair."

"That's their right if I sell my app to them." Nichole pushed the folder away. "Their largest client is my only competitor." And just like that, her future as an authentic and talented app designer with a program successful on a national level was ruined.

Had Chase known last night? She'd seen him talking to Drew Harrington.

"Why didn't Chase tell you?" Josie read through the paperwork in the folder.

"I wouldn't have listened," Nichole admitted. She'd needed to believe in Glenn and Vick. Needed to believe she could secure her own family's future. "But Chase offered me money today to launch *In A Pinch* myself."

But he hadn't offered her his heart. Or his love. *I don't even know who I am.* Nichole squeezed her eyes closed. She knew who he was. He was the man she loved. The man she wanted to share her life with. And the man who couldn't or wouldn't accept her love.

"Did you take it?" Mia asked.

"Please tell me you have the money," Brooke said.

"I refused." Nichole stood and paced away from the table and her friends.

She'd accepted the money from her ex, used it to start her new life with Wesley. She hadn't really wanted her ex's heart. She saw that now. But she wanted Chase's trust and his love more than his money. She could provide for her family and take care of Wesley like she had been for years. And now she finally understood her grandmother was right. Love was enough and all she'd ever really needed. Except she didn't have Chase's love.

"What if Chase actually wanted to help?" Josie rose and walked over to Nichole. "Maybe he thought he was giving you exactly what you needed for your future."

"I need him in my future, not his money." Nichole clutched Josie's hands as if pleading with her friend would make Chase understand. "But he doesn't believe me."

Josie held on to Nichole and looked into her eyes. "Maybe you have to show him."

"Show him what?" Nichole glanced at Brooke and Mia.

"That his love matters to you more than his money." Brooke stepped around the table. "More than football."

Nichole winced. "I possibly ruined his football career. Football was his life."

"Was his life," Mia repeated, and joined their group huddle in the middle of the kitchen. She held up the picture of Nichole and Chase. "But he could have a new life with you and Wesley."

"I don't know." Nichole skipped her gaze away from her friends. Another risk. Another jump. Could she take it?

"Do you love him?" Brooke's quiet voice pulled at Nichole.

She never hesitated. "More than I thought possible."

"Then you need to fight for that. You need to fight for a life together." Josie pointed at the picture. "Fight for the love in this photograph."

"I don't know what to do," Nichole confessed.

Her friends wrapped their arms around her and laughed. "It's a good thing then that we do."

CHAPTER TWENTY-FIVE

CHASE KNOCKED ON the office door, peered inside and skipped over any greeting. "Surgery is scheduled."

His sister spun her chair around and stood up. "Good to know."

Chase stepped into Mallory's office. Too restless to sit, he tapped the folder containing his pre-op paperwork against his leg. "It's next week on Tuesday."

"I'll check the schedule, see who's staffed that day." Mallory folded her hands together on her desk and watched him. "But our docs are the best. They'll take good care of you."

Chase stilled. The folder quieted against his thigh. "I've been down this road before." Just not without a recovery plan on the other side. Not without a strategy that would return him to the football field as soon as possible.

"You haven't been down this road with a broken heart before." Mallory frowned. "Unfortunately, modern medicine hasn't discovered a medical cure for that specific condition yet."

He had an injured shoulder, not a fractured heart. "I wasn't looking for a cure."

"That's good." One corner of her mouth tipped up, more annoyed than amused. "Because you're the only one who can fix it."

He was already fixing what he could: his shoulder. Wasn't that good enough? His sisters always pushed him. Always challenged him. The same as Nichole. *You could stick around and fix it yourself.* Then he'd have to pretend he belonged. But what if he really belonged? What if he accepted Nichole's love? Then he'd have to admit... "I should get going. Let you work."

"Chase..." She stopped him at the door. "You can fix everything if you wanted to."

He'd offered Nichole money to fund her app launch. She'd refused. Denied his help and him. He'd done the right thing. For once, he'd put someone else first and let Nichole go. "Things are as they should be. Leave it alone, Mallory."

His sister walked over to him and shook her head. "I love you, little brother, but you can be quite dense sometimes."

Chase stared down his sister. "That's encouraging."

"I'm not trying to be encouraging." Mallory set her hands on her hips. "You need the truth, not encouragement."

"What's the truth?" He straightened to his full height as if that had ever convinced his sister to back down.

Mallory set her hand on Chase's chest, directly over his heart. "You offered Nichole the wrong thing. You know it but refuse to admit it."

"There's nothing to admit." His heart pounded in his chest. Could he love Nichole like she deserved? He'd only ever loved football and his life on the football field. What did he really know about loving another person? He could fail. Hurt her even more than he already had. He'd hate himself even more. "We don't work. Nichole and I are too different."

Mallory stepped back. Her gaze wide, her voice surprised. "For such a risk-taker and thrill seeker, I've never seen you more scared."

Chase stared at the floor. Considered running out of his sister's office but knew the truth would only pace him every step. "I'm facing the end of my career, Mallory. Of course, I'm scared."

"We not talking about your career," Mallory countered. "This was never about football."

But it was supposed to be. It was only ever supposed to be about football. It was never supposed to be about finding his place off the field. Or seeing a future—the one he'd always wanted as a kid—the one that included a wife and children. And him being the dad he'd always wanted his own father to be. But this wasn't like throwing an interception in the first half of a game. In a game, he had two more quarters to correct his mistake. To find a way to win. They were talking about life. Real life.

And the probability of making a mistake quadrupled. The risks piled up like the defense on a loose ball. But the rewards…

Mallory adjusted the collar on his jacket and touched his shoulders, drawing his focus back to her. "Go home, Chase, and spend some time alone."

"How will being alone help me with the end of my career?" How would being alone help him win in the game of life? That would be if he wanted to play at all. His heart bumped against his ribs.

"It probably won't." Mallory kissed his cheek. "But you just might learn to like yourself again."

"I'm fine with who I am." *Then I guess we're done here.* He flinched at Nichole's words. All because he'd admitted he might not like himself. Now his sister expected him to like himself too.

"Keep telling yourself that." Mallory patted his shoulder. Her voice was strong and sure, unlike her indifferent affection. "And one day you might believe it."

Chase closed his sister's office door and shut off her suggestion. He'd already spent too much time alone, avoiding the press and his feelings for Nichole. Now his sister wanted him to be alone and actively aware of that fact. As if.

Pre-op bloodwork complete, lunch several hours in the past and the kittens worn out from chasing a feather on a string, Chase stretched out on his living room couch. The silver kitten kneaded his chest, the gray one curled into a ball beside her sister. He should name them, but nothing sounded right. Nichole would've come up with cute names. Or better yet, Wesley would've shouted his ideas until the kittens responded. Chase grinned. Indoor voices were always difficult to master. Or they could've had a contest for the best names. Or a board game tournament to earn naming rights. So many options and every single one included Wesley and Nichole.

Not Chase, alone in his house, adjusting to the silence.

His doorbell rang. Thanks to several texts from Travis, Chase already knew his agent intended to stop in. Chase called out, "It's open."

Travis appeared in the open foyer and studied Chase from a distance. "What exactly are you doing?"

"Learning to be with myself." Chase flicked the silver's claws out of his shirt and petted the kitten until she settled next to her sibling.

"How's that going?" Travis approached, skepticism shifting across his face.

Chase dropped his head on the back of the couch and looked at the ceiling he'd considered painting earlier. But he'd been overwhelmed by the different shades of white he'd discovered on his internet search. Nichole liked details. No doubt she could've explained the nuances in the colors. Still, he'd started a renovation list of ideas to make his place more of a home and less of a transient college dorm.

He shifted his attention to Travis. Surprise

lifted his own voice. "Really well. Turns out I'm not all that bad to hang out with."

Travis sat down on the longer section of the L-shaped couch and laughed. "You're just now figuring that out. We've known it all along."

"I'm not always the fastest on the insightful stuff." Chase propped a pillow behind his head and considered Travis. "I'm also not the best about revealing my true self, but here goes."

Chase opened with an apology to Travis, moved on to his struggle with dyslexia, the prognosis for his surgery and finally his thoughts on retirement. Travis listened, asked questions and listened some more. And he never judged Chase. A gift Chase would be forever grateful for.

Chase drew in a deep breath and exhaled. "Where does that leave us now?"

"The same place we've always been. Friends first." Travis leaned close to Chase and held out his hand. "How would you feel about a sports commentary position?"

Chase gripped Travis's hand, grateful for his friendship and his guidance. "You're serious."

"Camera loves you," Travis said. "And you love the game."

Chase nodded. "But teleprompters aren't my friend."

"That can all be worked out. It's a job, and it keeps you connected to football." Travis stood and touched the silver-streaked kitten. A smile drifted across his face. "But Nichole and Wesley—it's the ones you love that keep you connected to life. They're the ones that remind you to keep on living life."

"A sports agent and a psychologist." Chase frowned at Travis. "You couldn't have shared your insight earlier."

"You wouldn't have heard me." Travis smiled warmly and waved at the room. "You only recently started to listen to yourself."

Chase picked up the kittens and set them on the couch. He stood and hugged Travis. No more apologies were needed.

"Do you have a plan?" Travis asked.

"Not quite." Chase rubbed his chin and grinned. "But I have a family, a rather large extended one, and I think it's past time I show them what they mean to me." And what Nichole meant to him.

CHAPTER TWENTY-SIX

"GENTLEMEN, THIS CONCLUDES our business relationship." Nichole stood inside the private dining room of Sapphire Cellar and addressed the two partners of Fund Infusion and her former business associates. "*In A Pinch* is no longer available for sale."

"We had an agreement." Vick Ingram dropped his cocktail glass onto the table and rose from his chair. A bottle of champagne sat in an ice bucket and appetizers waited to be sampled, as if Vick and Glenn had already begun the celebration. Before Nichole's arrival.

"We had signed NDAs." Nichole remained steady and tall. "We never had a binding sale contract." For that, she was thankful for her impromptu ski-moon in Tahoe and the interference of her make-believe marriage.

"Was this another fake invention like your pretend marriage?" Glenn asked. A twisted frown emerged from beneath his thick mustache. "After all, we never were allowed to validate your code. I suppose it doesn't actually exist and you've wasted our time."

"The code exists. The app is built and functioning." Nichole lifted her chin, drawing on even more confidence. Her inner strength she fully embraced. And besides, the only time being wasted was hers.

"Then you should want to sell." Glenn stabbed his fork into a shrimp. "It would seem without Chase Jacobs to depend on, you'd be in need of the money."

She had her own money and knew could depend on herself. That didn't mean she wouldn't have liked Chase beside her though. "I want my app to launch nationwide. But that's the problem, isn't it? At least, for you and your main client and *In A Pinch*'s only active competitor in the market."

"Excuse me," Glenn sputtered, and wiped his napkin across his mouth.

"How do you know about our clients?" Vick smoothed his hand over his wrinkled tie.

"I have people like Chase Jacobs in my corner." And family and friends who had her back. Always. Just as she had theirs.

"Chase Jacobs is nothing but a fraud," Glenn claimed.

"Is that because he exposed your true intentions for my program?" Nichole took aim, hit her target. Controlled the meeting. Maybe it was the dress. Or the power color: red. Or perhaps it was simply Nichole. She'd found her own inner power and a confidence she didn't expect to ever give up again.

"We fully intend to acquire your app," Glenn stuttered.

"It's not available," Nichole said. "I won't allow you to pay me off and kill my creation."

Vick shifted his weight from one foot to the other, his face pinched into an unflattering shade of pink. "I'm sure we could come to some kind of agreement."

"There is no agreement if it includes shutting down *In A Pinch*." Nichole straightened, every part of her steady from her heels to her chin. Even inside, nothing swayed. Nothing faltered. "You can let your client know I will take *In A Pinch* to market and it will hold up against anything they develop."

Vick and Glenn exchanged an uncomfortable look.

"But they better hurry. *In A Pinch* has technology and offerings your client hasn't even come up with yet. And they've been in the market for several years." Nichole smiled and waved to the table of now-cold appetizers. "Enjoy your dinner, gentlemen."

Head high, shoulders straight, Nichole exited the private dining room. Never wobbled on her heels. Never looked back. *Welcome to the game, Nichole.*

She allowed her smile to extend across her face. Allowed herself to relish the moment. Allowed herself to own her victory.

She walked into the bar of the Glasshouse Inn, chose a stool in the very center and greeted the bartender. She had one more item on her to-do list. The most important task on her list.

She pulled out her cell phone, opened her text message app and typed:

Meet me for drinks at Glasshouse Inn. I'll wait as long as I need to.

Nichole put her phone to sleep and turned it over on the bar top. Now she waited. And for the first time all evening, she wavered. Worry clipped along her spine. But she refused to bend. Refused to give up now. She intended to fight, and she intended to win.

"Nichole."

She closed her eyes, soaked in her name coming from the one person she'd have waited all night for: *Chase.* And suddenly a calm assurance replaced the worry coursing inside her. She spun around. "Chase. You're here. That was really quick."

He tugged on his suit jacket and motioned toward the exit. "I was outside with the valet."

"You were here." He'd already been in the parking area. Already been on his way. Nichole rose, closed the distance between them to less than a hand's width.

"I was coming here to see you." He opened his arms. "Nichole, I'm…"

Nichole stepped into his embrace, set her finger over his mouth. She'd owned her newly discovered confidence with Vick and Glenn. Now she had to believe in her heart. "I've been thinking quite a lot recently."

Chase reached up, curved his fingers around hers and pressed their joined hands against his chest. Nichole felt his rapid heartbeat, heard her own—just as rapid. Just as fast. He waited. His gaze fastened on hers.

"We tried the pretend part of a marriage and it didn't work out." She'd forgotten they were only pretending. And if she believed in Mia's photographs like her friends did, Chase had forgotten too. She moved fully into him, stepping right into his personal you-can't-ignore-me space.

His arm locked around her waist and anchored her in place. Exactly where she wanted to be. She arched one eyebrow and enhanced the challenge in her words. "I'm proposing we try it for real this time."

"Do you think we'll have different results?" Teasing. But in the depths of his green eyes, she saw it. Recognition. Tenderness. Affection.

Her reply came in a breathless whisper. "Definitely."

"So do I." He released her and dropped onto one knee.

Nichole touched her throat, tried to catch her heart cartwheeling from her chest. She'd come to fight for Chase. For them. Now her entire body wanted to float. To dance on those clouds.

He pulled a ring box from his jacket pocket, opened the lid and revealed a square-cut sapphire, her birthstone, surrounded by sparkling diamonds. "Nichole Marie Moore, I love you. I loved you the day you challenged me to be more than a cheater. I loved you for remembering I liked red licorice. And I love you even more now."

Tears fell from her cheeks; her hands trembled. Her voice went missing. She struggled to locate even the smallest sound. Something to acknowledge she'd heard him. Something to express the love bursting inside her. But Chase wasn't finished.

"You showed me how to like myself— every part of myself—and it's a gift I'll never be able to repay. But I want to try for the rest of our lives." He paused, but there was nothing unsteady about the breath he drew. Nothing hesitant in his words. "Nichole, will you marry me?"

"Say yes, Mom!" That familiar exuberant shout came from across the hotel lobby. "I already did."

Nichole covered her mouth, trapped her gasp against her palm. Wesley stepped into the bar area, his grin wider than Nichole had seen in far too long. More tears soaked her cheeks. She glanced at Chase. How could she possibly love him any more?

"I brought backup," he admitted.

"You asked Wesley if you could marry me." A tremor snaked up her legs. The good kind. The kind that anticipated being swept off her feet, then being caught safely.

"He's part of our team." Chase's one-sided grin returned, tripping delight up into his gaze. He tipped his head toward the entrance. "I might've asked the rest of the family too."

Nichole gaped. Brooke, Dan, Ben, Josie and the rest of her extended family walked into the bar. Chase's family followed, Travis and Elliot included. His mom wiped the tears from her eyes. Wesley helped Nonna, holding on to her arm and beaming with pride.

"Has she said yes yet?" Nonna patted Wesley's hand, then pushed her glasses up. "I'm ready to celebrate. Haven't been here in an age, but I recall the bartenders make a delicious Shirley Temple."

Happiness surged through Nichole, uncontainable like those stardust sprinkles on the clouds. She launched herself into Chase's arms, confident he'd never let her fall. "Yes. Yes, I'll marry you. I love you."

Chase caught her and spun her around. Their kiss ended too soon. He pulled back, touched her cheek. "You should know I've drafted my retirement statement and scheduled my surgery."

"You should know we'll be there with you every step." Nichole framed his face with her hands. "Always right beside you. We're a team."

Chase set his forehead against hers. "We're a family. It's the strongest team there is."

Nichole fell into another kiss, then leaned back. A tease in her own voice. "Does this mean you can share your grilled cheese recipe now?"

His laughter shimmered around the chandeliers. "I love you more than you can know. And I'm quite fond of you in the color red."

"I quite like it myself. I think red suits me." Nichole curved her arm around his waist and forgot about recipes and dresses. She saw only Chase, her family and her future.

EPILOGUE

Three weeks later...

CHASE ADJUSTED HIS shoulder splint and stepped around to put his good side next to Nichole. He reached over with his left arm and stopped Nichole from dumping her cup of flour into the mixing bowl. "You need to scrape off the extra flour from the top of the measuring cup."

Nichole frowned. "With what?"

Chase handed her a butter knife. "Just a smooth slice across the top."

"I could slice cheese even better." Nichole cleared the extra flour from the measuring cup and grinned at him. "I haven't forgotten about the grilled cheese recipe."

"We aren't making grilled cheese." Chase tweaked the tip of her nose.

"Yeah, Mom. You're supposed to be making sugar cookies." Wesley laughed from the far end of the table. He'd pulled up a chair beside Nonna. The pair had decided to devise a kitten-naming challenge to begin after dinner. A dinner that had grown to include more than just them. Nonna and Wesley were currently detailing the rules and regulations of the challenge on a whiteboard.

"Nonna and I already made those last week and ate them all," Wesley added.

Nichole aimed her measuring cup at the duo. "I have a rule to add. The winner gets full naming rights. There will be no veto powers handed out."

"That's two rules." Wesley frowned at her.

"And we really must reserve the right to veto." Nonna winked at Wesley. The two had become quite the united front. Nonna continued, "After all, we can't have the kittens running around with poorly chosen names."

Wesley nodded, his face and voice somber. "They'll feel really bad if we give them bad names."

Chase covered his mouth and his laugh. They'd been debating the best names for more than two weeks. He'd heard Nonna and Wesley already calling the kittens, Misty and Trixie. Both names Nichole had come up with after she'd won the first board game contest to determine naming rights. Chase guessed that now Nonna and Wesley simply enjoyed their game nights and joking with Nichole.

"Fine, but I want veto power too." Nichole set her hands on her hips and looked at Chase. She missed Nonna and Wesley silently sharing a giggle. Nichole asked, "What's next?"

The flour on Nichole's chin distracted him. He reached over, rubbed her jaw and leaned in for a soft kiss.

She laughed and stepped away. "You're supposed to be teaching me to bake. Stop diverting my attention."

"We don't really need cookies." Chase adjusted his shoulder splint. But he had needed another kiss.

Nichole fended him off with her measuring cup. "I'm supposed to be learning to cook while you recover from surgery. So I can help out in the kitchen."

She'd already helped him. She'd been with him every step of the way, from the time he went into pre-op to the moment he opened his eyes in recovery. She'd held his hand. Made him laugh. Brought him red licorice and kept her promise to always be beside him. Just as he would be for her.

The doorbell rang.

"I'll get it." Wesley jumped up from the table and shouted, "It's the rest of the family!"

Chase curved his good arm around Nichole's waist, tucked her into his side and kissed her. Voices and laughter vibrated through the house, extending into every corner and filling every part of Chase.

Elliot and Travis challenged Dan and Drew to a car race on the video game console in the family room. Ben and Wesley shouted advice and driving tips. Josie and Brooke each cradled a kitten on the sunporch. Theo, Josie's boyfriend, shook his head at Chase and grinned at Josie after her suggestion that they adopt some kittens too.

The doorbell rang again. His mother and sisters swooped into the kitchen, carrying casseroles and dessert trays. More family and friends crowded into the house. More laughter and warmth surrounded him.

Nichole touched his cheek, drew his attention to her. She asked, "Are you sure you're up for this?"

"There's no place else I'd rather be." He kissed her again, allowed their love to flow through him. "What about you?"

"You're beside me and then there's all this family." She placed her hand over his heart. "I'm home and it's better than any dream."

Home. He lifted her hand, pressed his lips

against her palm. He finally understood Non-na's words.

The only home he ever wanted to run to was Nichole.

* * * * *

For more great romances in the
City by the Bay miniseries from
Cari Lynn Webb, visit
www.Harlequin.com today!